Vexed 3:

The Final Sin

Vexed 3:
The Final Sin

Honey

URBAN BOOKS

www.urbanbooks.net

Urban Books, LLC
300 Farmingdale Road, N.Y.-Route 109
Farmingdale, NY 11735

ISBN 13: 978-1-64556-164-4
ISBN 10: 1-64556-164-X

First Trade Paperback Printing May 2021
Printed in the United States of America

10 9 8 7 6 5 4 3 2 1

Distributed by Kensington Publishing Corp.
Submit Orders to:
Customer Service
400 Hahn Road
Westminster, MD 21157-4627
Phone: 1-800-733-3000
Fax: 1-800-659-2436

Chapter One

"I'm about to lose my damn mind, Zach!" Venus wiped the heavy flow of tears from her eyes with a crumpled napkin and sniffed. "I swear to God I don't know what's going on with my baby. It's like she's possessed or something. All of the talking back and cussing—"

"Cussing? Who the hell does she be cussing at?"

"Me, of course. It's like she hates me, Zach. And I can't figure out why. At first I blew it off, thinking it was just her little teenage hormones going wild and maybe she had boy fever. But now I believe it's much deeper than that. What if she's on drugs or caught up in some crazy-ass cult? Oh God! My . . . my poor baby girl!"

Zach reached across the kitchen table and squeezed Venus's hand tenderly. "Be strong, sweetie. I got you. We'll get through this together as a family like we've always done. I promised you the day Nahima was born that I would always be there for you and her no matter what happened between you and Jay. That was almost sixteen years ago. Have I failed you yet?"

Venus shook her head as tears continued to stream down her face over a weak smile.

"Damn right I haven't, and I never will. That's why I'm sitting up here in your kitchen at seven thirty-six in the morning after pulling a twelve-hour shift. My ass is tired as hell, too. But Uncle Zach is about to fix this shit."

"I hope you can. But Nahima ain't the same little girl you used to bounce on your knee and give piggyback rides to around the block, Zach. She don't even look the same. That child came in here the other day with all of her long, thick, beautiful hair chopped down to an Afro. I almost had a heart attack. She's so damn disrespectful and defiant. It's like she's channeling—"

The double chirp from the security system, followed by the sound of the front door closing, interrupted Venus. She and Zach turned toward the entrance of the kitchen.

"Go get her, Mommy," said Zach. "I'll chill right here. Holla if you need me."

"Okay."

Venus stood up, seemingly nervous, and tightened the belt on her paisley bathrobe. She dabbed her eyes with the napkin again and swallowed hard before she made slow steps toward the kitchen door.

Zach couldn't imagine raising a child—biological or adopted—who he'd one day be afraid of. Zach Jr., Zion, and Jalen were no angels, but he would kill them dead before he'd allow them to rise up and go rogue on him and his wife, Jill. *Oh, hell nah!* That was why when Venus sent him a text message right after midnight, informing him that his niece, Nahima, hadn't returned home from school since she'd dropped her off that morning, he decided to head straight over to their house after completing his shift at Grady Memorial Hospital.

Zach felt kind of bad that he hadn't been more involved in Nahima's life in recent months, but the job promotion he'd busted his ass to get was so stressful that sometimes he barely had the energy to spend time with his own kids on his days off. It was true that success brought pleasure and pain for a brother in America. But the mega pay raise, new benefits package, and the authority that had come along with the upward move were worth it.

After completing the pediatric nurse practitioner program at Emory University's Nell Hodgson Woodruff

School of Nursing, Zach had been promoted to third-in-command at Grady, under only the two doctors over-seeing the neonatal intensive care unit. That was when the vultures and demons had come out bold and fierce. A little redheaded, green-eyed "Karen" had been his stiffest competition for the promotion, and she probably would've scored the damn bag if her little anorexic ass hadn't been so evil and temperamental. Hardly anyone in the unit liked her because she was a young girl from old Southern money with an Ivy League education who looked down her nose at the older and more experienced nurses, especially the black ones. The little bitch didn't think her shit stank.

Cool, smooth, and always the professional gentleman, Zach, with his years of experience and great rapport with not only the other nurses but with the unit's support staff as well, booted her ass right out of the game. And when she landed on her flat ass, her white privilege fueled her rage. Now she was on a mission to make Zach's life pure hell. But she had the right one, because boss brother number one was that nigga. Not even his three degrees and nearly fifteen years of experience on the same job had erased the hood from his blood. Hell, Zach's street cred was still good. Money and success hadn't changed him one bit. One could just ask all of his homies around the way. They had mad love and respect for Zachary Sean King because he'd stayed faithful to his roots and his peeps.

Zach had the same barber, Jaterrius "Jatty" Walker, who was still serving up fresh cuts six days a week. He'd been in the same shop in the Ridgewood community since the late eighties. Zach's dry cleaner, mechanic, favorite soul food restaurant/pool hall, and lifelong church were all located in that same neighborhood. Zach knew every dope boy and street hustler on the blocks. If he were a snitch on the police's payroll, he'd be one rich motherfucker because he could point out all the traps and bootleg houses. But he wasn't that type of cat because the Ridgewood street code was very much a part of his DNA. And it always would be.

A lopsided smile crept across Zach's face even as exhaustion tugged hard on his eyelids. Thoughts of the neighborhood his aunt had raised him and his sister, Jay, in always gave him a warm and fuzzy feeling on the inside because of the fond memories. He had come a long way, and he was proud of all he had accomplished over the years in spite of his circumstances.

As visions of Zach's childhood flipped through his mind's eye like pictures in a family photo album, he drifted off to sleep. It was a brief doze, though, because the sound of Nahima's voice on high volume calling her mama a bitch slapped him fully awake.

"I am your mother! You better stop talking to me like that!"

"You ain't my real mama! You turned your back on her, you selfish-ass bitch!"

Zach was on his feet, through the kitchen door, and in the front foyer with superhero speed that shocked even him. He blacked out for a few seconds after that, but when a fragment of his good sense returned, his hands had a death hold on Nahima's neck, squeezing the life out of her with her back against the wall. "Who the hell do you think you're talking to, huh? Have you lost your goddamn mind?"

"Zach, please let her go!" Venus tugged on his right arm. "She can't breathe! Lord, have mercy! You're going to kill her! Please let her go! Let her go, Zach!"

Zach was in a tunnel zone. No one else was in the room but him and the spawn of the evilest creature to roam the earth's surface. The eyes his eyes bore into held wickedness from the deepest pit of hell. She had no soul. Decent humanity escaped her. Only death could save her from herself.

"Before I allow you to become like Jay, I will kill you!"

Zach was so spazzed out that he had no idea that Charles, wearing only a towel on his lower body, had rushed downstairs to help Venus save their daughter from death by asphyxiation.

"God, please don't let him kill my baby! Let . . . let her gooo!"

"Zach, let her go. Come on, buddy," Charles said calmly in an even tone directly in his ear, grabbing him from behind.

By nothing but the grace of God, Zach's sanity fully returned, and he allowed Charles to pull him away from Nahima. The sea of red rage that had temporarily blinded him was replaced by white walls covered with pictures, sunlight shining through the windows, and the little girl he had loved since the day she was born gasping for air in front of him.

"Uh . . . ah." Nahima doubled over with saliva dripping from the corner of her mouth. "Uuuh . . . ah huh." She broke out in a coughing fit.

Venus wrapped her arms around her child and kissed her beet red face. "It's okay, baby. Just breathe in and out slowly. Don't try to talk. Just take deep breaths."

Nahima fell to her knees and pressed her palms on the hardwood floor, still struggling to take in air. Venus was right there on the floor with her, rubbing her back and shedding tears that matched hers.

After the blur of his fury had subsided, Zach was remorseful, but at the same time, he couldn't help but feel that there was a hint of justification for his actions. Maybe if someone had choked the shit out of Jay when she was younger, instead of spoiling her out of sympathy over the absence of their parents, she wouldn't have turned into the hellacious monster she was. She wouldn't be in prison rotting away in sickness and self-pity, either. Zach didn't want that kind of life for Nahima, but if she didn't get her shit together, she would end up just like Jay. He couldn't allow that to happen, could he?

"I . . . I'ma call the . . . the police."

Zach removed his cell phone from his hip pocket and kneeled down next to his niece, who was still gasping for her every breath. "Use my phone. But you might want to change out of that THOT outfit and take a shower before they get here, because you smell like two grams of strong weed and stank-ass pussy. Ain't no badge going to arrest me or feel sorry for a disrespectful fifteen-year-old girl who busted up in the crib reeking of Kush and raw sex after staying out all damn night without her parents' permission." He placed his phone on the floor an inch away from her hand and stood. "Call five-o, Nahima. I want you to."

The penetrating glare she gave Zach when she lifted her head didn't faze him at all. He wondered who the fuck she thought she was giving him the evil eye with her nostrils flaring like a raging bull. Her little defiant ass needed to concentrate on breathing before she passed out. If Nahima wanted to do grown-folk shit, he was going to handle her like an adult. That didn't mean he didn't love her, because he actually did. He was just tired of her funky-ass attitude and the shitty way she treated her mother.

"Look, I'm sorry I got carried away," Zach finally said to Venus as he stood up with his phone. "I snapped when I heard her call you a bitch, I guess. I don't know, but I'm here for you and Charles whenever y'all need me. Right now what I need is a hot shower, some food, and my bed. I'm out."

Venus nodded and smiled even as tears continued to spill from her eyes, but she didn't speak. Zach knew it was best that she not say anything, because it might set Nahima off when it seemed like she was in the grips of reality about what she had done.

"Thanks for coming, Zach," Charles said, following him to the front door.

"She's my niece, man, and I love her. I'm trying to keep my word to Venus. I promised I would help her raise Nahima until she turned eighteen, but I'm not sure if I can now. I might catch a case fooling with that girl. I think I'm going to have to step back for a little while."

"I understand."

Chapter Two

Nahima rolled over onto her side in bed so she could look out the window. "And Charles with his punk ass didn't do a damn thing. All he said was some lame-ass shit like, 'Let her go, buddy.' Can you believe that shit?"

"That's foul, bae. Your family is fucked up for real."

"Yeah, they're all fucked up except for my birth mom and my nana. The rest of them can eat shit and die for all I care, especially Uncle Zach and fake-ass Jill. I can't stand that mud black bitch. She's the one who ruined our family. How the hell you go from licking pussy to deep-throating dick? And that nasty ho kept it in the family, hopping from my mom to her brother! Who the hell does ratchet shit like that?"

"Hold up now, bae. Your birth mom switched from clit to dick, too. I'm just sayin'." Santana laughed.

"Whatever." Nahima sucked her teeth. "That was a whole different situation, and it didn't involve relatives, either. Anyway, since you got jokes, I'll holla at you later."

"Oooh, so now you big mad at a nigga for shootin' it to you straight? Fuck that shit."

"Nah, fuck you!" She ended the call and tossed the phone on the other side of her queen-size canopy bed.

Nahima was brain-dead in love with her boyfriend, Santana, but she didn't appreciate him talking shit about Jay. In her eyes, her only living biological parent could do no wrong. She was a victim of an unfair God and an unjust legal system. Five years ago, Nahima learned that

Jay and Uncle Zach had lost their mother when they were very young because their father had shot her in the heart after catching her fucking his best friend in a motel room. And the dude had been a pastor at the time when he killed his wife.

Then, later on in life, Jay had fallen in love with Venus, who had only used her for her eggs so she could have a baby because her own eggs were all dried up. Sadly, that baby was her. And as if that weren't enough bad luck, after her mom had tried to start a new life away from all the pain she had survived in Atlanta, the poor bitch she'd taken off the streets of Kingston, Jamaica, and placed in the lap of luxury betrayed her. Yeah, when Jay was busy trying to provide for Jill and send her to school once they moved to Atlanta, the ungrateful slut fucked her brother, Zach. Now, he and Jill were married and living their best life with three children in the 'burbs in a phat crib they'd built from the ground up four years ago. Their shady asses even had a vacation home in Jamaica and four late-model whips parked in their garage.

It wasn't fair that Zach and ho-ass Jill were enjoying wealth and good health while Jay was in prison serving seventeen years on some bogus charges as she battled kidney failure and cirrhosis of the liver. What was worse was that the whole damn family had hidden all of this information from Nahima. For years, she'd been led to believe her birth mom was a monster who had put out a hit on her own brother and kidnapped Jill in Jamaica with the intent to kill her. In fact, everybody in her family believed all that bullshit, as well as the DA and jury who had convicted her. All of them busters and the judge must've been hella stupid to have fallen for all the lies Zach, Jill, the phony-ass hit man, and a bunch of other evil witnesses had told to trap Jay. Nahima couldn't believe her family had helped the system convict their own blood. What the fuck?

Well, not everybody had turned against her mom during the trial. Her nana, Jackie, had stayed in her corner, and so had her grandfather, the gun-toting preacher. They had told the judge about the hardships Jay had experienced growing up without her parents in the hood. Yet their testimonies weren't enough to convince the wack-ass jury to return a not-guilty verdict. Now Jay was in prison fighting for her life with no family support except the letters and emails she got from Nana every now and then. She put money on her books, too, from time to time, which was cool. But four months ago, when Nahima asked Nana for her mom's address at Leesworth Women's Federal Corrections Facility so she could start a relationship with her, she'd refused to give it to her.

"Your mother made some bad choices regarding you, Nahima. Jay doesn't have a relationship with you because she chose not to. I'm afraid she'll hurt you by not responding to your letters if you reach out to her without a heads-up from me. Let me ask Jay if she wants to hear from you, okay?"

Nana wasn't a liar. Nahima knew that for sure. If Jesus was real, and she strongly doubted He was, Jackie Dudley Brown was His ride-or-die, period. She prayed a hundred times a day, went to church twice a week, and read her Bible more than anybody Nahima knew. Nana sang praises to her God every Sunday at church, too, with her beautiful voice. And no matter what was going on in the family with her sisters, their crazy kids, or Uncle Zach and Jill, she always spoke the truth and stood on the right side. However, she never gave Nahima Jay's address at the prison, nor did she tell her if her mom wanted to receive letters from her. Maybe she forgot to ask her. Nahima would never know because she didn't bother to follow up. Instead, she took matters into her own hands.

One Saturday when Nahima was at Nana's house helping her set up her new smart TV, she took a break to eat a Philly cheesesteak sandwich and check her social media pages and school email account. Since her phone was on the charger, she decided to fire up Nana's laptop computer to shake the dust off of it. She hardly ever used the damn thing except to email Jay whenever she reached out to her from the prison. But Nana was in love with her Dell UltraSharp touch-screen computer because it was a Mother's Day gift from Uncle Zach.

After Nahima finished scrolling through the Gram and Twitter, she decided to be nosy and check Nana's browser history. It was right there in plain sight in her Gmail account like she was supposed to see it. Jay had sent Nana a message thanking her for the money she had sent her earlier that week, and she updated her on her failing health. Nahima jotted down Jay's email address at Leesworth and put it in her pocket.

Although she wouldn't reach out to her right away for many reasons, when she finally got up the nerve to do just that, the world as she had known it all her life would change. Nahima would no longer live in the darkness of her family's lies and grimy secrets. Jay would shed light on all of them motherfuckers and their sins.

"What's up, Kang? You feelin' a'ight today?"

Jay brought her electric scooter to a stop in front of the commissary and secured the brakes. "I ain't dead yet, so I must be okay. Why are you worrying about me, old lady?"

"Damn, a friend can't be concerned 'bout you? I know you saw Dr. Dalrymple yesterday, and I want to know what's up."

"My bad, Gracie. You know how it is around here. Everybody's got an agenda, including Warden Sheftall with her shady ass. Major Herndon ain't no better, but at least he's real about his shit."

Gracie leaned over the counter and looked Jay dead in her eyes. "Forget about these corrupt people in here and tell me what the doctor said. How is your liver, and what's up with your kidneys?"

"Ain't nothing changed. The kidneys are maintaining between twenty-five and thirty percent even with dialysis and meds, and as far as my liver goes, I might as well not even have one. Cirrhosis is eating it up."

"I'm sorry to hear that, Kang. I was hopin' for better news. But how come your kidney function is so low? I thought your brother gave you one of his."

"He did, but lately it's been showing signs of rejection for some strange reason. Plus, it's overworked because the other one is so badly diseased. The damn thing don't work at all."

"Damn! Kang, I'm so sorry."

Jay waved her hand dismissively and sucked her teeth. "It is what it is. But don't worry about me, because I'm at peace. My daughter is in my life, and my little boy is doing fine. If God calls my number today, so be it, as long as my children are all right."

"Well, I hope God will let you hang around a li'l bit longer so you can have some time with your kids outside of this hellhole."

"That ain't happening, Gracie. I've served almost nine years of my sentence, but I've got eight more to go. Do you really think I'll still be alive in eight years? Honey, please."

Gracie checked her surroundings before she came around the counter and kneeled next to Jay's scooter to whisper, "You need to speak with one of them law school students who come here the first of every month. They helped Lewis up in C8 get out early 'cause of her low IQ.

And some chick down in C3 only did two of her five years
'cause they found somethin' her attorney did wrong on
her case."

"And?" Jay asked, totally unimpressed.

"Kang, you is medically fragile, as they say. Plus, you
ain't been in no trouble since you been in here, and
Sheftall really depends on you to keep the inmates'
money straight 'round here. You need to talk to them
students when they come next time. I bet'cha they can
get you up outta here on account of your bad health."

"I ain't wasting my time on that shit. It won't do me any
good to get my hopes up and then get crushed when I find
out they can't help me. I'd rather maintain a relationship
with my daughter and auntie until God calls my number
and hope He'll have mercy on me on Judgment Day. I'll
holla at you later, Gracie."

"A'ight, Kang. I'll see you at dinner."

Jay powered up her scooter and maneuvered her way
down the hall toward her office. She was still the inmate
accountant/business manager at Leesworth after all
these years. She'd maintained that position under two
wardens before the current one, Iris Sheftall, who had
taken over two years ago.

Jay smiled thinking about Gracie's nonsense. She
didn't have the time or energy to waste on some wannabe
attorneys on a mission to become famous for helping
throwaway inmates. Jay wasn't the type who believed
in miracles anymore anyway. She knew God was real
and He loved everyone, but she was also familiar with
His wrath. As the daughter of a Pentecostal preacher,
who had grown up in the church, she had come to terms
with her past sins and the effects they'd had on so many
people, especially her family. God didn't owe her any
favors. People had died because of Jay's wicked ways.
She couldn't escape that painful reality. The father of her

son, a pastor, and his wife had lost their lives behind her interference in their marriage and her selfishness, as well as a female deputy who had left her children behind to mourn her after she had been manipulated and used.

Because of her dark and gloomy past, Jay had no hope for any blessings coming her way. She didn't deserve any miracles, and unlike the Clark Sisters, she wasn't looking for a miracle or expecting the impossible, either. Jay had finally taken responsibility for all of her transgressions and accepted her fate. She was going to die in Leesworth. There was no way around it. It was the hand that life had dealt her. But it wasn't so bad because at least she had her daughter in her life now. That was a miracle. Jay couldn't even explain how it had come to pass. All she knew was that, out of the blue about four months ago, she'd received an email from Nahima. And from that day on, they had been in constant contact with each other via email and phone calls.

In the beginning, Nahima had had many questions that Jay had been more than happy to answer. The family had told a bunch of lies about certain past situations, too. Nahima was confused about her conception and the breakup between her biological mom and the woman who'd given birth to her. And the child was way off on the facts about the Jay-Jill-Zach love triangle as well as how her how little brother had come into the world while her birth mom was in prison. It had taken many email exchanges and phone calls between Jay and Nahima before the confused teenager was finally able to fully grasp her family history. Thanks to her real mother, she was no longer in the dark or dumb to the facts. Now Nahima knew every damn thing she had a right to know about Jay, Venus, Zach, Jill, and the rest of the King family. It was Jay's version of the truth, though.

Chapter Three

Just as Nahima finished ironing all of her outfits for school for the following week, her cell phone rang. She glanced at the clock on the dresser and smiled. It was seven o'clock on the dot, so she knew it was Jay. She dove on the bed and slid across it to answer her phone before the third ring.

"Hello?"

"What's up, baby girl?"

"Nothing much. I'm grounded again. I swear that woman makes my ass itch sometimes. What did you ever see in her?"

"Never mind all that. What did you do to get grounded this time?"

Nahima released air from her cheeks in frustration. "I missed curfew."

"Oh, yeah? How late were you? An hour or two?"

"Nah."

"Well, exactly how late were you past your curfew then? And don't lie to me, damn it."

"I stayed out all night."

"Say what? Girl, what the hell were you doing out all night, and who were you doing it with?"

"I was with Santana, my man. We were hanging out at his boy's spot, chillin', watching movies on Netflix, and playing cards. Nobody was checking for the time. At the end of the card game, it was after three in the morning and I was hungry. So we hit up the Waffle House to pick up some food and got a room at a motel afterward because we were too sleepy to drive all the way out here to the 'burbs. And either way Venus and Charles were gonna flip out, so I just said fuck it."

"You shouldn't have stayed out all night, baby girl. That shit ain't cool. You're only fifteen. Venus is a selfish bitch, but she does love you, so I know she was worried."

"Man, whatever."

"She does love you, Nahima. I can't even lie about that."

"Well, if Venus loves me so damn much, how come she let Uncle Zach put his hands on me, huh? That fool tried to choke me out, and she and Charles didn't do shit about it."

"Zach? He was at your house? When did he put his hands on you?"

Nahima heard pure rage in Jay's voice, and it served as the motivation she needed to paint the worst picture possible of her parents and uncle. A better actress than Viola Davis or Angela Bassett could ever be, she turned on the faux waterworks on demand, panting and sniffing pitifully. "I guess Venus called Uncle Zach while he was still at work, because he was already here dressed in scrubs when I got home."

"And he just started choking you?"

"Nah, nah, it didn't go down like that. Venus met me at the door and started going in on me, asking me where I had been and who brought me home and all kinds of dumb shit. But I wasn't trying to hear all that, so I told her to fall back and get outta my face. Then I called her a bitch when she grabbed my arm and started yanking me around."

"Nahima!"

"She had no business snatching on me! Anyway, your lame-ass brother ran into the front hall trying to be a gangster when he heard me call Venus a bitch. That fool went to choking me and slammed my back against the wall real hard. His eyes were all stretched wide, and he was growling like a wild animal or a monster."

"Oh, my God! What did Venus do, and where the hell was Charles? Why didn't they make Zach stop?"

"Venus was boo-hooing like a weak-ass bitch, begging him to let me go, but he didn't care. He sounded like a goddamn demon. You know, like a person who's possessed. He told me before he'll let me end up like you, he would kill my ass!"

"That low-down, dirty, evil motherfucker!" Jay fell silent, like she had been robbed of words.

Nahima seized the opportunity to turn up the heat by breaking down in a phony fit of sobs.

"Don't cry, baby girl. It's okay. Tell me how it ended. Did Venus knock the shit out of Zach?"

"Uh-uh. Charles finally ran downstairs in a towel and begged him to let me go. Then he pulled him away. I was going to call the police on Uncle Zach because that was assault. But . . ."

Nahima caught herself before she said too much. She couldn't tell Jay the real reason why she didn't call the police, that Zach had blasted her out for smelling like weed and sex. That would make her look bad in her birth mother's eyes. It would mess up the image she was trying to create of a misunderstood teenager all alone in a fucked-up world the adults in her life had thrown her into before she was even born. She was too smart to crush her sympathy game.

"Nahima? Are you still there? Why didn't you call the police, baby girl? Hell, why didn't Venus call them?"

"I love Uncle Zach, and even though he tried to kill me, I didn't want him to go to jail."

"Uggghhh! That bastard had no business putting his hands on you! And he needs to stop throwing low-key shade on me when I ain't even thinking about his evil ass. And what the hell does he mean that he'll kill you before he lets you end up like me? What kind of shit is that? I would rather you take after me than his disloyal ass. Ol' backstabbing-ass motherfucker."

"He said it. I swear to God he said those exact words while he was choking me."

"I feel like calling Zach and cussing his punk ass out. He ain't nothing but a bully. Damn, I wish I could call Aunt Jackie and tell her what he—"

"Jay, you can't! Nobody knows you and I are in contact. We can't let anybody find out, because they'd go all kinds of crazy and put a stop to it."

"I know, baby. I know they would. So don't worry yourself sick. I won't say anything to Auntie Jackie. But sooner or later, we're going to have to let the family know we're communicating. I'm your mother, and I have every goddamn right to be a part of your life no matter what. I want Jalen to know me at some point, too. It's only fair."

"You're right. We just need to keep our situation on the low for now until we figure out how to break the news to Venus, Charles, Zach, and Nana. That's going to be the most explosive day in history for the King family. Watch and see."

"Yeah, I bet it will."

"When are you going to hit me up again?"

"I'll try to call you Monday evening at the regular time."

"Okay. Do you need anything?"

"Ummm, yeah, you can send me some of those cookies I like and some panties. I'm so damn fat now that every pair I have is too small. They're cutting into my stomach and thighs. Buy me some white cotton granny panties in a size nine and send them to me, okay?"

Nahima smiled, no longer chasing her first Academy Award. "I got you, Jay."

"Thanks so much, baby girl. Well, my time is almost up. Let me scoot on back to my cell. We'll talk Monday."

"Okay. Bye."

"Bye-bye."

"I love you," Nahima whispered after the call ended.

"Nana! Nana! Nana!" Jalen ran through the den and hopped in Aunt Jackie's lap as she sat comfortably in her favorite recliner.

"Hey, Nana's sweetie pie." She kissed the child's cheek and ran her fingers through his curly Afro. "How are you?"

"I'm good. I made an A one hundred on my spelling test yesterday."

"Oh, my goodness, I am so proud of you. You're so smart."

"Auntie, put that big Negro down. He ain't no baby," Zach fussed, crossing the threshold with Jill, Zion, and Zachary Jr. right behind him.

"Shut up, Zach! Jalen will always be my baby just like your other two children and Nahima."

"Speaking of Nahima—"

"Now is not the time, baby." Jill rolled her eyes at her husband before she leaned down and gave Aunt Jackie a hug. "How are you today, Auntie?"

"I'm fine, sweetheart." Aunt Jackie kept her eyes on Zach as she received greetings, hugs, and kisses from Zachary Jr. and Zion before they took seats on the sofa.

"Nana, can we turn the TV to Disney Plus please?" 11-year-old Zach Jr. asked. "We want to watch *Marvel's Runaways*."

Zion, a year and a half her brother's junior, sucked her teeth and rolled her eyes at him. "No, we don't. We want to watch *Black-ish* reruns on BET. Don't we, Jalen?"

"Yeah!" the youngest of Zach and Jill's kids jumped down from his nana's lap and pumped his little fist in the air, agreeing with his big sister.

"Okay. How about we do this?" Aunt Jackie stood up, grabbed the remote control from the coffee table, and offered it to Zion. "You and Jalen can watch BET in here, and Zach Jr. will watch Disney Plus in my bedroom while I talk to your mom and dad in the kitchen. Now who can complain about that?"

Chapter Four

Zach placed his glass of sweet tea on the table after he took a sip. "I swear she smelled like pussy and weed. I ain't lying."

"Will you please stop using ungodly language in my house before one of the kids comes in here and hears you, Zachary Sean King?"

"I'm sorry, Auntie, but I'm just keeping it one hundred. Nahima is doing the nasty, and she smokes happy grass. And based on how strong it was, I'd put my money on Kush or some of that loud."

"Lord Jesus, help us today right now, Father!" Aunt Jackie shook her head with tears in her eyes. "How did such a sweet and polite child turn into a . . . a . . ."

"A weed-smoking ho?"

"Zachary! Don't call our niece such an awful thing. Mind your manners, eh?" Jill picked up her fork and took another bite of her slice of sweet potato pie.

"I'm just speaking the truth. Venus said Nahima has been coming in late for weeks now smelling like weed. It broke her heart when I told her I believe she's having sex. But my nose don't lie. I know the smell of funky pus . . . um, vagina when it hits my nose."

"We need to pray, y'all."

"Nah, Auntie, we need to tell Venus to put Nahima on birth control and take her to Narcotics Anonymous. That's what we need to do."

"Zach, can you talk to her? You and Nahima used to be so close. What happened?"

"She grew up and some little thug took my place. Then again, I may have spoiled her too much. To be honest, we all did. But I'll admit I went overboard. In my heart I felt it was my duty to give her the love, attention, and all the things Jay never gave her. So I think I gave her too much, and instead of being grateful, Nahima created a false sense of entitlement like everybody owes her the world."

"Maybe," Jill chimed in. "But I don't really agree with your way of thinking, Zachary. Nahima was the perfect teenage girl until a few months ago. Then all of a sudden, she lost interest in her little brother and no longer wanted to spend weekends at our house so she could be with him. And she stopped calling us and Aunt Jackie. She started acting mean and became disrespectful out of the blue. It's like she snapped and turned into a monster."

"Jill is right, Zach. Nahima has been spoiled rotten all her life, but she didn't start acting a fool until a few months ago. Something happened. Lord, I wish I knew what it was."

"I'm telling y'all, some thugged-out knucklehead done popped her li'l cherry, and now she thinks she's in love. Nahima is sprung on the ding-dong. I wonder who the little punk is. And I hope like hell he's got enough sense to strap up before he goes deep. Otherwise, Venus and Charles better get ready for a grandbaby, or worse, Nahima is going to contract HIV or some other sexually transmitted disease."

"No! The devil is a liar!" Aunt Jackie locked eyes with Zach from across the kitchen table. "I need you to talk to her. I'll fast and pray, but I need you to go over to Venus and Charles's house and talk to your niece to—"

"Nope." Zach folded his arms and shook his head. "I ain't going over there to talk to that child. I'll end up shooting her."

"I ain't asking you, boy. I am telling you to go and talk to your niece."

"I'm not going near Nahima, because she's too disrespectful. And if she says something out of her neck to me, I'll kill her. Then I'll end up in the pen like my crazy sister, her demonic mama, and my children will be fatherless. Sorry, Auntie, I will not sacrifice my children's stability to save Jay's child. I have cleaned up my sister's messy mistakes over and over again all my adult life. Hell, I even gave her vindictive ass a kidney after she paid a man to kill me and kidnapped my wife and planned to kill her. And y'all know I didn't want to adopt her son. But didn't I do it? Did I not adopt Jalen as my own?"

Jill reached over and grabbed her husband's hand and squeezed it as she nodded her head.

"Yes, you did, Zach. We all know you've sacrificed a lot for Jay." Aunt Jackie was in tears at this point.

"Yeah, I have. So I think I've done enough for my sister and her children. That's why I'm done. I ain't doing nothing else unless God breaks me down and tells me different."

"Okay. I'll talk to Nahima and pray for her," Aunt Jackie uttered just above a whisper. "She's my flesh and blood, and I love her. I won't give up on my precious great-niece just like I would never give up on you."

"Daddy, I want my big, big sister to come to our house and help me make cookies again. Will you call her for me?"

Zach closed the EllRay Jakes book he'd just finished reading to Jalen and placed it on the nightstand. He looked down at his sweet baby boy and got lost in his big ol' steel gray eyes. They always turned his heart to ice cream at the wrong damn time. Two days ago, Zach had sworn off Nahima, fearing that any contact with her would cost him his freedom. That was just how much her foul behavior and stank-ass attitude got under his skin. He simply didn't want her in his presence right now. It was too risky. But Nahima was his niece, whom he loved dearly in spite of her flaws, and she was Jalen's biological sister. The love in Zach's heart for both of them wouldn't allow him to keep them apart.

"Please, Daddy?"

"Okay, buddy, I'll call Nahima and ask her to come over and bake cookies with you."

Jalen instantly started giggling. Then he balled up his little hand into a fist, tapped his heart three times, offered it to his daddy for a pound, and said, "You my dawg."

"You're Daddy's dawg too, my man." Zach mimicked his son's gesture and bumped his little fist with his. "Good night, Jalen. I love you."

"I love you too, Daddy."

"He told me before he'll let me end up like you, he would kill my ass!"

Zach's threat to Nahima was messing with Jay's head. The little speck of peace that she had finally found in the middle of the lowest point in her life had been slipping away from her ever since she'd learned about him choking her child and screaming hateful bullshit to her. Venus was wrong as hell to have allowed a grown-ass man—uncle or not—to cuss out her 15-year-old daughter and assault her without reporting the incident to the authorities. And what kind of father was Charles? He should've kicked Zach's ass for what he did to Nahima. That was what any real father would have done.

Jay flipped over on her newly approved air mattress to lie on her back. It wasn't hurting as much tonight as it had been earlier in the week. Sheftall had finally received permission from the powers-that-be to allow Dr. Dalrymple to prescribe her the pain medication she'd needed for her back. It was about damn time. Being in prison with poor health was punishment enough. Living in excruciating pain every damn day had made it inhumane.

Thank God for Aunt Jackie, who had signed paperwork agreeing to pay for 20 percent of her medications every month. Otherwise, Jay would've been in deep shit. Zach wouldn't even fart on her if she needed to stink in order to live, and it had been so long since she had reached out to her father that he had probably written her off too. So her aunt was the only person on God's green earth besides Nahima who gave a damn about her. And they were the only two people plus her baby boy who she truly cared about.

As the pain meds tugged on Jay's eyelids, she started her nightly routine of imagining what her life would look like today if she hadn't made certain decisions. She wondered every day if she and Venus would still be together if she had tried to love Nahima and given parenthood a fighting chance. Would she and Jill have lasted if they had stayed in Jamaica? Maybe if they hadn't moved in with Zach when they got to the States, they would've made it. Jill damn sure wouldn't have found out that Nahima was Jay's biological daughter, and she never would've been seduced by her disloyal brother. Then there would've been no need for her to steal from her job to pay for the hit she'd taken out on Zach. So in retrospect, leaving Jamaica to stop Venus from marrying Charles was the biggest mistake of Jay's life. That one decision was the beginning of her darkest days.

Jay allowed that thought to sink in deep as sleep began to swaddle her like a warm blanket. No matter how much she wanted to blame others for her downfall, it was her fault that she was in prison. There were no two ways about it. Of course, she would never say it out loud to another living soul, but it was the gospel truth. And looking back on it, Jay's plan to throw a monkey wrench in Venus's plan to marry Charles had been stupid as hell. How in the world was she supposed to have won her ex back when she'd brought her current bitch to Atlanta with her? Jay had acted on impulse back then without a plan. And because of that, she would live the remainder of her pathetic life in Leesworth. Or would she?

Medical science and the federal justice system said she would, but . . .

Jay's eyes popped wide open against the force of gravity on her heavy eyelids. Maybe Gracie's idea wasn't nonsense after all. If a dumb bitch could be sprung from the pen because of her low IQ, why couldn't Jay's sentence be cut short because of her failing health?

Chapter Five

Nahima trotted down the stairs wearing a light blue denim miniskirt, an orange halter top, and a pair of gold strappy sandals with a medium wedge heel. The designer backpack she had begged Charles to buy for her was hanging from both wing straps on her left shoulder. Recently, she'd begun to experiment with makeup, and the YouTube tutorials she constantly watched seemed to be paying off. Nahima's thick eyebrows had been arched to perfection above her flawlessly applied eye shadow in three brilliant earth tones. The bronze, nutmeg, and rust complemented her light brown eyes while the gold lipstick gave her mouth that shiny, pouty appeal that white girls had been paying plastic surgeons a grip to create for them for decades. Those high King cheekbones were accented with golden bronze blush like a pro makeup artist had worked his or her magic. The child looked gorgeous.

Venus cleared her throat as little Miss MAC Counter headed for the front door. "Remember if you aren't back in this house by nine o'clock sharp, your daddy and I will take your phone, laptop, iPad, and both of your game consoles. And instead of going to Orlando for a week in July with Yashia and her family, you'll be in Raleigh with your grandfather while Charles and I enjoy the trip without you. I'm not playing, Nahima. You got it?"

"Yeah, I got it."

Venus walked over to her daughter and pulled her into her arms for a hug. "No matter what you're going through, please know that your daddy and I love you very much. Nothing will ever change that."

Nahima's petite body stiffened in her mother's embrace, but Venus didn't care. She held on to her only child anyway because she truly did love her. Although Nahima's behavior and the venomous words she had starting spewing from her mouth lately were making it more difficult by the day for her mother to express her love, she was hopeful that it was just a teenage phase that would soon pass. If that weren't the case, Venus didn't know what the hell she and Charles were going to do.

Zach, who had been a major player in Nahima's village since the day she was born, had decided to take a break from his uncle/godfather duties. Venus couldn't blame him though, because he had his own children to raise and a wife. No man in his right mind would put up with a bunch of ratchetness from his teenage niece when he didn't have to. So his decision to step away from Nahima for a while was completely understandable.

The sound of a car horn pulled Venus out of her thoughts. She took a backward step with her arms still encircling her daughter. She smiled at Nahima when she looked into her eyes despite the scowl on the child's face. More than ever before, she was determined that whatever was causing her baby girl to act out would not win. Venus would fight for the soul of her child by any means necessary. She would not give up and let drugs, sex, bad grades, and a nasty attitude destroy Nahima. With God's help, she and Charles would do everything they could to help her make the turnaround she so desperately needed.

"That's Yashia," Nahima said softly.

"Okay. Go on. I'll see you at nine o'clock. I love you, baby."

"Bye."

Nahima opened the door and rushed outside with Venus right behind her. She even started running up the walkway and waving her hand like a maniac at her BFF, Yashia Taylor. Nahima was acting like she hadn't seen the girl in ten years even though school had been dismissed only two hours ago. Surely, they had spent plenty of time together throughout the day. After all, the two girls took advanced fashion design and creation together, which was their third-period class that led into lunch. That was their downtime when they always shared a table with the other members of their small clique.

Once Nahima was in the passenger's seat of the black late-model Toyota Corolla, Venus smiled and waved at the girls. Yashia honked the horn before she pulled off. The BFFs were on their way to the studio owned by their sewing mentor, Mrs. Marsha Stephens, to work on their big project, which was due in a little less than a month. Nahima had come up with the great idea to design and create a jumpsuit that could be worn interchangeably. One side was going to have silver sequins, and the flip side would be black faux leather. Nahima had bragged that this original garment would allow a woman to have a casual and formal outfit in one piece.

Venus sighed as she made her way back inside the house. How could such a beautiful, smart, and talented girl have turned into a rebellious gangster in a matter of months? It was like someone had cast a wicked spell on her precious little girl, turning her into an alien or a beast from hell. Venus couldn't wrap her mind around the sudden changes in Nahima. But a faint yet powerful voice deep down inside her soul had often reminded her over the years of one simple truth that could not be ignored. It was a fact that Venus had never spoken to anyone, not even Charles and especially not to Zach. The connotation was much too heavy to even think about, painful even. But it had constantly nagged at her from the first moment she'd held Nahima in her arms nearly sixteen years ago.

Venus shivered and gasped out loud against the mysterious chill that crept up her spine as she headed toward the kitchen to finish preparing dinner for Charles. She tried to block out the words that persistently haunted her regardless of how great a life God had blessed her with. Some things were simply inevitable and could not be avoided. Genetics was real and superseded acquired characteristics and learned behavior. The realization hit Venus like she had just run headfirst at full speed into a mountain, causing tears to spill like a waterfall from her eyes.

Nahima is Jay's biological daughter!

"Make a right at the next traffic light."

Yashia took her eyes off the road for a hot second to peep at Nahima. "For what? That ain't the way to Mrs. Stephens's studio."

"I know," Nahima agreed with a sheepish grin on her face. "I told Santana I would swing by his boy's spot to holla at him for a minute on our way."

"Oops, you lied about that."

Nahima jerked her head in her bestie's direction. "Are you for real right now?"

"Dead-ass," Yashia snapped and drove straight through the traffic light instead of turning right.

"I would've done it for you, but I guess you forgot about all those times I covered for you so you could lie up with Dondrae."

"No, I haven't. I remember and I appreciated it, but you can't compare Dondrae to Santana."

"So you think Dondrae is better than Santana? Is your man some kind of angel or superhero? Girl, bye!"

"First of all, Dondrae is a senior in high school who is only a year older than me. He makes good grades and plays baseball like a pro, which landed him a scholarship to Georgia Southern. Santana is a twenty-two-year-old thug with a record and warrants who sells weed, steals cars, and trains pit bulls for a living. Did he even finish middle school?"

"Not every girl wants a lame-ass virgin mama's boy for their man." Nahima busted out laughing. "You were Dondrae's first fuck, and he was yours! That is some pitiful shit right there."

Yashia pulled into a parking space in front of the studio and killed the engine. Then she looked at her friend and wrinkled her nose as if somebody had just shit in her car. "Nah, what's some pitiful shit is that you lost your virginity to a street nigga in a stolen car in an alley over in Ridgewood and was bleeding so bad because he rode you like you were an animal that you had to lie and tell your sweet old auntie that your period was on so she could buy you some sanitary napkins because that nigga said he didn't have time to take you to the store!"

"You didn't have to go there, Yashia. That's real fucked up. I trusted you with my business."

"And I haven't told anybody, either. But you ain't gonna sit up in my car and talk shit about my man without me coming for your ass. And anyway, I care about you, Nahima. You're my girl. I just think you are making a big mistake by sneaking around with that Santana dude. You're way too pretty and smart for him. Do you know how many fine-ass guys at our school wanna get with you? Rashawn Gibson is feeling you deep, and every dude at Westwood Park knows it."

"Yeah, but I don't like him or any other little silly boy at our school."

"Look, bestie, you need to let that fool Santana go, because he ain't been nothing but trouble for you since y'all hooked up. Where did you meet him anyway?"

Nahima smiled with a dreamy, faraway look in her eyes. "I saw him showing off a dog he had trained on the Gram. He posted videos of the dog before he trained him and afterward. Bae got skills, girl. He turned that dog from a wild animal into a family pet. The owner paid him seven hundred dollars, too."

"Whatever. You still didn't tell me how y'all met. You saw him on the Gram and then what?"

"I shot him DMs with some pictures from my birthday photo shoot when I saw he was from Ridgewood. Then we started messaging each other back and forth until he asked for my number. That's when we started calling and FaceTiming every day. We finally met face-to-face at Dave & Buster's when we met Kela and her crew there for Cole's birthday party. I sat outside with him in a fire-ass Escalade the whole time except for the first ten minutes after my daddy dropped me off."

"And it was love at first sight, huh?"

"Kinda," Nahima said with a big smile on her face. "We kissed and I let him suck my nipples and eat my pussy. It felt so—"

"Ewww, so this nigga just runs around licking random bitches' pussies? That shit is nasty as hell! Yuck!"

"No, he doesn't do that. He ate my pussy because he knew I was a virgin. Bae said I was special and he wanted to be my first everything. Santana really loves me, Yashia. I know you don't believe it, but he does."

"No, I don't believe that buster loves you. And if you believe it, you're a damn fool. Come on, let's go inside and work on our project."

Chapter Six

"Aw, thanks so much, Zach." Venus swiped at her tears with her fingertips. "I understand. You were already exhausted and pissed when you got here because Nahima hadn't come home. And when you heard her call me a bitch, you just snapped. I get it. So you shook her up a bit, but you didn't kill her. To tell you the truth, I think you put the fear of God in her, and I appreciate it. So there ain't no need for you to apologize to me, because Charles and I understand."

"Yeah, but I still needed to clear the air. And I definitely owe Nahima an apology for choking her. No grown man should ever put his hands on a little girl, period. That's the only reason why I want to take her to breakfast before school tomorrow. I want to tell her I'm sorry."

"I appreciate your concern and the gesture, and so will Charles. Now I don't know how Nahima is going to feel about your invitation for her to spend the weekend with you, Jill, and the kids. She usually likes to hang out at Yashia's house so they can meet up with their friends at the mall or the movie theater. Are you sure you and Jill can handle her for a whole weekend?"

"Yeah, we can handle her. We've got plenty of movies, all the game consoles, and I'll cook or order her favorite foods like I used to do. Uncle Z will show Nahima a good time."

"All that stuff was cool for the old Nahima. It's hard to please the new version of my child no matter how hard you try. That girl is something else."

Zach sighed deeply, and Venus could feel his frustration over the phone. "I know, but I've got to try. I ain't doing it for Nahima, though. She don't deserve my time or attention right now. I'm doing this for my baby boy. I swear Jalen is one of the best things that ever happened to me. I love him so much that it makes my heart hurt. I'll do anything to make my li'l man happy. And a visit from his ratchet-ass big sister will make him happy."

Venus switched the phone from her left ear to the right one. "Okay, let's cross our fingers and hope for a miracle."

"No worries. Aunt Jackie is already praying on it."

"Well, it's already done then. Hallelujah!"

"Thank you, Jesus!"

Zach and Venus shared a laugh.

"Who is it?" Nahima snapped in response to three quick taps on her locked bedroom door.

"It's Uncle Zach. Can I come in please?"

Why is Ike Turner here so early in the morning? He's probably here to jump me again.

Nahima applied one last coat of pastel pink gloss to her lips and turned away from the mirror before she took her sweet time making her way to the door. She unlocked it, turned the knob, and cracked it to stare at her uncle like he was a complete stranger there to do her harm.

"Good morning. I came to take you to IHOP so we can talk before I drop you off at school. Is that cool?"

Surprised, Nahima nodded her head. "I'll meet you downstairs in five minutes."

It was unusually quiet in the cafeteria. Tuesday morning was biscuit-and-gravy day. The ladies at Leesworth always looked forward to the homemade biscuits and brown gravy Ms. Gertie, Mr. Bud, and the rest of the crew served them. They were light, fluffy, and buttery, and they tasted good as hell. Every damn inmate should've been down on her knees thanking Jay for those biscuits and gravy because it was her expert budgeting skills and ability to seal deals that had secured the contact with a company to ship the ingredients for the kitchen crew to prepare the best breakfast of the week. Those biscuits were made from White Lily self-rising flour and buttermilk. Everybody, including the kitchen crew, had hated those bootleg frozen biscuits that tasted like cardboard and the gross powdered milk. Jay had worked like a Hebrew slave and negotiated like Warren Buffett to get Ms. Gertie and her workers what they'd needed. She had made it happen at a cheaper price than the nasty shit they used to use, too.

Jay was damn proud of that accomplishment and many others she had secured for her fellow inmates. Because of her, they now had real sanitary napkins, thick socks, Colgate toothpaste, and other items that incarcerated women never thought they could have. Basic shit like that probably meant nothing to folk on the outside, but to the Leesworth women, they were better than birthday gifts.

"Damn, KiKi, slow down. You over there soppin' up that gravy with that biscuit like you ain't gon' ever eat again."

Jay blinked out of her drifting thoughts and laughed at Gracie. "Leave that girl alone. You know she don't eat no meat, so at least let her enjoy that good ol' gravy." Jay leaned close to her friend and whispered, "Even though Ms. Gertie made it with the grease from that fried bologna we had for dinner last night."

"Aw, man! For real, King?"

Jay didn't confirm or deny her statement. She was too busy laughing and nudging Gracie in her meaty side with her elbow.

KiKi shoved the plate of gravy to the middle of the table with a deep frown on her freckled face, but she continued devouring that biscuit.

"Tell me again how come you don't eat no meat, honey." Gracie smiled at her young vegetarian friend.

"It was the way Asaad was raised. He ain't ate no meat since he was thirteen. So when we got together, I just picked up his ways. I joined the Messiah's Messengers faith. That's Assad's religion. I embraced his political views, took on the vegetarian diet, and everything. And that's how we chose to raise our son, Diali, and our daughter, Iwawae."

"'Cept you ain't raisin' them chirren now 'cause you committed fraud by runnin' them crazy credit card and bank scams 'cause Asaad told you to. Now you in prison while he and his other wife are raisin' your babies."

"You're absolutely right, Ms. Gracie. Thanks so much for reminding me how stupid I am." KiKi grabbed her plate and water bottle and hauled ass from the table with nearby inmates snickering at her back.

When Gracie turned and looked at Jay, she flinched. If a mean mug was money, she'd be paid for life. Jay's expression was hard and ugly on purpose. A blind man could tell she was pissed with her friend.

"Wh . . . what you lookin' at me like that for?" Gracie stuttered.

"You were dead-ass wrong, G. Don't pretend like you don't know, either. You didn't have to go there."

"Well, I didn't lie, did I?"

"Nah, you didn't lie. But just because something is true, you don't have to say it. You're too old for that tenth-grade mean-girl shit. Hell, your ass is old enough to be KiKi's grandma. Instead of stepping on her back while she's already facedown in the dirt, you should be teaching her how to survive in this shithole. You've been in and out of here since the sixties, so you damn sure know the routine." Jay laughed.

Some other inmates sitting near them started laughing as well. They were high-fiving and mumbling to each other, too.

"Go to hell, Kang," Gracie snapped, clearly pissed.

"I'm already here. Tell me to go someplace else, old lady. Hawaii is beautiful all the time even with the volcanoes." Jay placed her hand on her friend's forearm. "You need to find KiKi and apologize to her because she didn't deserve for you to tease her like that. Every bitch in this prison is here for something they're not proud of. We shouldn't rub each other's noses in our shit. Prison life is already hard enough without us being mean to one another for the hell of it."

"Okay, I'll stop by the laundry room later today and tell KiKi I'm sorry. I've gotta meet with them law students first, though."

"Oh, yeah? What are they working on for you?"

"Well, since I'm sixty-two years old and I got a disabled adult child back in Savannah, they may be able to get me outta here early. My baby boy needs me."

Jay twisted her lips and shook her head. "That ain't going to happen, old lady."

"How come?"

"Ain't Robert still with your ex-husband and his wife, where he's been since he was sixteen?"

"Yeah, but my middle daughter, Glenda, said every time she goes over to his daddy's house to see him, he whines and tells her he wants to move out and get his own place so he and his girlfriend can live together. I believe Ray and his wife won't let Robert move out because they don't want to give up his check. That bastard and that tramp he married think they slick."

"Or Ray and his wife may be scared for Robert to move out because of his diabetes, high blood pressure, and the seizures he has sometimes. They can't take care of him if he's living somewhere else than under their roof."

"It don't matter! I'm Robert's mama, and I need to get outta this goddamn place so I can take care of him myself. I want my baby to be happy. Nobody can take care of a child better than his mama. That's how come I'm gonna talk to them law school students to see if they can help me get outta here early. And if they can, I ain't ever comin' back. I swear to God I ain't." Gracie started crying. "And if you have any sense, you would talk to them too, Kang. I done told you they can help you get out on account of your health. You want me to come to your office before I meet with them?"

"Nah, I'm good."

Chapter Seven

Zach's black G 550 SUV rolled to a stop directly in front of Westwood Park Academy. He sneaked a peek at Nahima with a slick side-eye while facing forward. His apology to her over pancakes, cheese eggs, and bacon had landed on a good note. At least, it had seemed like it. But the votes were still being tallied on his invitation for his niece to spend the upcoming weekend with him and his family. Zach was kind of butt hurt that Nahima hadn't agreed to visit her baby brother right out of the gate. A few months ago, he and Venus had found it hard to keep his sister's two biological children apart. Now it felt like he needed to place a bribe on the table in order for Nahima to come and spend time with Jalen.

"I enjoyed hanging out with you," Zach finally said softly when the silence between them became unbearable.

"Yeah, it was cool."

"Call me before Thursday afternoon with your answer so I can get everything ready for your visit. It'll mean the world to Jalen, but if you're not comfortable coming over, I'll understand."

"I'll text you Wednesday night."

"Cool." Reluctantly, Zach leaned over the console and squeezed Nahima's knee and placed a kiss on her cheek at the same time. "No matter what, I will always love you, pumpkin."

"Me too. I'll hit you up Wednesday."

A heavy-hearted uncle watched his one and only niece—a child he had devoted his all to—exit his car before he drove away. Zach wanted to cry and drown himself in his pain over the spirit of Jayla Simone King that had somehow sneaked inside of Nahima and taken control. It was burning a hole straight through his soul and ripping his heart into a billion pieces. Indeed, it was the harshest reality he'd ever had to face. Regardless of the never-ending love, energy, time, and resources Venus, Charles, and the entire Dudley and King families under Zach's influence had invested in Nahima, it had not been enough. Jay's blood and her spirit, the very essence of her, were much too powerful. There was nothing the people who truly loved the child and wanted the very best for her could do to kill or even weaken what had been passed down to Nahima from her mother's genes through her DNA.

Nahima was as much a part of Jay as Jay was a part of her even though they hadn't met or touched each other in almost sixteen years. And even then, the innocent baby who'd been deliberately rejected and denied the love of her biological mother was believed to have been divinely protected and immune to the vexed spirit hidden deeply in the blood pumping through her veins. However, their connection was natural, super innate even, created by the hands of Almighty God. Jay's spirit had defied the odds, mysteriously reaching through the barriers of time and distance to settle in the depths of Nahima's soul. The family had been deceived to believe that love and separation could protect her from the seed that had created her.

Tears that Zach hadn't even realized he was shedding reached his lips. The taste of salt rescued him from sinking deeper into the dark reality that had come to haunt him. He had never seen it coming. God knew he hadn't. Surely, the countless prayers Aunt Jackie had lifted up to heaven on behalf of her family had covered Nahima too. The power of man could never compare to the matchless, sovereign power of the one and only true and living God. Or were they all being punished for how Nahima had been conceived and because of the type of relationship Venus and Jay once shared?

"Nah. No way," Zach mumbled as his tears continued to fall. "Evil won't win. I'll kick the devil's ass and bury him in hell to save my niece."

"So how old are your minor children you wish to be reunited with if the Justice Unlimited Project's efforts result in your early release, Ms. King?"

"Um, actually, I'm only interested in my baby, a little boy. He's seven years old. I named him King, but my brother changed his name to Jalen when he and his wife adopted him. So his legal name is Jalen Gavin King. I only got to spend one day with him before that goddamn social worker ripped him out of my arms. It was the worst day of my life. I swear to God it was. I wanted to die. In a lot of ways, I did."

Every word Jay spoke before she broke down in tears was true. Of all the terrible experiences she had encountered over her forty-two years on the planet, losing her baby boy had definitely been the one that had killed her spirit. The death of Gavin, the child's father, had hit her pretty hard, too. But his death was like a mosquito bite on the arm compared to the silver dagger straight through the heart she'd felt when she lost her newborn son. Jay could hardly catch her breath at the moment just thinking about it after all these years.

"Okay," the young brunette with deep raven eyes mumbled as she typed fast, entering more information into her computer. "Little Jalen was adopted by his maternal uncle and aunt. Have you maintained contact with him? Does your brother or his wife bring the child here to visit you? Do you and your son exchange letters, or does he draw pictures at school and send them here?"

"No. To tell you the truth, after the system took my baby away from me, I got real, real down. I fell into a deep depression and withdrew from the whole damn world. It's a terrible thing for a woman to give birth to a baby in prison when she's struggling with a medical condition that's getting worse every day and most of her family has turned their backs on her. Then my baby's father got killed, which felt like somebody had tied cement blocks to my legs when I was already drowning in the ocean. Hard times in life like that make you weak, damn near kill you. So I'm not about to sit up here and lie to you. I didn't want to see my son because it was too damn painful."

"I totally understand, Ms. King. No one within the JUP will judge you for your past decisions. We're only concerned about your current situation, and from everything you've told me so far, you appear to be an ideal candidate for our services. Your poor health, along with some other key factors, increases your odds. Of course, we'll have to do some research on your case before we accept you. This interview today is the first step of our intake process. So please continue. I'd like to hear more about your son."

"Like I said, my mind was so messed up after giving birth to my baby and the death of his father, I told my aunt to tell my brother to never bring my son here. It would've put the final nail in my coffin to hold him and smell that fresh new-baby scent and see his perfect smile for a two-hour visit every now and then, only to have to watch him leave without knowing when or if I would see him again. I couldn't handle it, so I refused to put my baby boy on my visitation list. So my brother's wife, the raggedy bitch she is, started sending me pictures of him. My sweet baby boy was so pretty and growing fast. At first, those pictures made me happy. I used to actually smile, and I would look forward to hearing my name during mail call because I knew I was going to get a new picture of Jalen. Then my health dipped lower, so I had to face reality. I accepted the fact that I was going to die in this godforsaken cage. What good was it going to do me to keep torturing myself with pictures of my beautiful baby when he would never get to know me, huh? So I stopped going to mail call and eventually told my aunt to let my brother and his wife know I didn't want any more pictures, updates, or anything else pertaining to my son. I even tore up all the pictures of him I had posted on my wall. I was done. I let him go."

After a few seconds of deafening silence, Jay wiped her eyes and nose with the sleeve of her sweatshirt and looked up to stare at the law student. All of a sudden, there was a distinct shift in the atmosphere as the sound of her fingers tapping the computer's keyboard filled in the quietness. Jay was shocked when saw tears rolling down the young lady's cheeks when she finally lifted her head. Her thin body was trembling with emotion, no doubt in response to what she'd just heard. Jay hadn't meant to push the law student's sympathy button at all. She had simply told her the truth. The story was sad for sure, even though Jay had brought all of the misfortune into her life. Every bad decision, evil plot, and vengeful act all belonged to her. But if the law student could find sympathy for Jay somewhere among the wreckage of her destroyed existence, she would gladly take it.

The young lady cleared her throat. "Like I said earlier, our team will thoroughly research your case to determine if you fit the criteria to receive our services. Until that time, I need you to identify a family member or a close friend on the outside who would be willing to serve as your resource person or liaison, if you will. He or she will be expected to gather certain documents, make contact with key individuals beyond our reach, and contribute financially to your cause. Of course, there is no charge for our services because we are a nonprofit organization. However, the work we do sometimes requires filing fees, postage costs, copying, and other small things of that nature. So we tap a client's resource person in the event our funds are low."

"I understand."

"Great. Do you know someone on the outside who'd be willing to act as your resource person, like maybe your brother or another relative? What about a friend or your pastor?"

"Can I get back with you on that?"

"Sure, you can." The young lady removed a card from her purse and offered it to Jay. "Take this. My name is Amanda Lewis, and you can reach me at this number and email address once you confirm a resource person. If you can't find anyone, we may be able to assign you an advocate."

Jay took the card. "Thanks."

Chapter Eight

Nahima's dream to become a world-renowned fashion designer was very much attainable because the girl was super talented. Her love for quality apparel and her keen eye for fashion were like no other. Nahima had the ability to throw together an outfit suitable for any runway around the world with her eyes closed. Thank God Venus had noticed her child's gift early on, because the discovery had prompted her to invest in private sewing lessons and amateur design classes for her daughter whenever and wherever they'd been offered.

Now Nahima was the fashion icon at Westwood Park Academy. Not only did a large percentage of female students seek the freshman fashionista's wardrobe advice, but even some of the teachers as well. Mrs. Caroline Garrett, one of the guidance counselors, did too. The future fashion designer to the stars could wear a pair of riding boots with a sundress and an African head wrap smack dead in the middle of December, and her loyal following at Westwood Park and on social media would mimic the look in droves the next day. Nahima was a natural-born stylist and highly regarded trendsetter.

God had blessed her to design and create, too. She could sketch and sew any garment for females of all sizes, body shapes, ages, and cultures. And it was a good thing she had such a gift, because there were times when the fashion diva just couldn't find the right piece to complete a certain look for a specific occasion. Those were the times when she would work her magic with her sketchpad and her fancy, computerized, state-of-art, professional sewing machine that was so damn expensive that it was her only gift from Santa two Christmases ago. Nahima would create the perfect article of clothing to fulfill her fashion fantasy in the blink of an eye.

The interchangeable jumpsuit she'd envisioned for the class project she and Yashia were working on was one of her dreams. Even their design teacher, Mrs. Moran, was impressed with the idea, the sketch, and the mock sample the girls had submitted a few weeks ago. She was so encouraging of Nahima's efforts and had told her more times than she could count how talented she was. But it was time for lunch, and Mrs. Moran wanted her star student and Yashia out of her classroom so she could lock up and enjoy the remainder of her forty-five minutes of leisure time. She had already warned them twice.

"Just give us five more minutes, Mrs. Moran. I want to finish sewing this beaded appliqué in the sleeve."

"You asked me for five more minutes ten minutes ago, Nahima. I appreciate your enthusiasm, darling. Believe me, I do. But I've got a tuna fish sandwich waiting for me, and I'd like to eat it while I read the final chapters of my Germaine Solomon romance novel. So pack up and get out."

Nahima and Yashia laughed at their favorite teacher as they placed the unfinished jumpsuit in the leather garment bag and cleaned up their work space. They then headed out the door en route to the locker they shared on the 11B hall of the building. After that, the BFFs would make their way to the cafeteria, where they'd join their clique at their usual table. Of course, Nahima would visit the deli bar to grab a turkey sandwich with two slices of provolone cheese and light mayo on wheat bread, while Yashia would go through the line to check out the special on the hot bar for the day. She knew the Tuesday menu by heart and would more than likely choose the tacos over the meatloaf and mashed potatoes.

When Nahima and Yashia reached their designated table, their girls Kela and Ryan were pigging out while deeply indulging in animated conversation. They took their usual seats.

"Where y'all heifers been?" Ryan asked before she bit into her greasy chili dog.

Yashia rolled her eyes. "We stayed behind a few minutes to work on our design project."

"Are you talking about the secret masterpiece y'all won't tell us about?" Ryan laughed. "It must be made of platinum, because not even your classmates know what it is."

"I ain't mad with y'all," Kela chimed in. "I admire the way Nahima handles her fashion grind. She's gonna make us rich and proud one day."

"True dat! True dat! The House of Nahima International Inc. is gonna be all that and then some. I'm gonna be paid, and every little girl around the world will be rocking my style, and their mamas too!"

The whole clique cracked up laughing and exchanged fist bumps, all agreeing with their girl's prediction of her very successful and financially sound future. They always spoke of their dreams and supported each other's endeavors.

"Oh, snap!" Kela blurted out behind the hand she'd placed in front of her mouth. "Here comes Rashawn again. He done walked past this table three times already looking for you, Nahima. Please give the brother a chance. Damn."

"I ain't got nothing for Rashawn, so he needs to keep it moving."

Yashia's smirk and sharp eye roll didn't go unnoticed by her BFF, but Nahima decided to let it slide. The other clique members must've noticed the vibe and body language bouncing between the two girls, because they all got quiet seconds before Rashawn reached their table.

Damn, this nigga looks good in them black jeans and red Falcons jersey. But he ain't Santana.

"What's up, Miss Lawson-Morris? You good?"

"I'm fine, Rashawn. What's going on with you?"

"Nothing much. I'm just trying to confirm if Quay is really doing a concert for the home team next month. Have you heard or what?"

"Yeah, he'll be at State Farm Arena one day next month for two shows," Ryan, the gossiper of the crew, announced. "My uncle is good friends with a man named Breeze, who is Quay's manager. He's Lieutenant Governor Ebony Robinson's brother, too. Anyway, Breeze told my Uncle Flip that Quay is gonna kick off his world tour right here in the A next month."

"Well, thank you, Gayle King, for that very detailed report. Girl, your nosy ass knows everything and everybody!" Kela teased.

All of the girls started kee-keeing and slapping hands at their girl's expense, but Ryan didn't seem the least bit fazed. Everybody at Westwood Park knew she was their one-chick media source, and she had proudly embraced her role.

Rashawn licked his lips coolly and smiled. "Thanks for the tip, Ryan the reporter. Now I know to look out for a pair of front-row tickets so I can take some lucky honey."

"Oooh, girl, did you see how he was looking at you when he said that, Nahima?" Kela screeched the moment he walked away. "The tall double-fudge cupcake wants you. I could smell the lust slicing though his Polo Red cologne."

"That's too bad, because like I said, I ain't got a damn thing for Rashawn Gibson. Plus he can't hardly afford no front-row seats to the Quay concert, so he needs to stop trying to flex like he's ballin' out like that."

"Humph, his daddy is a doctor, a pediatrician, and his mom is a housewife who dresses so fly that not even you can style her bougie ass, Nah-Nah," Ryan reported.

"I don't care. I ain't feelin' Rashawn, so let it go."

"Fuck all the nonsense. I wanna go to that concert. I hope Dondrae and I can scrape up enough coins to buy two cheap tickets way up high somewhere in the ghetto section of the arena. I don't care if we have to sit on top of the damn building. I just wanna see Quay with my bae."

"I ain't got no bae, but I wanna see Quay too." Kela looked at Ryan. "Let's go together. My granddaddy will probably buy us some tickets for a couple of welfare seats close to Yashia and Dondrae if I sneak him some sweets and a pint of gin."

"Yeah, I'm with it," Ryan shot back, laughing. "But don't blame me if your papa falls into a diabetic coma from all that sugar and alcohol."

Kela giggled and slapped hands with Ryan before the table fell silent.

Three pairs of eyes immediately zoomed in on Nahima. She returned the group's stare, unblinking. It was just like her girls to try to pressure her to do something they wanted her to do without considering what she wanted. She was cool with Kela and Ryan pushing for her to go to the concert, because they had no clue that she wasn't feeling the idea because Santana wouldn't be able to tag along. There was no way in hell that he would want to hang around a group of silly-ass high school kids. He had to check her sometimes for acting like a little girl, so he would go off on Ryan for running her mouth and Kela for giggling about every damn thing all night for sure. And no doubt, Santana would end up slapping Yashia in the mouth for her slick tongue before the concert even kicked off. And he wouldn't give a damn if Dondrae was there with her, either. Hell, he would throw hands at him too. That's just how gangsta Santana was.

With her thoughts sorted out, Nahima mentally dismissed her girls, especially Yashia with her shady ass. Pissed, she left her clique and her untouched turkey and cheese sandwich at the table even as her stomach growled loud as hell.

"Who was that, Zachary?" Jill asked the moment her husband ended his phone conversation.

"It was Nahima. She wants to spend this coming weekend with us. I can't lie. I'm shocked shitless."

Jalen giggled and pointed an accusatory finger at Zach. "Daddy, you said a cuss word. Now you gotta put a dollar in the potty-mouth jar."

Zach reached into the pocket of his green scrubs pants and pulled out a folded stack of cash. "Daddy needs some change. All I have is a five-dollar bill."

Zion walked over, quickly snatched the crisp bill bearing Abe Lincoln's somber mug, and ran off with it laughing.

"Girl, get your butt back in here with my money!"

"Why? You're going to cuss at least four more times before you leave for work. So I'm going to drop it in the potty-mouth jar in advance." The sassy lone daughter in her sibling group flashed a smile so cute that the only thing her dad could do was shake his head and smile back.

"Zachary, don't mind the children and their shenanigans. Tell me what Nahima called to say."

"I told you I invited her to spend the weekend with us when I took her to breakfast before school the other day. Jalen had asked me to invite her over to bake cookies with him. She didn't answer right away, but she promised to let me know later."

"So she called to say she's coming over tomorrow for a weekend visit, eh?"

"Yeah, and I'm excited."

"Me too, Daddy," Jalen said in his tiny, raspy voice as he eased up next to Zach from out of nowhere and wrapped his arm around his long legs. "I love my big, big sister."

"Since Nahima is coming over, I need to go grocery shopping because she'll want jerk chicken and spicy beef patties."

"And don't forget about the plantains and ginger roots for the ginger beer."

"I won't. I'll get all of her favorite things. We're going to have fun this weekend like we used to before life changed."

"Yeah," Zach agreed, smiling. "It'll be like old times."

Chapter Nine

"I'm only going over there so I can get some money from my uncle since he's feeling all guilty and shit for how he treated me the other day."

"How the fuck you know that nigga's gonna just throw money at you all willy-nilly?"

"I know my uncle, bae. I saw that special look in his eyes he used to have for me when I was a little girl while he was getting all mushy and humble at IHOP. He still loves me, and I believe he's sorry for putting his hands on me and talking all that shit about killing me for acting like Jay. Trust me, Uncle Zach is about to make all the right moves with me this weekend."

Santana looked over at Yashia sitting in her car after she blew the horn and gestured for Nahima to come on. Clearly, she didn't appreciate him eyeballing her, so she leaned on the horn and stuck her head out the window with a smirk on her face. Santana flipped her off before taking a long drag on the Black & Mild he'd lit a few minutes ago.

"I can't stand that high-yella bitch. You need to axe her ass. Ain't you got some other friends with their own rides?"

"Nah. Me and Yashia are the only two in our crew whose families got money. Kela and Ryan don't even have fathers, and they live in Section 8 housing in the same crime-infested neighborhood. Ryan's mama is a hairstylist, and she makes good money because she's got mega clients. But she's raising six kids by herself with no money from either one of her baby daddies. At least Kela can depend on her granddaddy sometimes to help her mama with her and her two little sisters."

"Damn. So you stuck ridin' with a bougie-ass, high-yella bitch with no respect for your man?"

"Yashia ain't that bad. We've been riding for each other since we were little kids at church. Her parents have always been cool with my parents and my uncle, so we've been tight forever. Yashia's cool, and she's always got my back."

"Well, I don't like her."

Nahima moved in closer to Santana, pressing her breasts into his chest before she kissed his lips. "She's the only person in my life who I can depend on to help me see you, bae."

"Whatever. Anyway, all I'm worryin' 'bout right now is you gettin' money from your uncle so I can get my burner outta the pawn shop. Sarge let me hold some old piece-of-shit .45 to do a few jobs. But that shit is old as fuck. It's a good thing I didn't run into no trouble. That nigga got me workin' with heat the cowboys used to fight the Indians back in the Old West. That's some bullshit. I need my Glock outta hock, so you better get me some money from your uncle."

"I got you, bae, but I got to go now so I can beat my mom home. She'll start trippin' if I ain't at the house when she gets there. I'll call you."

"Bet."

Nahima power walked across the Church's Chicken and got into Yashia's car. "You didn't have to keep blowing your horn like that."

"Look, I did you a favor by bringing you here to see that nigga in the first place, so don't say shit to me about me blowing the horn in my car. This sneaking-around shit is getting old. If that nigga loves you so much, maybe he needs to start picking you up and taking you to his house so y'all can hang out."

"Did I clown you when you were dragging me around everywhere to throw your parents off so they wouldn't know you were fucking Dondrae?"

"No. But I didn't have you in the hood in gang territory sitting in no damn car, either, did I? We were either at Dondrae's house or at his cousin's spot where you were comfortable in front of a TV with food."

"My situation with Santana is different from yours and Dondrae's, and you know it."

"Yeah, I do. Our situations are different as hell. One is a regular teenage, high school sweetheart deal, and the other one is a toxic relationship involving a grown-ass man with a record making a fool out of a fifteen-year-old girl who ain't got a clue. Now I'll let you figure out which one is which."

Nahima shut down mentally as she always did whenever she and Yashia argued about her relationship with Santana. She turned her entire body to the right to stare out the window to see old, abandoned houses, buildings covered with gang art, and children balancing backpacks on their bodies as they walked past dope boys on the corners with the bass of rap music booming in the background.

Yashia didn't understand what it felt like to be in love with a man. What she and Dondrae shared was puppy love. That's why she was always hating and talking shit about her and Santana. She was just clueless. And so were Nahima's parents, especially her mom. Instead of asking her only child if she was having sex and discussing it with her, Venus had made her a doctor's appointment for next week to get on birth control. That was cool, though. Now she and Santana wouldn't have to worry about finding money to buy condoms anymore. Nahima smiled at the thought, because she had been wondering how it would feel to have unprotected sex with Santana. She would find out as soon as the birth control kicked in in her system.

Jay couldn't keep her mind on the monthly expenditure report she had been working on all day. Usually, she would knock it out in two or three hours, but not today. A million thoughts about the meeting she'd had with Amanda, the law school student, were distracting her from the simple task. Jay kind of hated that she had let Gracie talk her into sitting down and telling her story to the young girl. She had come to grips with her plight a few years ago, realizing she would never leave Leesworth alive. But since the meeting with Amanda, a tiny spark of hope had been ignited. What if she could actually get an emergency medical release? Should she even try?

Jay was still mentally weighing the pros and cons of even putting forth the effort. It wouldn't be easy for sure, because Jay didn't have anyone on the outside who would be willing to grind for her. Aunt Jackie was too holy and righteous to sign on to her scheme to use Jalen as a pawn to spring her out of prison. She, more than anyone else alive, knew the truth about her son's conception, birth, brief stay in foster care, and adoption. Aunt Jackie also had knowledge about Jay refusing to see Jalen even after Zach and Jill had adopted him, because she had volunteered to bring the child to the prison for visitation many times. All offers had been rejected.

Jay leaned back in her chair and stared at the ceiling, recalling how Amanda had told her she wouldn't be penalized by the organization for any of her past decisions. The girl had even cried after hearing her story. That had to be a good sign. All Jay needed was one person on the outside to sign on to help her, but the truth was she didn't have anyone. Besides Aunt Jackie, she only maintained contact with Nahima. Jay had cut ties with everyone else, including her father. When she was wallowing in self-pity after Gavin's death, she'd stopped calling Wallace and had allowed his letters to be returned to him by her corrections counselor.

Jay opened her desk drawer and found Amanda's card. As the official inmate accountant and business manager, she had certain privileges. She didn't have to stand in line to use one of the few computers in the library like all of the other women. She could check her email in her office anytime she wanted Monday through Friday between the hours of eight in the morning and five in the evening. Her phone privileges were on point, too, since she had one in her office. However, Jay's call reach was limited and subjected to preapproval by the warden's office. So she couldn't just pick up the phone on any given day and hit up her family members and friends whenever she wanted to. It didn't work like that.

As luck would have it, Sheftall had been kind and lenient toward Jay when it came to her phone privileges ever since she'd learned that her trusted numbers cruncher and her daughter were now in constant contact. Obviously, the warden realized that a happy inmate made a happy worker. So to keep Jay content, Sheftall had given her the green light to make all of her allotted fifteen-minute personal calls on the phone in her small office on Mondays, Wednesdays, Fridays, and most Saturdays, as well as on holidays and family birthdays. That way, she could avoid the long lines and fights with the other inmates over the ten phones in the communal area.

Today was Thursday, so Jay wasn't allowed to make a personal call without facing the consequences of a demerit on her behavior report. But she could shoot Amanda an email. Without a second thought, she logged on to her Leesworth email account. After typing the email address from the card on the addressee's line, she inhaled a long, deep breath and exhaled it slowly. With a clear head and her heart filled with emotions of all kinds, she placed her fingers on the keyboard and began to type.

Dear Amanda,

This is Jayla King, the inmate at Leesworth suffering from renal failure, cirrhosis of the liver, and depression. I am reaching out to let you know that my daughter, Nahima Lawson-Morris, will be my resource person. She will do anything to help with my case. She is young, so she may need some assistance, like an advocate like you mentioned. If that isn't possible, I don't know what I'll do.

Chapter Ten

"Nahima! Nahima! You came to bake cookies with me!" Jalen ran down the steps and leaped into his sister's arms.

After making a perfect catch, she lifted his little body to her chest, closed her eyes, and squeezed him so damn tight that he shrieked and giggled. Nahima loved her little brother more than any other person in the universe. Shameful tears slid through her closed eyelids when she thought about how she had allowed her ill feelings for Uncle Zach and Jill to keep her from visiting Jalen for so many weeks. She quickly made a vow to never let anyone or anything come between her and her baby brother again.

Jalen placed a palm on each of Nahima's cheeks and gazed into her tearful eyes. He flashed a snaggletoothed grin. "How come you're crying? Am I too heavy?"

"No. You are perfect. I'm just happy to see you." She kissed his pointy nose and smiled. "Where are your two front top teeth, li'l man?"

"Mommy pulled them out because they were wiggly and wobbly, and I couldn't bite my food. I was a big boy, too. I didn't even cry. I wouldn't let Daddy pull my teeth because his hands are too big and strong. The tooth fairy came and left ten dollars under my pillow when I was sleeping. I put it in my Black Panther piggy bank."

Nahima couldn't help but laugh. Jalen's smile was contagious, missing teeth and all. He was the cutest little boy ever, and she could listen to him talk all day long in his sweet, raspy voice. She just couldn't stand to hear him call Jill his "mommy," because she wasn't. The sound of it irked the shit out of Nahima.

"What's up, Nahima?" Zachary Jr. greeted his cousin as he made his way down the steps.

She placed Jalen on his feet and smiled at him with her hand extended for a fist bump. "Dude, you are getting tall. What'chu eating, yo?"

"I eat my veggies and lots of fruit, and I drink milk."

"Where is Zion?"

"She's upstairs in her room." He turned around and yelled, "Hey, Z, get off the computer and come downstairs! Nahima is here!"

"I'll go get her," Jalen said before he broke out running like the Flash and dashed up the stairs.

Nahima walked toward the great room, and Zachary Jr. followed her. They sat down on the love seat together.

"So what's up, Junior? What'chu been up to? You got a girlfriend?"

He looked toward the kitchen door with a sly smile on his face. "There's this one girl at my school named Apple who likes me. We text all the time, but we're just friends. My dad said I'm too young to have a girlfriend."

Nahima rolled her eyes to the ceiling and twisted her lips in defiance of her uncle. *Uggghhh! He's always in somebody else's business. He needs to worry about that Jamaican ho he married after he took her from Jay.*

"I guess your dad's right. You're just eleven. Wait until you turn fifteen before you start dealing with the honeys, because love is complicated."

"How do you know? Do you have a boyfriend?" Zach Jr.'s eyes ballooned while he waited for his cousin's answer.

"I sure do, and he's a lot older than me, so my parents and Uncle Zach don't know about him. So don't speak on it. Okay?"

"I won't say anything to anybody. I know how to keep a secret, but Zion runs her mouth all the time. Dad said she can talk the milk out of a cow." He laughed. "So what's your dude's name? I told you about Apple, so—"

"I need to let you all up in my business, huh?"

"Yeah, kinda."

"Well, his name is Santana Bridges. His mom is Puerto Rican, and his dad is African American. He's twenty-two and—"

"Whoa! Are you for real? Dude is really twenty-two?"

"Yeah. I told you he was older than me. What's the problem?"

Zachary Jr. wasn't smiling anymore. His serious expression made Nahima feel some type of way. She immediately regretted discussing her love life with her kid cousin. What the hell kinda shit had she been on? She'd definitely made a big mistake, but she had no one else she could talk to about Santana besides Yashia, and she hated him and always gave her major attitude whenever his name came up in their conversations.

"Hey, you ain't gonna snitch on me, are you? Remember, you promised to keep it on lock."

Zachary Jr. eyed Nahima with a somber look that made her feel dirty. "I won't snitch, but I don't think a teenage girl should date a twenty-two-year-old man. Why can't he date a lady his own age?"

Before Nahima could give her cousin an answer, Jalen entered the great room and flopped down in her lap, giggling. "I brought Zion downstairs to you."

Nahima and Zachary Jr. looked over their shoulders to find Zion smiling at them.

"What's up, Z? Come give me a hug. It seems like I haven't seen you in a thousand years. You get prettier and prettier every time I see you, li'l mama." She opened her arms to her little cousin.

"I'm glad you came to spend the weekend with us," Zion whispered, hugging Nahima. "I changed the color of my room and got some new pictures and stuff. I hope you'll like it."

"I know I will, pretty girl."

"Man, it smells good in here!"

"We're baking cookies, Daddy! That's why it smells so good in Mommy's kitchen." Jalen smiled from his seat on top of the center island before he licked cookie dough from the wooden spoon in his hand.

Zach walked through the kitchen happier than he'd felt in a long time. Having Nahima in his home spending time with Jalen made his heart tap dance. His li'l dawg was on top of the world too, which gave him life. He and Jill were going to have one hell of a time getting his little ass to bed tonight. He didn't want Nahima out of his sight. With or without Zion's approval, Jalen would be an extra guest in her newly redecorated bedroom this weekend. Zach pinched his li'l dawg's nose before he turned and placed a hand on Nahima's shoulder.

"The aroma is making my mouth water, pumpkin. What kind of cookies are y'all baking?"

"Those are sugar cookies in the oven. We're mixing peanut butter cookies now."

"Humph," Zach grunted as he opened a bottle of Heineken beer. "I didn't know you were going to bake peanut butter cookies, pumpkin. Please be careful, and make sure you clean up good. Keep the sugar cookies totally separated from the peanut butter cookies, too."

"No problem. But why do I have to keep the cookies separated?"

"Your cousin, Zion, is allergic to most nuts but especially peanuts. If she even touches something with peanuts in it, she breaks out with itchy hives and her tongue swells up, which makes it dangerously hard for her to breathe. It's really scary. So please be extra careful, all right?"

"I promise to be careful, Uncle Zach. Trust me."

"Okay, Daddy, I won't let Zion eat any of my peanut butter cookies."

"That's my li'l dawg."

Jalen giggled and gave his daddy a pound. "And you're my great big dawg."

"I'm so glad you and Nahima made up and she's spending time with y'all this weekend, Zach."

"I figured you'd be happy. You want to come over and let's make it a mini, weekend family reunion? I'll come and scoop you up."

"Um . . . er . . . this won't be a good weekend. Let's do it another time. I've got some things to do, baby."

"What kinds of things, Auntie?"

"Zachary Sean King, don't you be asking me no questions! It ain't none of your business what I gotta do! If I have to roll pennies, that's my business! I'm grown! Goodbye!"

"Auntie? Auntie!" He flipped the phone over and looked at the blank screen as if the dial tone in his ear weren't enough. "She hung up on me. What the hell?"

Zach laughed, leaning back in his designated chair that he called his throne, located in his basement man cave. It was a custom-built brown Italian leather deluxe recliner with a lower lumbar-roll feature, a heating system, a thermal cup holder, an electrical socket, and an extended leg rest. Physically, he was quite comfortable, but he had a brain pinch that had him feeling a bit uneasy on the mental side.

Aunt Jackie didn't spend the night at Zach's house often because he rarely asked her to. He saved his invitations for whenever he and Jill needed to get away from the kiddies for some "grown-folk time." It had been a minute since Zach had taken wifey on a sexcation, which meant Aunt Jackie hadn't crashed at King's Kastle, the nickname he'd given his home, in a while. But this weekend was a special occasion. Nahima had decided to leave her stank-ass attitude at home and was at her uncle's house baking cookies with her baby brother. Aunt Jackie should've been running over to Zach's crib to see her, shouting hallelujah, but she wasn't coming, and he wondered why the hell not.

Chapter Eleven

"Goodbye!" Aunt Jackie pressed the button to end the call and stuffed her cell phone inside the pocket of her apron as her heart raced.

Zach had ticked her off, questioning her about her weekend plans. Who the heck did he think he was? The last time she'd checked, she was still his aunt, the woman who had raised him and his sister, which gave her rank over him. Therefore, he had no right or business to ask her a doggone thing about her personal life.

After a quick glimpse in the mirror on her dresser, Aunt Jackie left her bedroom to check on dinner. The heavenly aroma of her famous stuffed Cornish hens met her before she even reached the kitchen. She smiled, knowing she had outdone herself on the special meal. Her turnip greens were scrumptious per usual. She had already done a little taste test. The baked seven-cheese mac and cheese she was known for all around her neighborhood and her church was in the warmer. That thing was the best kitchen gadget ever. It was a Christmas gift from Zach and Jill. In addition to the mac and cheese, the warmer also held the fried corn, candied yams, and black-eyed peas. The potato salad had been chilling in the refrigerator since last night. Dessert would be Aunt Jackie's award-winning pecan pie and her mama's whipping-cream pound cake. Both would taste mighty fine with the French vanilla ice cream she'd picked up from Kroger at the last minute. For sure, this was a feast fit for an African king.

Sneaking a peek at her beautiful golden brown Cornish hens, Aunt Jackie's thoughts floated back to Zach. Maybe she'd acted a little too snippy toward him. He had only been trying to include her in the family fun going on at his house this weekend. She couldn't deny he'd sounded excited. But that gave him no right to pry into her business or imply that her weekend plans weren't important. If only he knew . . .

Aunt Jackie glanced down at her watch. Instantly, she caught a case of the bubble gut. It had been more years than she could count since she'd felt like this. But she liked it, sweaty palms, heart flutters, and all. Just because she was a chaste woman of a certain age, nobody could judge her for having natural feelings and enjoying life on her own terms. In fact, she deserved to have a little fun in her golden years. After all, she had made plenty of sacrifices and denied herself lots of pleasure for others, more specifically, Zach and Jay. Now it was time for her to spread her wings and soar.

"Jesus!" Aunt Jackie gasped when the doorbell rang, startling her.

Nervously, she untied her apron, removing it from her waist before placing it on the countertop. She took a deep breath and left the kitchen feeling excited with a hint of anxiety. As far as she was concerned, her solid size-sixteen frame looked good in the simple black jumpsuit with short cold-shoulder sleeves she'd ordered from Roaman's online catalogue. If God hadn't wanted her to be short and voluptuous, He wouldn't have made her that way, she concluded as she got closer to her front door. Out of habit, she raked her fingers through her salt-and-pepper shoulder-length sister locks before she unlocked the door and opened it.

"Good evening, Jackie."

The rich, bottom-bass timbre would be her undoing someday. God, help her. But at the moment, it just made her heart do a hallelujah dance and her cheeks flush. His cologne was the devil. Its woodsy-citrus scent made her weak in the knees, as if her arthritis weren't enough.

"Good evening, Oscar. Come on in," she half sang and half spoke as she stepped aside to allow him to enter the house.

"These are for you." With a smile, he handed her a dozen long-stemmed pink roses wrapped in green cellophane.

"Awww, thank you, Oscar. They're so pretty." She accepted the flowers and inhaled their aroma. "And they smell like the Garden of Eden."

"You're welcome. A pretty woman deserves pretty flowers." He leaned down and kissed her lips softly.

You better be glad I'm saved, sanctified, and filled with the Holy Ghost, or I would probably jump your bones!

"Um, why don't you make yourself comfortable in the dining room, Oscar? You know your way around the house. I'm going to find a vase for my pretty roses. I want them in the bedroom so I can smell them as I fall asleep every night as long as they live."

"All right, but I'm going to stop by the bathroom to wash my hands first."

"That's fine," Aunt Jackie said before she walked toward the den.

Oscar was a blessing from God. He was tall, handsome, and smart, he had his own money, and he loved the Lord with all his heart. The brother still had all of his original teeth, too, and he had huge hands and feet. The icing on the cake was that sexy bald head of his. Oscar's dark complexion reminded Aunt Jackie of a brown M&M. And just like the popular candy pieces, he was sweet to her every day the good Lord gave them. What more could a mature Christian woman ask for? The retired high school principal had an old sista ready to go back to school to learn a few things.

Have mercy!

Aunt Jackie found an empty vase on the bookshelf in the den. She hurried to her bedroom with it and her roses in tow, where she went into the en suite bathroom and filled the vase halfway with water from the sink. Then she arranged the roses inside the oblong crystal vase before placing it on the nightstand on the left side of her bed. Aunt Jackie admired her flowers as a vision of the man who'd so graciously given them to her appeared in her mind's eye. Dinner and quality time this evening would be the highlight of her weekend. And Zach wanted her to come over and hang out with him, Jill, their three children, and Nahima? Not tonight!

"I thought we were supposed to be sharing this cake, baby." Oscar looked down at Jackie's fork sitting unused on the table. "I already ate the pie and ice cream by myself. Now I need your help with this slice of cake so it won't go to waste."

Aunt Jackie followed his eyes to her clean fork. Sighing, she explained, "I had every intention to help you eat the cake, Oscar, but there's no more room in my stomach. I shouldn't have eaten that second helping of potato salad, huh?"

"Nah, I can't blame you for that, honey. That was the most delicious potato salad I've ever tasted in my life. As a matter of fact, I hope you'll put a healthy helping of it in my doggie bag if you don't mind."

"You know I will. I'll even put the rest of this cake and a few more slices in as well."

"Thank you, sugar." Oscar placed his fork on the table and picked up a napkin to wipe his mouth. Eyeing his dinner date, he grinned like he had just struck oil in Saudi Arabia. "I thank God every day for allowing me to find you. Of course, I thank Him for Wallace, too, because he was the vessel God used to bring us together. You're everything he told me you were and so much more."

"I'm blessed to have you in my life too, Oscar. And I agree with you. God definitely used Wallace, of all people, to hook us two old crows together." Aunt Jackie laughed. "It's strange that Wallace King actually played Cupid for me."

"Why is that so strange, Jackie? Is it because he was once your brother-in-law?"

"Yeah, that's one of the reasons. The other one is hard for me to admit, but I might as well say it because God already knows my heart."

Oscar lifted Aunt Jackie's hand from the table and laced his long fingers through her much shorter, stubby ones. "Say it, sweetheart. You know you can tell me anything."

"It's just that I spent so many years harboring ill feelings in my heart for Wallace. I didn't have it in me to hate him, but God knows I tried. I resented him so much that I wouldn't even let Zach say the word 'Daddy' even when he was too young and innocent to understand what was going on all around him. My poor, sweet baby. All Zach knew was he missed his mommy and daddy. I was wrong to keep him from talking about Wallace, Oscar. I was dead wrong."

"I would never judge you for the way you felt back then. Wallace killed your sister. It was a mistake, but that didn't make it hurt any less. You were young and living a carefree life you'd planned for yourself, and then all of a sudden, you were the caretaker of two babies. Your world got turned upside down. I understand."

"I thank God for bringing me and those two babies through our tragedy to the other side."

"Amen. And I thank Him for restoring your relationship with Wallace. Otherwise, we wouldn't have ever met." Oscar lifted their joined hands to his lips and kissed the back of Aunt Jackie's. "The moment I told Wallace I was leaving Raleigh to move to Atlanta so I could spend the rest of my years near my daughter and grandchildren, the first thing he said was, 'I might need to set you up with my former sister-in-law, Jackie.' I was a little skeptical initially, but then he showed me a picture of you, and I fell in love."

"Stop playing, boy." Aunt Jackie felt her cheeks getting warm.

"I ain't playing. I saw those curvy hips and pretty brown eyes and lost my righteous mind. I was ready to get down here to Georgia to meet you. I rushed the sale of my house and gave most of my furniture away. I left Raleigh with just my clothes, shoes, a few keepsakes, and some mementos that belonged to my late wife."

"Oscar, we've been dating for nearly six months, and you've never told me that."

He laughed and squeezed Aunt Jackie's hand tenderly. "I didn't want you to know how desperate of an old man I was. But now that I have you, I don't mind you knowing you got your hooks in me, girl. In fact, I'm so addicted to you, baby, that I want you to meet my daughter and her family. And I'm ready to meet Zach and his wife and kids, too."

"Now, Oscar, you know—"

"Uh-uh, Jackie, I don't want to hear it this time. I'm a grown man. This sneaking around in secrecy like teenagers is getting on my nerves. It's time to tell your nephew you're in a serious relationship with a man who loves you. My daughter knows all about us. I even showed her the picture we took at Calloway Gardens. She's dying to meet you, but I won't let her until you agree to let me meet Zach."

"Oscar, Zachary Sean King Senior is a little rough around the edges. He might show his natural black behind when he finds out I've been dating a man for six months and didn't tell him."

"I ain't scared of Zach. He doesn't look too tough to me. I watch him at church with his gorgeous wife and their kids every Sunday. Why do you treat him like he's your daddy when he's really your nephew? Are you afraid he'll give you a whipping for courting a man you love?"

"No, I'm not! It's just that Zach is very overprotective of me, and he doesn't know you. Once he meets you, he'll have all kinds of questions about why I didn't tell him about you from the very beginning, how we met, and blah, blah, blah. Not only will I have to deal with all his prying, Wallace will too. Remember, he's in on the secret as well. I made him promise not to tell Zach anything about you, and he agreed." Aunt Jackie closed her eyes and shook her head. "Lord Jesus, that boy is going to have a fit."

"Zach will be just fine once you introduce us. I'm ready for it. Now you and Wallace can act like chickens all you want, but I'll continue to be the man God made me to be. I'm in your life because I love you and I enjoy your company. And to tell you the truth, I want to take our relationship to the next level, but you're letting your nephew stand in our way." Oscar stood up and started gathering the dirty dishes from the dining room table. "I'm giving you until next Sunday to tell Zach about us and introduce me to him. If you refuse to do it, I'll just walk over to him after church and do it myself. It's up to you, sweetheart."

"Oh, my God! You wouldn't do that, would you?" Aunt Jackie challenged with her eyes bucked.

"Oh, I'll do it. I'll step to him with my hand extended for a handshake and say, 'Zach, I'm Oscar Floyd Wilson from Raleigh, North Carolina, and I've been courting your aunt, Jacquelyn Elaine Dudley Brown, for about six months now. I'm in love with her, and we're getting married real soon.'"

"Please don't do that, Oscar. I would have another heart attack." She pinned him with narrowed eyes as he continued clearing the table. "You wouldn't dare."

"Try me."

Chapter Twelve

Jill had expected a showdown at the end of the night, but she'd had no idea that a certain little boy would put up such a robust fight. Her little man was holding his own like a seasoned lawyer, determined to have his way.

"There will be no more arguing, Jalen King. Now leave Zion's room and go to your room, little boy. It's bedtime."

"But, Mommy, I want to sleep in here with Nahima. I have to tell her a bedtime story about how the Black Panther took me to Wakanda for my birthday."

"He's always making up all kinds of stories about the Black Panther," Zion said from her seat at the foot of her bed. She rolled her eyes. "The boy is going to be an author when he grows up. Watch and see."

Jill tried her best not to smile as she folded her arms and shot her baby boy a stern look. "How do you know Nahima and Zion want to be bothered with you, eh?"

"He's my little brother," Nahima spat, wrinkling her nose. "I want him to sleep with me."

"Okay." Jill reached down and lifted Jalen into her arms for a quick kiss on each cheek. "Good night, sweetie. Sleep well. Mommy loves you."

"I love you too, Mommy. You're the best mommy in America, Jamaica, and Wakanda." He giggled and tapped the tip of Jill's nose with his finger.

"And you are the sweetest little boy in the whole wide world."

"Come on, Jalen. I want to hear my bedtime story."

Clearly excited, he wiggled out of Jill's arms and hopped down, hitting the carpet and running directly to Nahima. He flung himself into her open arms, causing her to fall backward on Zion's guest bed, which matched hers on the opposite side of the huge Oriental rug. He squealed and laughed when she started kissing him all over his face.

Jill eased out of the room and closed the door behind her with a smile on her face that she did not feel in her heart. There were some things one could hide by pretending and speaking lots of kind words at all the right times. However, just like a bug when it is smashed, whatever is on the inside will ooze out. Jill's keen instincts told her that Nahima was a bug. She hadn't missed her subtle eye rolls, smirks, and edgy tone of voice whenever she addressed her. Everybody else seemed clueless to it, but Jill was much too sharp for that. Right now, in the eyes of Zach, Zachary Jr., Zion, and Jalen, Nahima was a pretty, innocent butterfly with brilliant colors they all adored. But in due time, she would show them all what she truly was—a bug.

"Mi nuh believe ev'ryting mi yeye dem si," Jill whispered as she walked down the dark hallway to the master suite.

"What the fuck?" Nahima dropped her cell phone to the bathroom floor and reached for her towel on the counter to cover her naked body. "Don't you know how to knock?"

"Sorry! Sorry! Sorry!" Zion covered her eyes with both hands and started stumbling as she walked backward toward the bathroom door. "I didn't know you were in here. The door wasn't locked."

"Get out!"

Zion turned and ran out of the bathroom, slamming the door behind her.

"Yo, shawty, who the hell was that? What's goin' on?"

Nahima rushed to the door and locked it before she snatched up her phone from the fluffy hot pink rug. "That was my little cousin, Zion. Ugh, kids."

"Is she retarded or somethin'? How come she bustin' in on you and shit while I'm tryin' to see that pretty pussy?"

"Bae, this is her private bathroom in her bedroom. I forgot to lock the door. Damn! What the hell was I thinking?"

"So you forgot to lock the fuckin' door. No biggie, right?"

"I don't know. What if she saw what I was doing? That would be so fucked up."

"How old is she?"

Nahima sucked her teeth. "She's only nine. But Zion is smart. Both of my little cousins are whiz kids, and so is my baby brother. If Zion saw me masturbating, she might snitch. That would be so embarrassing."

"Man, that nine-year-old li'l girl don't know what you were doin'. Hey, but you can teach her!" Santana laughed like crazy. "Go find her li'l ass and lock her in the bathroom with you. Tell her you'll give her some money if she show me her li'l pussy."

Nahima was pissed the hell off and grossed out at the same time. Why the fuck would a grown-ass man, her man, want to see a little girl naked? That was some sick shit.

"I'm gonna pretend like I didn't just hear you say that, Santana. That was some disgusting shit to say about a little girl. Are you on some pedo shit or what? I don't fuck with child molesters. I'm out."

"Hey! You better not hang up that goddamn phone! Who the fuck you think you talkin' to anyway? I'ma knock the shit outta your raggedy ass when I see you. Your mouth done got too damn slick. Now put the damn phone back down there and open your legs again so I can bust this nut. Get freaky like you did before that li'l girl busted in there on you."

"What you readin', Kang?"

Jay looked up from the papers she'd been reading in the inmate library all day and glanced at Gracie. She took off her glasses and hooked them on the collar of her long-sleeve T-shirt. Rubbing her tired eyes, she tried to clear her head of all the medical and legal jargon fighting for room inside her head.

"I've been going over my medical records and my case file since this morning. I got an email back from Amanda, the law student, yesterday. She told me to look for a few things that may help increase my chances for her organization to take me on as a candidate for early release. But even if I find what they're looking for in my file, I still need a resource person on the outside."

"I thought you said your daughter would be your outside contact."

Jay shook her head. "She can't because she's not eighteen. That's their policy. My resource person must be at least eighteen years old with no criminal record. And they've got to be willing to come to Leesworth to meet with my case manager and law student rep whenever they request it, which means the person must have a valid driver's license and reliable transportation."

"Damn," Gracie drawled, pulling out the chair next to Jay. She sat down next to her friend. "So what'chu gon' do?"

"The hell if I know. Nahima is the only person I've got who'll be willing to help me out. Aunt Jackie ain't about to go along with any plan that involves my baby boy. If the plan was just about my medical situation, I wouldn't need Nahima at all."

"Huh? I don't get it. I thought you had lost all your legal rights to your li'l boy. Didn't your brother and his wife adopt him?"

"Yeah, but I really didn't want them to. I wasn't in any mental condition to make such a serious legal decision at the time."

"What'chu mean, Kang?"

"I had just given birth to my baby boy, and then his father was brutally killed. After that, my health took a turn for the worse. That was a lot of heavy shit to deal with at one time for anybody in or out of prison."

"Ain't that the truth?" Gracie touched Jay's shoulder and looked her square in the eye. "I bet your mind was messed all the way up, huh?"

"Hell yeah, it was! Psychologically, I was incapable of making rational decisions. I was clinically depressed, Gracie. I just read it in my medical records. Amanda said any lawyer worth his or her credentials could easily stir up some trouble for Zach and Jill regarding the adoption if I could find a mental health diagnosis in my records to prove they may have taken advantage of me."

"It looks like you done found it. Hot damn, Kang, you 'bout to get up outta here!"

"Slow your roll. I want an early release, but it ain't that simple. On the legal side, I can definitely have the legitimacy of Jalen's adoption questioned due to my mental health diagnosis at the time. But it'll piss Zach off, and he'll come at me swinging hard and bring up my past. I don't know if a judge will overturn my baby boy's adoption and restore the parental rights of a mother who took out a hit on her brother who legally adopted the child in question."

"Oh, shit, that is kinda bad. But you gotta try, Kang. Hell, fight Zach back just as hard. He didn't even want that baby at first. Didn't you tell me Jalen almost got adopted by a couple because your brother refused to take him?"

Jay stretched her eyes wider than the Atlantic Ocean and grinned at Gracie. "Yep. That's true. But he made up for that and became active in Jalen's life even before his daddy was killed. Then he gave me one of his kidneys. He did it out of guilt, but he still did it."

Jay put on her thinking cap and considered a few different scenarios while Gracie sat quietly watching her with her chin resting in the palm of her hand. As far as she was concerned, she didn't owe Zach a goddamn thing. Yes, he had taken Jalen and was raising him like a little prince in his mini mansion in the 'burbs, and one of his kidneys had saved her life. So she really didn't want to bring trouble to his front door, but she wanted out of Leesworth in the worst way by any means necessary. What was an incarcerated, terminally ill bitch to do?

"Let me study some more of this legal shit and my medical records over the rest of the weekend. I'll get permission from Sheftall to call Amanda Monday morning and have my regular talk with Nahima that evening. I should be able to come up with the perfect plan after then."

"That sounds like a good plan, Kang. One thing about it, you's a smart, educated woman. If anybody can find a way for them law school students to get them up outta Leesworth early, it's you, honey."

"You ain't ever lied, my friend."

Chapter Thirteen

"What the hell is Nahima doing? It shouldn't take no fifteen-year-old girl that damn long to get dressed and primped for church."

As usual, Jalen giggled and pointed a "shame on you" finger at Zach when he heard him curse. "There you go cussing again. It's Sunday, so you owe the potty-mouth jar double, Daddy. I'm going to tell Pastor Broadus and Aunt Jackie to pray for you really hard and really loud today." The child couldn't stop laughing.

Zach stopped eating his plate of grits, eggs, and sausage links and placed his fork on the table. Shaking his head, he reached into the pocket of his navy blue slacks and pulled out a wad of cash. After peeling a few crisp bills off, he offered them to Jalen. "Here you go, buddy. Daddy's got to stop cussing so much around you. It's getting too damn expensive."

"Daddy, you cussed again!"

"Lord, have mercy, Zachary! You curse like a drunken sailor. Are you a heathen, eh?"

Zach Jr. and Zion looked at each other and burst out laughing.

Without trying to defend himself, Zach sighed loudly and gave Jalen some more money. The child took all the cash and hopped down from the kitchen table, laughing his cute little face off along with his mom and siblings. But before he could leave the kitchen, Nahima entered wearing a very fashionable lime green sundress with large daisies all over it. It was beautiful and fit her slim figure perfectly, but it was strapless and extremely short. The flowing swing hem hit her at mid-thigh.

"Come back, Jalen," Zach called out.

"Huh? You want your money back, Daddy?"

"Nah. Here you, go, li'l dawg." He pulled out the stack of money again, removed a few more bills, and offered them to Jalen.

The child scrunched up his face, clearly confused, but he turned around and accepted the extra money anyway before he left the kitchen. The moment Jalen was out of sight, Zach eyed Nahima from head to toe as she stood at the stove fixing her breakfast plate. Not only did she look like she was on her way to a THOT convention instead of church, but her rude ass hadn't said good morning to a soul in the kitchen.

Zach cleared his throat. "Good morning, Nahima."

She turned around with a sheepish grin on her face, holding the plate of piping hot food. "Oh, my bad. Good morning, Uncle Zach. Hey, everybody."

After the rest of the King family returned Nahima's delayed greeting, she joined them at the table and started eating without blessing her food. Zach was the cussing champion of the world without a doubt, but he would never partake of food without thanking God for it or asking Him to purify it for his health and nourishment. That was just basic Christianity, which Nahima knew all too well. Aunt Jackie had made sure to teach her the fundamentals of their Pentecostal faith before she could walk or talk. The child knew better. Zach didn't know what the hell was wrong with her, though.

"You need to hurry up and finish your breakfast, pumpkin, because you've got to change out of that ho-girl dress into something decent before you walk out of my damn house."

Nahima looked up from her plate and stared at Zach like he had a slimy green booger hanging out of his nose. Her eyes traveled around the table, but everyone avoided her direct gaze. Jill was obviously doing the most to stay clear of the situation by opening her Bible and pretending to read it as she sipped her coffee.

"Are you for real? This is an original design I made for my clothing line. My mom lets me wear stuff like this to church all the time."

"Your mom is Catholic, girl. You can wear a see-through catsuit to mass and the priest would be happy. Pastor Broadus will throw you on the altar and pour a whole bottle of blessed water all over you and Aunt Jackie will be right there with him speaking in tongues if you bust up in Refuge Pentecostal Temple in that getup. So hurry and eat and then go change."

"But, Uncle Zach, I—"

"There ain't shit else to talk about, Nahima. Finish your breakfast and go upstairs and take off that ass-popper."

Everybody turned and looked at the entrance of the kitchen when they heard Jalen snickering. With the exception of Nahima, they all laughed at him as he wagged a finger in Zach's direction.

"Don't worry, Daddy. The extra money will cover those two cuss words. Okay?"

Later that evening, after a huge Jamaican feast and two Netflix movies with the King clan, it was time for Nahima to head back home to prepare for school for the week. Although her uncle and his wife had gotten on her last frigging nerve from time to time over the weekend, she couldn't deny how much fun she'd had with her baby brother and cousins. And she was glad that she wasn't going home empty-handed. Uncle Zach had given her

$100 before they'd climbed in his G-Wagen for their drive across town. Nahima almost felt bad about dipping into the potty-mouth jar for fifty bucks after church once her uncle surprised her with the C-note. She had only stolen the money from the jar because Santana was expecting her to come with some cash for him so he could get his burner out of hock. And besides, what was Jalen going to do with all of that money anyway? His Black Panther piggy bank was loaded with cash too, but it was $25 lighter now. His big, big sister had hit his stash also. But he was too little to even miss the money. Little man was just happy that his big, big sister had come to his Black Panther–themed bedroom to check it out and play with him for a while.

Nahima smiled and looked over her shoulder at her baby brother as Zach drove with his Bose stereo system blasting some old dead dude named Luther singing a lame song about having a party and everybody singing. The music was so boring that it had put Jalen to sleep with his mouth wide open. He was even snoring with his cute little self. Damn, she loved that kid to death. No matter what, she would spend more time with him so he would grow up knowing he could always depend on her.

"Hey, pumpkin, I got a surprise for you."

Nahima turned around and looked at Uncle Zach. "You do? What for?"

He took his eyes off the road for a split second to meet her curious gaze, grinning. "You made Jalen's weekend. Zach Jr. and Zion enjoyed your company too. I know things aren't the way they used to be between you and me, but your visit was the first step to fixing that. Don't you think?"

"Yeah. I felt like your pumpkin again. I like that. I promise to spend one weekend out of every month at your spot from now on."

"Damn, girl, you're about to make an OG cry." He patted her knee. "You just confirmed that the surprise I got for you was the right move."

"Okay, I'm about to lose it, Uncle Zach! What is my surprise? Where is it?"

"Look inside the glove compartment. There's a blue envelope inside for you. Check it out."

With nervous excitement, Nahima wasted no time following her uncle's instructions. When she picked up the blue envelope, her heart was beating so damn fast and hard that she could hear it in her ears. Her hands were shaking to the point where she had to force herself to calm down and breathe slowly so she wouldn't rip the damn thing. Uncle Zach's laughter was adding a buzz to the special moment.

"Oh, my God! Oh, my God!" Nahima screamed with tears blurring her vision as she made out what she was holding in her right hand. She got a little bit dizzy when she read the bold font a second time. "Two front-row center seats to the Quay concert! Aaahhh! Aaahhh! I'm dead! I can't believe it. I'm dead!" She reached over and wrapped her arms around her uncle and squeezed him, placing kisses all over his face. "Thank you! Thank you! Thank you! I love you so much, Uncle Zach! Thank you! Thank you! Thank you!"

"You're welcome, pumpkin. I love you too. But if you don't let go of me, you're going to make me run off the road."

Nahima released him and wiped her eyes as she gazed at the tickets through her tears. Yashia, Kela, and Ryan couldn't top her ticket swag. While they were hunting for coins and begging their parents, grandparents, and everybody else for project seats a thousand miles away from the stage, she already had a pair of front-row center tickets. Maybe she should let Uncle Zach choke her ass again if he was going to give her $100 and prime concert tickets to make up for it. Her girls weren't going to believe this! Putting up with that ho-ass, mud black bitch Jill over the weekend and the embarrassment of having to change out of her dress this morning had been worth the trouble after all.

"Did you have a good time with the Huxtables?"

"Yeah, it was cool. I told you that already."

Nahima looked at Santana's eyes though her phone screen and could tell he was high off of weed, and no doubt he had been drinking, too. But even toasted, he was still hella cute to her. She wanted to lie and tell him Uncle Zach hadn't given her any money. Now that she and Yashia were going to the Quay concert for sure, she wanted to use her money to buy some fabric to create an original to wear, and she needed to send Jay some panties and cookies, too. But she wasn't going to lie to him if he asked, because he needed his gun to make money working for Sarge.

"So how is Eminem doin'?" Santana laughed before he lifted the bottle of Cîroc to his lips and took a sloppy swig with the liquor spilling out the corner of his mouth like a typical drunk.

"Hey, don't call my baby brother that bullshit, okay? His name is Jalen."

"I don't give a fuck what that li'l cracker's name is. Shit, he white."

"I'm hanging up."

"Nah, hell you ain't." He took another swig and started coughing. "Did your unc give you some money? You know I need some to get my shit outta hock. So what's up, bae?"

"He gave me little bit. How much you need?"

"Shit, how much you got?"

"A hundred dollars," she lied.

"Hell, that's all? I thought he was like a doctor's assistant or some shit like that."

"He's a nurse practitioner, Santana, not a physician's assistant."

"Whatever. His ass coulda gave you more money than a hundred dollars. Shit, I'ma need all of that and then some. Tell that high-yella bitch to bring you by Church's Chicken tomorrow after y'all get outta school so I can get the money. Ask your mama and daddy for some money, too. I need at least two hundred dollars to get my gun. Work on that, a'ight?"

"Yeah. All right." Nahima faked a yawn, covering her mouth with her hand. "I'm sleepy. I'm about to crash."

"A'ight. I'll see you tomorrow."

"Good night."

"Later."

Chapter Fourteen

"This surprise better be worth all the hype. I can't believe you made us wait 'til lunch to tell us."

Nahima rolled her eyes at Yashia and took a big bite of her turkey burger and chewed it slowly. She looked toward the deli and spotted Kela and Ryan in the salad bar line. She wouldn't pull out the tickets to the Quay concert until the whole crew was seated and she had everyone's attention. So Yashia could bitch all she wanted, but Nahima was going to do things her way.

"Nahima, are you serious right now?"

"I will show you my big surprise as soon as Kela and Ryan get to the table, so just chill the fuck out already. And it will be worth every damn bit of the hype. Trust."

"Ugh, you make me so damn sick!" Yashia stole a French fry from Nahima's plate and bit into it.

Just then, Kela and Ryan arrived at the table and took their usual seats next to each other across from Nahima and Yashia. But before the clique could get into the surprise reveal, Dondrae walked by. He placed his fingers over his lips, signaling for the other three girls to be quiet as his other hand covered Yashia's eyes.

"I know it's you, D. I can smell your Hilfiger cologne."

"What's up, bae?" He leaned in and kissed her cheek.

Nahima smirked and crossed her eyes all goofy at Kela and Ryan, and they laughed at her silliness.

"I got a surprise for you," Dondrae announced, sitting in the vacant chair next to Yashia.

"Damn, everybody got a surprise today. What's up with that?" Kela asked.

Dondrae removed something from the breast pocket of his green ROTC shirt and waved it in Yashia's face.

"What is that?" Ryan asked with her nose wrinkled.

Yashia grabbed two card-like items from Dondrae's hand and read them. "Oh, snap! These are tickets to the Quay concert! We're going to see Quay!" She turned and kissed Dondrae's lips. "Thanks, bae!"

"You know I always got you. The seats ain't on the floor. Shit, they way up in the EBT-card section, but at least we're going."

"I wish I had a man to take me to see Quay's fine ass."

"Me too, Ryan. Shit, I wanna go to the concert." Kela poked out her bottom lip.

Annoyed, but not to be outdone, Nahima quickly whipped out the blue envelope that contained her two tickets. "Well, Dondrae almost shit on my surprise, but those bootleg tickets ain't got damn thing on these," she sassed with a serious neck roll, holding up her tickets. "Front-row center seats, bitches, and you too, Dondrae. Eleven hundred dollars apiece."

Kela leaned forward. "Whoa!"

"How the hell did you get those?" Ryan looked like she was about to cry.

"Damn, those are up there in the Buckingham Palace section!" Dondrae offered Nahima a fist bump. "That's what's up."

"Thank you. One was supposed to have been for my bestie, but now, I've got to find someone else to go with me since her man came through for her."

"Take me!" Kela and Ryan yelled at the same time and burst into a fit of laughter like two old, drunk ladies.

Yashia's face was cold, hard, and blank as a statue. And she didn't say a word about her girl's surprise front-row tickets, which told Nahima she was not happy at all. But she was going to be more pissed than ever when she found out her BFF was going to take her man to the concert now that she had an extra ticket. Who else would she take? Evidently, the universe wanted Nahima to take Santana. Why else would things have unfolded the way they had?

"Fuck!" Santana threw his cell phone with so much force that it bounced off the coffee table and landed on the floor. He flopped down hard on the raggedy sofa, causing the old springs to creak under his weight as the whole thing shook.

He was pissed the hell off because he needed his gun out of Smitty's Pawn & Loans, and Nahima's li'l bougie-ass, high-yella friend wouldn't bring her to the spot to give him the money he needed to make it happen. Now he was desperate. He needed money badder than a crackhead needed a rock like yesterday. How the hell was he supposed to lift cars or slang without heat? With no gun, he was broke without hope. That was fucked up, because his daughter needed diapers and food, and the rent was due. And he didn't have a single dime to help his girl pay it again this month. That bothered him more than anything because she was pregnant and had to work like a slave to cover his ass because he couldn't keep a real job.

Santana knew he was a piece-of-shit nigga who didn't deserve a good, loyal, hardworking, thick-ass, pretty bitch like Indigo, but he loved her. She had been riding with him for three years through all of his bullshit. No matter how many times he had been to jail or with the side pussy he smashed from time to time, she had stayed loyal to a nigga. That was why he would always be there for her and their daughter, Music. That little girl was his heart, his whole world all day long. Their unborn daughter in Indigo's womb, who they had already named Adore, would get all of Daddy's love too. But Santana didn't want her to be born prematurely and have to fight to survive because her mama was on her feet twelve to sixteen hours a day doing hair at her cousin's shop. The doctor had said it would go down just like that if Indigo didn't cut back on her work hours, control her high blood pressure, and get her iron level up.

Needing to clear his mind, Santana picked up the remote control from the coffee table and turned on the TV. The dull picture with floating lines all over some local news anchor's face reminded him that the cable and internet were off. He couldn't watch shit—not ESPN, Netflix, VH1, or even fucking BET. Once again, his anger and aggravation rose above his level of control. He just couldn't keep his shit together, so he hurled the remote across the room against the wall, where it crashed hard and shattered apart. Batteries and pieces of the gadget flew in all directions.

"Fuuuck!"

"What took you so long to answer the phone? This is my third time calling you."

Nahima sat her wet body wrapped in a towel on the edge of her bed. "I'm sorry. I've got a lot going on, Jay. I was in the shower, but I ran out as soon as I heard the phone."

"Okay, but what were you doing earlier, like around six o'clock?"

I was getting cussed out by a nigga who claims he loves me.

"Ummm, I had left my phone in my purse after school by mistake, and I forget to take it out before I started my homework and studying. So I didn't hear it ringing."

"You didn't check your messages before you got in the shower? That don't make no sense, Nahima."

"I'm sorry, Jay. I told you I got a lot of shit going on. Cut me some slack, yo."

"Cut you some slack?" She sucked her teeth and laughed, but Nahima could tell she wasn't the least bit amused. Jay's tone was dripping with mad sarcasm. "I'm sitting up in this fucking animal cage losing my mind over the fact that I'm dying and my son may never meet me, and you say you got a lot of shit going on? That's fucking hilarious."

"Okay, I messed up. Forgive me for my bad choice of words. I know my little problems can't compare to your situation. But I'm here for you, Jay. Please believe me on that."

"I'm glad to hear you say those words because I need you to do me a huge favor. It's the biggest and most important thing you could ever do for me. You're the only person in the world who I can trust and depend on to do it, so please promise me you got my back, baby girl."

"I promise I got you, Jay. You know that already. What do you need me to do? You need some money? If so, I can—"

"Nah, I don't need no money. Aunt Jackie just put seventy-five dollars on my books last week, and she paid the balance on my meds, too."

"Oh. Well, what do you need then?" Nahima got up and grabbed the bottle of cocoa butter from her dresser and returned to her seat at the edge of her bed. "It don't even matter, because whatever it is, I got you."

"Look, I have a pretty good chance to get out of prison early through a special program called the Justice

Unlimited Project. It's a group of law school students, physicians, and mental health providers who have a contract with the State of Georgia to take on inmates who were poorly represented by their lawyers or have pressing circumstances—mainly medical issues—to make space in the prison system for harder criminals and save taxpayers money at the same time."

"Wow! So you can actually come home?"

"Maybe. I need your help, though."

"Tell me what I have to do."

"First, I need you to find an adult, someone eighteen or older, who'll be willing to bring you and Jalen to visit me and to meet with my case rep if the organization decides to take me on as a candidate for early release."

"Why not ask Aunt Jackie?"

"It's a long story, but trust me when I tell you she won't do it."

"Okay, I trust you. I think I can find somebody." Nahima snapped her fingers. "Santana, my boyfriend, can bring me up there. He'll help me do whatever I need to do to help you."

"Didn't you tell me he's been to jail before, like a few times?"

"Yeah, but he's never been to prison, just county jail three times for petty shit."

"He has a record, Nahima. That disqualifies him from being my resource person. Damn!"

"But he can still bring me up there to see you. He'll just have to drop me off and hang out at a restaurant or store or someplace while I visit you."

"That won't work. You're a minor. You and Jalen can only come to Leesworth accompanied by an adult. You've got to find someone to bring y'all up here. And the person must be willing to come and meet with my rep from JUP, too. I need a visit with Jalen soon. Find a way to get him to Leesworth in the next few weeks."

"I'll ask my friends about their mamas or aunties."

"Thank you so much, baby girl. I appreciate your help."

"I told you I got you. I can't wait to see you, Jay." Nahima swallowed hard, trying to figure out the best way to say her next sentence. "About Jalen . . ."

"What about him?"

"I don't see Uncle Zach and Jill letting me bring him to the prison. I've never even babysat him before. How am I supposed to make a visit with him to Leesworth happen?"

"Do whatever the hell you have to do, Nahima! That's how! Jalen is your baby brother, my son. Tell Zach you want to take him to see a movie or to Chuck E. Cheese or some other kiddie place. You're good at lying and scheming. You do it all the time to hang out with that Santana nigga. Use your skills to get my baby up here. I already put his name and yours on the visitation list. And my resource person will be added as soon as you find me one. Make it happen. My time is about up. I'll call you Wednesday at the regular time. Answer the damn phone."

"Okay."

Chapter Fifteen

"Zach, what are you doing here?" Aunt Jackie stepped aside to give him room to enter the house. She smiled when he kissed her cheek as he crossed the threshold.

"Today is my off day, and I wanted to see you. So I decided to drop by and surprise you after I left the barbershop, but I left my key at home. That's why I had to ring the bell. Jetty told me to tell you hey, by the way. I'm hungry. What do you have to eat?"

Aunt Jackie followed Zach to the den, wringing her hands all the way. She took a seat in her recliner while he sat close to her on the love seat. Still shocked by his pop-up visit, she started humming and tapping her left foot on the carpet nervously.

"Auntie, I asked what you got to eat."

"Oh, yeah. Uh, I can heat up some leftovers from this weekend for you."

"That's fine. What did you cook?"

"I have stuffed Cornish hens, some turnips, mac and cheese, potato salad, fried corn, and candied yams. I also cooked a roast, some yellow rice, green beans, and yeast rolls. I even got half a pecan pie and a few slices of whipping-cream pound cake. Choose your poison."

"Damn. Auntie, why the hell did you cook all that food over the weekend?" Zach cocked his head to the side with a big grin curling his lips. Stroking his goatee, he said, "Better yet, tell me who you cooked all that food for, because I know you didn't cook it for yourself."

Aunt Jackie got up nervously, although she was trying her best to play it real cool. "When have you ever come over here and I didn't have enough food to feed the entire neighborhood, boy?"

Zach got up and followed his auntie into the kitchen. She could feel his body heat radiating from his chest to her back as he dragged his feet like she had asked him not to do all his life. It had gotten on her last nerve when he'd continuously done it as a child, and it still did now. But she was too close to her mental edge to fuss at him at the moment. His accusing question about the food in her refrigerator had thrown her off her game, and she didn't like it one doggone bit.

Aunt Jackie's big mouth had put her on the spot. Everybody knew she cooked big meals all the time just because she could, and she was often asked about the contents of her refrigerator. So it wasn't unusual for her to rattle off the deliciousness she could serve on a whim like she'd just done. But Aunt Jackie hadn't expected to be grilled by her wannabe daddy for having a smorgasbord in her kitchen. Zach should've been happy he had food options to choose from since his black behind was so hungry. But instead, he was using it against her, trying to be nosy.

When she opened the fridge and started removing the bowls of leftover food, Zach released a high-pitched whistle and started snickering like he'd heard a funny joke. Only the precious Holy Ghost kept Aunt Jackie from turning around and slapping the devil out of him. She was glad when he sat down at the square four-seat dinette table, where her half-eaten plate and glass of sweet tea sat on an African mud cloth placemat.

Without looking at Zach, Aunt Jackie asked, "What do you want, baby?"

"I'll take a little bit of everything you got, including both desserts. And can you make it to go, Auntie? I want to surprise Jalen by picking him up an hour early from school so I can take him to get some ice cream."

There you go surprising somebody else. You need to stop popping up on people. I raised your behind better than that.

"Sure, I can make you a couple of plates to go. I can use some of those takeout containers Sister Broadus gave me when we were giving away food after Minister Hudley's mother's repast."

"I appreciate that, Auntie. But you still never told me who the lucky person was you cooked this mega feast for." Zach laughed and clapped his hands.

Zach called his best friend, Dex, as soon as he settled in his whip. As the phone rang, he looked at the North Carolina license plate on the white Cadillac Escalade parked behind Aunt Jackie's silver Buick LaCrosse. He had never seen this particular SUV parked anywhere on Southwest Chappy Drive in the Ridgewood community of Atlanta before in all of his 47 years. Zach's stomach was flipping and twisting, doing all kinds of acrobats and shit and making noises. But none of that had anything to do with the aroma of the buffet of food Aunt Jackie had warmed up and packed in a box for him and was now on his back seat making him hungry. Nah, that wasn't it.

Just like on a particular day forty years ago when his stomach was making weird monster sounds and rolling, telling him something was wrong as soon as he entered his house and saw his grandparents and all of his aunties and uncles sitting in the living room looking like hell as they watched Jay play with her baby doll, Zach knew something was way off today. His stomach had warned him of an unspoken truth that god-awful day when he was just an innocent first-grader who liked to eat his grandmama's chitterlings smothered in hot sauce with his granddaddy and was in love with his beautiful mama and the shiny green bike she'd just surprised him with. Zach wondered what the hell his stomach was warning him about now.

He started his SUV when Dex's voicemail message filled the car from the dashboard speaker, telling his buddy and all other callers he wasn't available and he would hit them back at his earliest convenience. Zach ended the call without leaving a message and pulled away from the house his late Uncle Julius had bought for the family right before he married Aunt Jackie. He smiled at the memory of the day she moved them in. It was just his auntie, Jay, and him because it was on a Friday, only twenty-four hours before the small house wedding, and Uncle Julius had explained that the Lord wouldn't appreciate him moving in with them until after he and Aunt Jackie had become husband and wife. They all were so damn happy, even though Jay had cried herself to sleep in her new bedroom because she was scared her new uncle, the only father figure she'd ever had, wasn't going to keep his promise and move in the next day. Moving from their small two-bedroom apartment in the projects into their three-bedroom home in Ridgewood was one of the most exciting events in his life.

Zach honked his horn and waved at Coconut, Ridgewood's most beloved crackhead and drunk, as he swung a left onto Sunny Circle West. It still blew his mind that this Negro had actually graduated from high school one year behind Aunt Jackie and he was the star point guard on their school's basketball team. Dude had been offered a ton of scholarships from a bunch of HBCUs all across the South, too. Unbelievable bullshit like that made Zach want to smoke a rock and down a pint of cheap-ass gin, Coconut's preferred cocktail. He couldn't wrap his mind around how someone with major athletic talent and so much opportunity had ended up as the neighborhood addict. Then again, even with a list of advantages, it was still hard for a black man in America to make it, because there were countless systemic obstacles, hidden and head-on, for them to overcome. Maybe ol' Coconut had run into one roadblock too many on his journey to success and he didn't have what it took to beat the odds.

Zach's phone rang, and he abandoned his thoughts about what Coconut's life would've, could've, or should've been. It was Dex calling him back, and he was glad because he was the only person he felt comfortable enough to bounce his suspicions off. Zach pressed the button on the dashboard to answer the phone.

"Talk to me, Dex."

"What you doing calling me in the middle of the damn day when you know me and Ramona are off work? Are you trying to block a nigga from getting a nut or what?"

Zach cracked up, causing his SUV to swerve an inch or two over into the opposite lane, which earned him a warning honk from the driver of a pimped-out, apple red Chevy Impala. He flipped him off and blew his horn back. "Fuck you!"

"No, thank you, bruh. Ramona just took care of that."

"Y'all keep playing church over there, you and wifey gonna end up with a new little tambourine-playing member. And that'll fuck up my finances for real, because I need a third godchild like I need gonorrhea."

"I hear you. That's how come I've been thinking seriously about getting the ol' snip snip."

"Ouch!" Zach grabbed his penis and leaned forward toward the steering wheel like he was really in pain. "Not the jewels, bruh. Say it ain't so!"

"I ain't lying, bruh. Ramona and I don't want any more kiddies, but she stays horny and refuses to take the pill. I'm tired of using condoms. The good kind are too damn expensive, and Mr. Viper can't feel that warm and wet pussy the way he wants to through a layer of latex. So—"

"So you're going to let the doctor turn you into a bitch-ass opera singer with a butcher knife and a pair of pliers because you don't want to spend money on Magnums? Man, lose me on that shit. If Ramona don't want to get knocked up, tell her ass to take the pill or get a shot or one of those IUDs. If she bitches about all of those, make her ass get spayed. That's better than you getting neutered, nigga."

"I'll present those options to Mrs. Cruz tonight."

"Good. If she rejects all of them, put her ass on a dick diet."

Dex laughed so loud that it made Zach's shoulders jerk with surprise.

"A dick diet? What the hell is that?"

"Ration the dick out to her ass. Only give it to her on Tuesdays, Thursdays, and Saturdays if she uses some kind of temporary female birth control like one of those things she can pop in and out."

"You're trying to have my ass up in divorce court fighting over custody of my daughters and my home theater unit. Let's talk about something else. What did you call me for in the first place?"

"I believe Aunt Jackie has a man."

"And?"

"And? I ain't met the nigga because she's seeing him on the sneak and hiding him from me."

"The last time I saw Aunt Jackie, she still looked like the sixty-something responsible and highly respected woman we all love. She's grown, dude. So I seriously don't think she's got a boyfriend she's hiding from you or anyone else."

"Then please explain why she didn't want to spend the weekend at my house with her grandkids and got mad with me when I asked why."

"She didn't feel like being bothered with her bossy-ass nephew and a house full of crumb snatchers when she could chill at her spot in peace."

"Wrong! Her sneaky ass wanted to cook for some two-bit, hearing-aid-wearing, social-security-receiving pimp and sit up under him all weekend! Damn, I'm pissed."

"Why?"

"Because she's creeping. How come she can't let him be a man and show his face? If the nigga is solid, he should want to meet me and the rest of the Dudleys and Kings. This is some bullshit, Dex! You should've seen all the food Aunt Jackie cooked for that antique son of a bitch. She had stuffed Cornish hens, a roast, and about a hundred different side dishes, plus two kinds of her best desserts. You ought to smell my truck right now. It smells like the Busy Bee Cafe up in here. I could cater two weddings and a ghetto family reunion with all the grub she packed up for me and my crew."

"If Aunt Jackie's got a man—and I ain't saying she does—it's her business, and I'm happy for her. If anybody deserves romantic love in their later years, it's her sweet self, period. And I'll bet my 401(k) that whoever this old cat is, he ain't no buster. Jackie Dudley Brown is a holy, righteous, and dignified woman who's easy on the eyes and can sing Saint Peter and Saint Paul to sleep every night of the week with just one verse of "Amazing Grace." So if she's courting, good for her and good for the lucky gentleman."

"Yeah, his ass is lucky all right. He's lucky I didn't search my auntie's house and find his punk ass hiding in one of those rooms. He was right in her spot while I was there. He ran and hid somewhere, but he left his plate on the table right across from hers. He was drinking water while she had her usual sweet tea. I can't believe she didn't catch me checking out the two plates."

"Word, bruh? Mister left his plate on the table to go play hide-and-seek?"

"Word." Zach frowned at himself in his rearview mirror before merging into the northbound I-75 traffic. "I wasn't sure about it until I saw his OG wagon, a smooth white Escalade, parked behind Auntie's ride when I was leaving. I didn't notice it when I first arrived, but I put shit together when I was about to leave and started thinking about all that food in Aunt Jackie's fridge, the extra plate and water glass on the table, and the way she snapped at me when I asked her about her weekend plans. She was acting kind of nervous today, too, especially when I asked her who she had cooked that restaurant buffet for."

"Aunt Jackie is some old dude's bae! I like that shit!"

"I don't. Whoever the old pimp is, he's got a Wake County, North Carolina, license plate on his truck. That's the same county Wallace lives in. Man, that's weird as hell."

"It's weird as hell for sure. Did you jot the license number down? Since Patricia is a lawyer and all, I'm sure she's got some cop buddies or she knows some investigators who can run the plate through a database. Call her and Wallace tonight. I bet stepmom will look into it right away for you."

"I'm already on it, bruh. I memorize the plate number before I pulled off. I'll hit up my folks after dinner. If Aunt Jackie wants to act like a sneaky little teenage girl, I'm gonna treat her like one and act like I'm her daddy."

Chapter Sixteen

Nahima spotted Santana's shiny red Impala as soon as her Uber driver pulled up at Church's Chicken. He had told her this morning he would be in Ridgewood all day training some killer pit bulls for a dude named Keno who owned a dog-fighting ring up in South Carolina. She loved dogs, so it had made her feel some type of way when he'd bragged about how vicious he could turn even a sweet little poodle with his killer training skills. He had said something about using a combination of fresh peppers, the hottest ones he could find at the international market on Old National Highway, to make the pit bulls lethally mean. Torture like starvation, electrical shock, and whippings with a leather belt were a few of the other methods he used to train the dogs to kill others. Nahima couldn't imagine how anyone could be that cruel to any animal, but her bae swore there was no other way to teach and control the dogs.

Santana blew his horn when Nahima stepped out of the car. She smiled and waved as she did her runway stroll over to his Impala. She couldn't spend a lot of time with him because she and Yashia were expected at Mrs. Stephens's studio in an hour to work on their design project. They were going to add the flip lining to both sides of the jumpsuit and do some beadwork on the sleeves of the denim side. Nahima was hyped about it. But she needed to give Santana the $100 he needed to get his Glock out of the pawn shop first. And she couldn't wait to see his eyes explode when she surprised him with the Quay concert tickets. She would figure out the logistics of their first real date while they sat in his car waiting for Yashia.

"Hey, bae," she greeted him and dropped down in his passenger's seat. She leaned over and kissed his cheek after closing the door. "How did the dog training go?"

"It was a'ight. I almost got ran off the road today in Ridgewood by some dope boy in a G-Wagen, though."

"I'm sorry, bae. I'm glad you're okay."

"Yeah, I'm good. You got my money?"

Nahima nodded her head as she opened her purse. "I sure do. Here it is." She pulled out five twenty-dollar bills and offered them to him.

"Good lookin' out." Santana quickly took the cash and stuffed it in his jeans pocket. "So when is your friend comin' to scoop you up? I need to get to Smitty's to get my burner."

"She'll be here in ten minutes. She stayed at school to watch her boyfriend's baseball game. It should be over by now, so I'm sure she's on her way."

"Cool. You gon' buy your man somethin' to eat? A nigga's hawngry."

"I ain't got no more money, Santana, but I have a surprise for you. Close your eyes."

"I don't want no damn surprise. I want three wings, some fries, and two jalapeño peppers."

"I told you I'm broke. Now please close your eyes. You're going to like my surprise."

Santana closed his eyes and held out his hand. "A'ight. What is it, that watch I told you I wanted?"

"Nope. It's much better than that." Nahima placed the tickets in his open hand.

He opened his eyes and stared at them for a few seconds before he grinned. "Damn, girl, we going to see Quay?"

"Yes." She giggled. "My uncle bought them for me."

"Quay is my nigga! Jay-Z, Lil Wayne, Drake, Jeezy—ain't none of them mothafuckas got shit on him! Quay is the king!"

"I know, right? Everybody loves Quay, especially all of us homies in the A."

"True dat. So your parents gon' just let us roll out and shit?"

"Nah. I ain't figured it all out yet, but I will. Yashia, her boyfriend, and two more members of our clique are going too, so I guess I'll ride with them, and you'll have to meet us there. You and I won't sit with them, though, because they got some cheap-ass seats way up high somewhere. We'll be right in the middle of the front row so we can smell Quay's sweat."

Santana nodded his head slowly as if he were running the scenario through his head a few times. "Damn, I ain't never been to no concert. This shit is gon' be sweet."

Nahima reached for the tickets, but Santana shoved her hand away.

"Give them back, bae. I don't want you to get drunk and misplace them."

"I ain't giving you shit! You said they were my surprise, so I'm keeping 'em. Your li'l bougie-ass friends may talk you outta takin' me and set you up with some lame high school baseball player, one of that high-yella bitch's boy's teammates or whatnot. You go 'head and ride with your crew, and I'll meet y'all there just like you said."

Nahima wasn't feeling Santana holding on to those tickets. She wished she hadn't shown them to him now. Maybe she should've just told him about them over the phone and left them in her locked box in her room.

"There goes your girl." Santana nodded toward Yashia's car as it entered the parking lot.

"Don't lose those tickets, bae. My uncle paid a grip for them."

"I ain't gon' lose the tickets, girl. I'ma put them in my safe. Now kiss me so I can go get my heat, and you and your friend can go do what y'all do."

Nahima leaned over and pressed her lips against his, and he grabbed the back of her neck and rammed his tongue down her throat. The taste of alcohol and weed nearly made her gag. She quickly pulled back and gave him a half smile as she looked into his glossy eyes with dilated pupils.

"I'll call you tonight before I go to bed. I have to study for my history test, so it'll be late."

"Cool."

Nahima opened the car door and got out. As she hurried across the parking lot to Yashia's car, she tried to force her mind to forget about Santana and the tickets and concentrate on the outfit she was going to design for her to rock at the concert. But before she sewed anything, she had to figure out which guy at her school she could use for a decoy date to fool her parents, since she had two tickets. Nahima was going to have to bring the whole damn clique together to work on that particular project.

Jay stood up from her electric scooter she'd parked right outside of the warden's office and knocked on the door. Her back was killing her. The pain was so excruciating that it nearly took her breath away. She knocked on the door again and pressed her back against the wall for support.

"Come in." Sheftall's voice was faint, crossing through the steel barrier, but Jay heard her clearly enough.

"Good morning, ma'am," she greeted her after cracking the door.

"Good morning, Ms. King. What are you doing walking? The State paid too much for your little scooter for you to leave it somewhere in this jungle. Where is it?"

"I left it right outside. Ain't nobody crazy enough to mess with it." She stared at her swollen, aching feet for a hot second before facing the warden again. "May I have a seat please? I need to talk to you for a minute."

"Sure. Rest your feet, Ms. King."

Warden Iris Sheftall was an attractive 40-something sista with smooth peanut butter skin and a cropped, blond Afro. She was short, no taller than five foot three, tops, and she weighed close to 200 pounds, which put her on the thick side. But she wore it well. Overall, the wife and mother of three was a cool chick, but she had some peculiar ways, and Jay didn't trust her.

"Ms. King, are you going to talk or are you just going to look at me?"

"I received an email from one of the law students in JUP this morning. It looks like they want to review my case more closely in an attempt to facilitate an appeal for my early release. But I need three references. Amanda—that's my case rep's name—thinks it would be a good look if you would be one of my references."

"Is that so?" Sheftall smiled, displaying the five-mile gap between her two front top teeth.

"Yes, ma'am."

"I will serve as a reference for you, Ms. King. It won't be a problem at all. Do you want to know why?"

Jay was so emotional that all she could do was nod her head. She was too choked up to speak. It was taking much restraint to hold back her tears.

"I have seen women and men die in prisons all across Georgia. Most of them were terrible people who had brutally murdered others, raped, and robbed grossly out of greed. I'm familiar with your case, Ms. King. You did some crazy shit that hurt a lot of people, especially your brother and his family. But I believe you hurt yourself more than anyone else. And because you've pretty much been a model inmate, other than getting pregnant by your counselor, I think you deserve to leave prison early so you can reunite with your family as your health declines. Who knows? There may be a doctor on the outside who can turn your medical condition around. Experimental drugs and other forms of treatment may be able to save your life."

"Thank you, Warden. I appreciate this more than you will ever know."

"You're welcome."

"I need one more favor please."

"All right, Ms. King, you're pushing it now." Sheftall cut her eyes at Jay.

"I need to make a few phone calls to round up the other two references."

"Fine. You may use the phone in your office, Ms. King."

"Thank you, Warden," Jay said, struggling to stand against the pain in her back. "Thank you very much."

"Are you okay? You sound winded, and your face is flushed."

"I'm fine. My back just kicks my ass most of the day. My pain medication makes me loopy, so I don't take it until it's time to go to bed so I can sleep. That special air mattress helps, too."

"Okay. Take care of yourself."

"I will. Thanks again."

Chapter Seventeen

"Son, before we get into whatever you called me to talk about, can I please spend some time with my sweet grandbabies and my beautiful daughter-in-law?"

"Pops, you ain't got no sweet grandbabies, but I can let you see the juvenile delinquents Jill and I have if that's what you want."

Wallace chuckled as he stared lovingly at the handsome face on his computer screen that was a younger version of his. Zach reminded him so much of himself that it was scary.

"I would love to see your little juvenile delinquents, as you call them. I want to see their mama, too."

"Okay, let me text Zach Jr. and tell him to round up the gang and come down here to my man cave. I don't let them visit my private domain too often because they don't know how to act, especially Zion. That girl talks too much. She's sweeter than a five-pound bag of Dixie Crystals sugar, but she can talk a genie back into its bottle. So if you have any secrets, you better not utter a single one to Zion Seantelle King, because sooner or later, she will spill all your tea."

Wallace waved a dismissive hand at the screen as he watched his son text his grandson. "Leave my little princess alone. Every girl Zion's age has a problem running her mouth, but it ain't necessarily a bad thing in all situations. My little princess's loose lips might be your saving grace someday before she grows out of it. Some tattling is good tattling, Zachary."

"It ain't good tattling when she tells Jill every time she catches me smoking one of my premium Cuban stogies out on the deck."

Wallace couldn't hold back his laughter when he imagined Jill fussing at Zach in her thick Jamaican accent about smoking cigars. "The child is just trying to keep you from getting lung cancer, boy."

"Whatever. Anyway, I hear the invaders stomping down the stairs. Let me go unlock the door to my sanctuary."

Zach left Wallace's line of vision, giving him a moment to ponder the purpose of this out-of-the-blue video call. They had just spoken that afternoon while he was en route to the barbershop in his old neighborhood. Zach had phoned his old man just as he was closing out his daily noonday prayer and devotion. Their conversation hadn't been a short one, either. Wallace recalled them covering many topics, including Zach and his family's weekend reunion with Nahima, which had gone well, and Wallace Jr.'s successful campaign for freshman class president at North Carolina A&T University last fall. Father and son were brainstorming a plan to finance the young future attorney/United States senator's next political bid. Wallace Jr. had already announced his candidacy for sophomore class president, and his dad and big brother were expected to foot his campaign bill.

"What's up, Papa?"

The sound of Zach Jr.'s voice and his handsome face filling the computer screen brought Wallace's heart joy. "Hey there, young man. How are you?"

"I'm fine. How are—"

"I'm fine too, Papa," Jalen interrupted, hopping in front of his big brother. "Did you get my email?"

"I sure did, baby boy."

"Papa, I was just talking about you to my friend Jossie," Zion said with the prettiest smile.

"Hello, Papa King!" Jill sang in her accent Wallace loved so much.

The lively family video call went on for a while with the three King grandchildren and their mother catching up with the patriarch they all adored. Apparently ready to have time with his father alone, Zach abruptly took over his computer and shooed his wife and kids out of his man cave and back upstairs. He then reclaimed the chair behind his desk and trained serious eyes on Wallace.

"I need to ask Patricia to do me a favor, but I want to school you on what's going on first. It's about Aunt Jackie."

"What's wrong with Jackie, son?"

Wallace's heart began to beat so hard and fast that he could hear it pounding in his ears while he waited for Zach to speak. He hoped Jackie wasn't sick again. Her heart attack six or seven years ago had brought him to his knees in prayer many days and nights. God forbid she was having health issues again. They had just reached a happy and comfortable place in their relationship in recent years after decades of estrangement. It took a special kind of woman, a godly woman, to forgive the man who killed her big sister and thrust her two small children into orphanhood. Jackie Dudley Brown was such a woman, and Wallace was blessed and honored to have her in his life after all the pain he'd caused her. It would break his heart if she was sick again.

"Ain't nothing wrong with her per se. I think she's secretly involved with some mystery man, and I don't like it."

Oh, shit! Oops. Lord, please forgive me for my sinful thought. I wasn't expecting this. Jackie and Oscar are down there slipping.

"Son, what makes you think your auntie is secretly courting, and why is it a problem for you if she is? But most importantly, why on God's green earth did you think it was so important for me, of all humble souls, to know Jackie's personal business?"

Immediately, Zach's countenance changed before his father's very eyes. He wasn't a confident, some-times-cocky, overprotective, and pushy alpha male any-more. Who Wallace saw now was a little boy genuinely concerned about the kind and beautiful woman who had sacrificed everything to raise him and his baby sister to be successful, God-fearing members of society with all the love in her heart. Zach was troubled and he wanted consolation.

"I . . . I don't want any man to hurt her or take advantage of her ever. Auntie has been through enough heartbreak in her life when she lost her sister, had to drop out of nursing school, lost Uncle Julius, and then went through Jay's foolishness. I almost lost her when she had that heart attack, Wallace. If this in-the-cut nigga does Aunt Jackie dirty, I swear I'll kill him. That's how come I hit you up."

Wallace's face wrinkled of its own accord in fear. Did Zach know he and Oscar were friends? If he did, why didn't he lead with that information? Better yet, if he knew, why was he still referring to him as a mystery man?

Wallace cleared the lump of dread from his throat with a hard swallow. "Exactly why did you call me, son?"

"After I left the barbershop, I stopped by to surprise Aunt Jackie, and she seemed nervous that I was there. While she was packing up some food for me to take home, I noticed two half-eaten plates of food on the table and two glasses. She didn't even realize I was checking out the setup."

"So Jackie had a lunch date, and they decided that you didn't need to meet him or her. Surely you didn't call me because of that." Wallace leaned back in his chair and crossed his arms over his chest. "Zach, what's really going on?"

"First of all, I know it was a man. Why would Aunt Jackie feel like one of her girlfriends or a sister from Refuge needed to hide from me? Even if it was a new friend or female church member, one I don't know, why the hell couldn't I meet her? Unless . . . nah. I know my auntie ain't hardly no les—"

"Hey, boy, don't you say it! You know better. Of course, Jackie ain't gay."

"Then it's some coward pimp she's creeping around with, and you and my stepmother are going to help me put a name on his ass."

"How are Patricia and I supposed to help you do that?"

"Dude is pushing a white Cadillac Escalade with a Wake County, North Carolina, license plate. I figure Patricia could get one of her friends in law enforcement or in private investigations to run the plate number and ID the owner or renter of the vehicle."

"Zachary, are you sure you want to go through all that to get into Jackie's personal affairs? I don't think she'll appreciate that."

"I don't care. Text Patricia, and tell her to join us on this video call. If you won't do it, I'll just hang up with you and call her myself."

"Okay, let's do roll call, y'all," Kela suggested. "We gotta make sure everybody is on the call and their volume level is on point. I'm here." She laughed.

"You know I'm here because I called you," Nahima announced. "Ryan, are you there?"

"Yes, ma'am, Ryan Dominique Mathis is in the house!"

"I'm here," Yashia said dryly.

"What's wrong with you, bestie?"

"I'd rather be talking to my man than talking to y'all heifers. Now what is the emergency, Nahima?"

"I invited Santana to the Quay concert, but you know my parents ain't about to let him come and pick me up."

"Who the hell is Santana?" Kela asked.

Ryan popped her lips. "That's what I want to know. I thought I had memorized the entire student body at Westwood Park, but apparently, this reporter was wrong."

"He's some thugged-out, twenty-two-year-old nigga Nahima has been sneaking around fucking with for about four months."

"Yashia!"

"Shit, I'm slipping on my job. How come I didn't know that tea?"

"I guess because our so-called girl only trusted her bestie with info about her secret bae, Ryan."

"I guess so, Kela."

"Whatever. Anyway, now that Yashia has taken over Ryan's job as the clique's news reporter, I'll pick up from where she left off telling my business if it's all right with her."

"Go right ahead."

"Thank you."

"You're welcome."

"Like she said, Santana is my boyfriend, and because he's twenty-two and my parents don't know anything about him, he can't pick me up for the concert. So I need a guy from school who's going to the concert alone and has his own ticket to pose as my date to throw off my parents. I figured we all could still ride together, split up once we get to the concert, and come back together afterward for post-show breakfast at IHOP."

"Tell me again why we have to do this now?"

"Kela, I have two tickets. My parents and my uncle, who bought them, will want to know who I'm taking to the concert, and I can't tell them it's Santana."

Ryan laughed. "That's why your ass should be taking me."

"I couldn't choose between you and Kela. It would've been too much pressure."

"True dat. True dat."

"And I would've killed you had you picked Ryan over me."

"I know. That's why I didn't invite either one of y'all. Now can we get back to the subject at hand please?"

"Yeah."

"Go ahead, Nah-Nah," Ryan said.

Yashia remained silent.

"What I need y'all to do is talk to your friends and people in your classes about the concert. Then listen out for the name of any black guy who's going to the concert solo, already has a ticket, and doesn't mind rolling with us. When you find one, let me know. Okay?"

"I'm in. What about you, Ryan?"

"I'm a reporter. Of course I'm on it."

"What about you, bestie?"

"Yeah, Dondrae and I got your back. Now can I hang up and call him?"

"Yes. I need to study for my history test anyway. Thank you, ladies. I don't know what I would do without y'all. I'll see y'all tomorrow."

"Bye-bye."

"Good night."

"Bye, bitches!" Ryan screamed and then laughed like an idiot.

Chapter Eighteen

Indigo got out of bed and waddled toward the living-room on terribly swollen bare feet when she heard Santana pull into his parking space right outside their bedroom. She was only five and a half months pregnant, but she was huge and irritable as hell because of her out-of-control blood pressure and anemia. And the fact that she had to work long hours on top of her serious pregnancy complications because Santana didn't have a real job only made matters worse. Hell, she was styling hair like a cotton-picking slave, taking care of their 18-month-old daughter, Music, and doing all the cooking and cleaning with no help from him.

Indigo's puffy hands went straight to her wide hips when she stopped a few feet from the front door. She wanted to make sure her face would be the first thing Santana saw when, at three o'clock in the goddamn morning, he stepped inside of the apartment she paid rent on month after month by her damn self. She knew his ass was high and liquored up, too. That was why it was taking him so long to unlock the door.

"Damn, baby! You scared the shit outta me. What you doin' up?"

"Where the hell you been, Santana? It's three in the morning, and you got the nerve to bring your high ass up in my house asking me questions? Fuck that, nigga!"

"I'm sorry, baby," he mumbled, stepping toward her with his arms open for a hug.

Indigo took a step back, pissed and turned off by the suffocating mixed scent of Kush and Cîroc. "Don't touch me, nigga! I'm sick of your shit, Santana! If you don't bring some money up in here by tomorrow, I'ma put all your shit outside in the grass! You gon' have to take your ass right back over to Ridgewood and live with Avila and her bad-ass kids. I ain't playing. Try me."

"Hold up, baby." Santana reached inside his pocket and pulled out a wad of cash and dangled it in Indigo's face.

She reached out and snatched it and immediately started counting every bill. She looked up when she was finished with a smirk bending her lips. "Three thousand dollars? That's a good start, but you got to follow up with some more next week."

"I will, baby. I promise. Oh, wait a minute. I got a surprise for you. Check this out." He whipped two tickets out of his pocket and offered them to Indigo.

Without hesitation, she accepted them and read the words. "Did you steal these, Santana? I ain't going to jail over no damn stolen Quay concert tickets."

"No, I didn't still 'em, baby."

"Are they even real?"

"Yeah, they real. How the hell do you make phony concert tickets? Stop playin', baby."

"I know your ass didn't spend twenty-two hundred dollars on some tickets instead of helping me pay the damn rent."

"Nah, nah. A junkie gave 'em to me for two ounces. I thought you would like to get dolled up and let me take you out on the town. The other stylists at the shop, 'specially Amari with her ho ass, gon' be hatin' on you when they find out your man got you front-row tickets to see Quay at State Farm Arena. Plus I'ma get you a nice outfit to wear, something custom-made and whatnot. We goin' out to a fancy dinner, too. Hell, that's some bougie shit right there."

Indigo slowly closed the gap between her and Santana, smiling. "That concert gon' be lit!" She threw her arms around his neck and kissed him as he grabbed a handful of her big ass.

"I love you, girl."

"I love your raggedy ass too." She kissed him again. "I want a pretty baby-doll maternity dress to wear over a pair of fuchsia Michael Kors leggings I bought hot from one of Peanut's boys at the shop the other day. It's gotta have a nice pattern like paisley or flowers or some geometrical shit or something. I just want it to blend with the fuchsia and fit comfortably over my big-ass belly. Okay?"

"Girl, I got you."

Jay's stomach churned violently for the third time since she'd joined Gracie, KiKi, and her other friends at their regular table in the cafeteria for breakfast. She was very nauseated and sluggish, like she hadn't slept a wink. It had taken her a while to fall asleep the night before because her back had been hurting more than usual after dialysis. Thankfully, the night nurse had given her a second pain pill that had knocked her out. Now she was trying to eat some oatmeal and bananas, but her stomach was giving her grief and so was her back. On top of that, there was a burning sensation in her pelvic area that was driving her crazy.

"What's wrong, Kang? You ain't lookin' so good. You want me and KiKi to take you to the infirmary to see Nurse Oye?"

"Nah, I ain't going around there until I get some food down. I'm hungry, but my stomach is acting up. Let me try to eat some more of this oatmeal, and then we can go see the nurse."

"Are you sure, King? You're sweating like a pig over there. And I know your eyes are yellow because of your liver disease, but I have never seen them look like that. They're deep yellow, almost like mustard."

"Don't worry about me, KiKi. If things go the way I've been praying for them to go, I'll be out of Leesworth soon and back in Atlanta so I can be with my son. My auntie will find me some doctors to try new meds and advance treatments to keep me alive. You'll see."

As soon as those words left Jay's mouth, all the oatmeal she'd managed to eat followed. She'd tried her damnedest to keep it down so she wouldn't ruin everybody's breakfast, but her stomach had betrayed her.

Gracie and KiKi jumped up at the same time and were at her side in seconds. A couple of their tablemates gave them napkins to wipe up Jay's vomit. She was slumped over trying to catch her breath and wiping her chin with her forearm. Her sweatshirt sleeve was soiled with the contents of her upset stomach, but most of it had landed in her plate and on the table.

"Let's get her out of here, Ms. Gracie."

"Nah, KiKi, you go and get her scooter and take her on. I'ma stay behind and clean up this here mess. Go on now."

"Gracie, go with KiKi and take care of King," a young Hispanic girl named Mariana told her. "I got this."

Big Baby, their other tablemate, stood up. "I'll help her. Get King to the infirmary. We'll be around there before work starts."

KiKi ran to the entrance of the cafeteria and hopped onto Jay's scooter and fired it up. Then she carefully maneuvered through the rows of tables like she did every day to pick up her friend who was sitting at their table looking like death.

"Come on, King, let's go, baby. Ms. Gracie and I are taking you to see Nurse Oye. She'll give you some medicine for your stomach, and we'll make sure you get some soup, crackers, and a war Sprite to replace that yucky oatmeal."

Chapter Nineteen

"'He is worthy! Soooo worthyyy! He keeps on blessing me continually though worthy I'll never beee! He is worthy! Soooo worthyyyy! Thank you, God, for being worthy! He is wor—'"

Greg, Refuge Pentecostal Temple's minister of music, stopped playing the organ without warning just when Aunt Jackie was about to go all the way in for the kill on the worship song he'd been teaching her. Perturbed, she looked at him, ready to chew him out, but he tilted his head toward the center aisle of the sanctuary, signaling for her to hold her tongue. Her eyes instantly floated in that direction.

Lo and behold, it was Oscar, making his way toward her in his smooth, even gait that made her want to shout hallelujah. The brother appeared to be gliding on a cloud. All six feet and three inches of his towering height supported his well-toned, medium build just right. Oscar was decked out in a pair of loose-fitting Levi's jeans and a white long-sleeved North Carolina Panthers tee. His dazzling smile was in place, but it didn't quite connect with his eyes. That rarity, along with a sheen of perspiration sitting on top of his chocolate dome, told Aunt Jackie that all wasn't well with her man.

Oscar took a seat on the front right pew like he was there to observe the jam session between the minister and his star soprano, but she knew better. He would never come up from underground on their secret relationship without a good reason. Oscar's unannounced visit to the church in the middle of the day was putting their privacy at risk, and Aunt Jackie wanted to know why.

"Give me five minutes," she mumbled, turning to Greg.

"Sure, I'll be in my office whenever you're ready." He exposed all thirty-two of his teeth in a wide grin. "You were walking in that song like Jesus walked on water, Sister Jackie. I can't wait to teach you the verses."

"Thank you, Greg. I'll be right back."

Aunt Jackie walked away from the organ and slowly walked over to Oscar. "Hey. What's going on?"

"Can we go and sit in my truck? We really need to talk. You know I wouldn't have taken a chance of Pastor Broadus or some other church member seeing us if it weren't important."

"I know. That's why I'm about to have a panic attack. You're scaring me, Oscar."

He took her hand in his and squeezed it. "Come on, let's go outside so I can tell you why I'm here."

Aunt Jackie and Oscar took their time walking through the sanctuary and out of the church. It was a beautiful early spring day with a slight breeze. The smell of flowers blossoming under a radiant sun filled the air. If Aunt Jackie weren't so nervous, she would stop and take a moment to admire God's awesome handiwork, but there was no time for that.

Oscar's truck was parked directly in front of the church. His key fob chirped when they were half a foot away. Always the perfect gentleman, he opened her door when they reached the truck and helped her inside before he walked around, climbed in the driver's seat, and closed the door.

"I got a call from Wallace this morning. It seems we haven't been as careful as we thought we were with our secret relationship. Apparently, Zach is on to us."

"How is that possible, Oscar?"

"Your nephew is a very smart man. He's observant, too. All that food you prepared for us over the weekend tipped him off. And I ran out of the kitchen so fast when he stopped by that I left my plate and glass of water on the table. Then when he was about to leave, he noticed this truck and the North Carolina tag. That slick joker memorized my plate number and called his daddy to ask him to get Patricia to have one of her friends run it through a law enforcement database."

Aunt Jackie couldn't do anything but gasp and cover her mouth with both hands.

"Naturally, Patricia agreed to ask one of the investigators at the law firm where she works to look into it for her. She would look mighty suspicious otherwise."

"We're busted. Zach is going to have ten different kinds of fits."

"I don't care. If this is how the Lord wants to introduce me to your nephew and his family, so be it. But I would have preferred that we had just done it ourselves, baby."

"Either way, Zach ain't gonna like me having a boyfriend."

"That's good, because I don't like it either. I'm sixty-three years old, Jackie. What do I look like being somebody's boyfriend? I'm tired of that." He lifted the lid of his console and removed a black velvet ring box while Aunt Jackie watched him curiously.

"Lord Jesus, Oscar Wilson, what is that?"

"Take it and open it up to see what it is."

Aunt Jackie's hand was shaking so badly that she almost couldn't grip the tiny box. But when she did, she opened it right away and nearly started speaking in tongues. Tears began to fall fast and heavy from her eyes. The simple round diamond set high on four prongs on a semi-wide fourteen-karat white gold band encrusted with smaller round diamonds hypnotized her. She couldn't speak or move or even think.

"I don't want to be your boyfriend anymore, sweetheart. I love you, and I want to be your husband. Please make me happy and be my wife, will you?"

Aunt Jackie nodded and handed the box back to Oscar. Then she extended her left arm, offering him her hand. "Yes, I will marry you and make you as happy as you make me."

Oscar slid the gorgeous engagement ring on her finger and smiled, looking into her tearful eyes. She returned his smile and leaned over just as he did until their lips met in a sweet and tender kiss.

Chapter Twenty

"What's up, Rashawn?"

He slammed his locker shut and turned around, smiling. "Hey, Ryan the reporter. I'm about to go holla at Mr. Klebo, my guidance counselor. My dad's been on my ass about taking the SAT again. What's up with you?"

"Nothing much. I'm just a sophomore, but should I take the SAT too? Is it hard?"

"Yeah, you should take it, and no, it's not hard. Actually, it's kind of like an academic game of what you know or don't know. But there are a million websites and workbooks you can use to prep for it. Come with me to Mr. Klebo's office so you can register to take it too."

"I gotta go meet my girls for lunch. I'll sign up tomorrow."

"Okay, but don't forget, because I'm going to ask you if you did it."

Ryan smiled, shyly realizing how damn fine Rashawn was. He had a pretty-boy face, too, and no other dude at Westwood Park rocked all the fly labels like he did. Plus he was smart and came from a good family with money and shit. Nahima was a fool for sleeping on him. Ryan bet that old thug she was lying up with didn't have shit on Rashawn.

"Are you going to the Quay concert?" Ryan blurted out.

"Yeah, I bought my ticket Saturday. Why? Are you trying to go?"

"You only bought one ticket? How come you ain't taking no date?"

Rashawn cocked his head covered with the prettiest shiny coils and stepped into Ryan's personal space. Instantly, the scent of the cologne she and her clique had grown used to him wearing made her nipples hard. Mr. Gibson was looking brand new all of a sudden in Ryan's light brown eyes. His smooth cocoa skin looked as soft as a newborn baby's ass.

"I decided to kick back and enjoy my favorite rapper, third row center, by myself. A couple of my boys and I are going to meet up for dinner before the show and part ways afterward. They couldn't afford tickets to see Quay so they're going to check out a movie with their girls and hang out at the Flow Room later. What's your plan for that night?"

"I'm going to see Quay too, but I won't be on the third row." Ryan laughed through the butterflies fluttering in her stomach. "Me and my girl, Kela, will be up in the project seats, wishing we were in the suburban seats with you."

"Had I known—"

"Ryan!"

Rashawn and Ryan turned around and saw Kela stomping toward them.

"Hey, Rashawn," she greeted him quickly before she trained angry eyes on her friend. "Everybody is in the deli line waiting for you! I am hungry, and you know we've got that business to take care of."

"Oh, yeah. Um . . ." she mumbled, eyeing Rashawn with new appreciation and regret that she couldn't finish their conversation.

"Go on with your girl, Ryan. But I'm going to check in with you tomorrow on what we talked about you doing, okay?"

"Okay."

Rashawn left his locker and strolled down the hall. Ryan walked away in the opposite direction, leaving Kela standing with her hands on her hips and her mouth wide open. Lunch and gossiping with her girls were the last things she wanted to do right now. Ryan would much rather have been in Mr. Klebo's office registering for the SAT with Rashawn.

Nahima and Yashia were in a heated argument, throwing plenty of shade and rolling their necks by the time Kela reached their lunchroom table. Ryan was sitting with her head flinging back and forth like a tennis ball, taking it all in as she giggled between pushing forkfuls of shrimp salad into her mouth. Kela didn't give a damn about that petty shit the besties were snapping at each other about. Her eye was on her homegirl who only ten minutes ago was kee-keeing with Rashawn and making goo-goo eyes at him like he had just licked her pussy. Kela wanted to call Ryan's ass out on it, but she decided to put it on mental hold until Algebra 2, the sixth period class they had together.

"Will y'all two hush?" Kela snapped as soon as her big donkey booty hit her chair. She had been standing watching the two best friends go at each other like enemies for a minute, hoping they would soon get tired and let it go. "What are y'all fussing about anyway?"

"I'm done trying to solve Nahima's concert issues, because she's being too damn petty. I found a guy who's already got his ticket and agreed to go along with her plan. Dude even volunteered to scoop all of us up and drive us to State Farm Arena to see the show and go to IHOP afterward in his granddaddy's brand-new Suburban!"

"Problem solved then. Who is it?" Kela took a big bite of her taco.

Nahima wrinkled her nose and made a gagging gesture without offering an answer. Ryan placed her hand over her mouth to keep from spitting shrimp salad everywhere when she laughed.

"Trey Asbury," Yashia announced.

"Trey Asbury . . . That name sounds familiar." Kela kept tossing the name around in her head as she chewed her food. "Oh, shit! Are you talking about Two-ton Trey?"

"Yes!" Yashia and Ryan screeched in unison through hysterical laughter.

"That boy got titties, big-ass double-D titties! And he stank! He smells like unwashed pussy and a turd of shit mixed in a jar!"

Yashia banged the table with her fist. "She didn't say nothing about what the nigga had to look and smell like. All she said was he had to be black, have a damn ticket, and be ready to roll with us."

"So I forgot to mention anything about good personal hygiene, and I didn't make it clear that I would prefer a guy who weighed less than four hundred pounds! But you and Dondrae had to know I would never be down with Two-ton Trey coming to my house for me to introduce him to Charles and Venus Morris as my date to the concert! Hell, I don't even want him to know where I live!"

"Who did you find, Nahima?" Then Yashia leveled her eyes at her two other girlfriends. "Did either one of y'all find somebody to help her cover for that loser she's willing to die on the cross for so he can go to see Quay with her?"

Kela shook her head and dropped her eyes to her plate.

Ryan kept on eating, her gaze never leaving her food.

"Well, it's either Two-ton Trey or Santana is going to have to clean himself up, put on his big-boy boxers, and meet your parents. You make the call, bestie."

"There is no way I'm even going to pretend like Trey Asbury is taking me anywhere. So we'll just have to come up with someone else."

"No, you are going to have to dig up some unlucky guy, because Dondrae and I are done with it, and these two heifers ain't got shit."

"You could always ask Rashawn," Ryan said a little too reluctantly for Kela's taste. "I was just talking to him at his locker, and he told me he bought his ticket over the weekend. It's in the third row. And he said he's not taking a date, so may—"

"Why you didn't tell us that when you first sat your ass down, Ryan? Me and Yashia wouldn't have been in here going off on each other over this mess."

"Yeah, that's what I want to know." Kela popped her lips and turned all the way to her left to stare Ryan down. *Why didn't you report that important news story, Ryan?*

Clearly nervous, Ryan fidgeted before she placed her fork on her plate and looked at her three closest friends. Her eyes lingered on Nahima. "You said you didn't want anything to do with Rashawn. I can't even count how many times you've told us you ain't got nothing for him. He's been stalking you for weeks, but you always reject him. So how was I supposed to know you would be cool with him pretending to be your concert date, Nah-Nah?"

"She's got a point, Nahima," Yashia rushed to agree.

Good answer, but I ain't buying it. I saw how you were looking at Rashawn. There's more to the story than you're letting on, Kela thought, but she held her tongue and continued to watch the scene play out.

"I still ain't got nothing for Rashawn, but I'll take him over Trey Asbury's funky ass any day. Can you please talk to him for me, Ryan? Run down my whole situation, and ask him if he'll help me out. But make sure he understands it won't be a real date, because I ain't—"

"I know. I know. You ain't got nothing for Rashawn Gibson." Ryan giggled.

Now that it appeared as if Nahima's concert-date issue was more than likely resolved, the clique resumed eating and fell into their normal lunchtime gossip session. Kela was pigging out and talking smack per usual, but she kept cutting a side-eye at her girl Ryan, because her gut told her she had been bitten by the love bug and now she had an itch that only Rashawn Gibson could scratch.

Nahima stood up abruptly as she checked her cell phone. "I've got to go, y'all."

"Where are you going?" Yashia asked.

"I have a doctor's appointment. Remember? My mom wants me on birth control."

"Oh, yeah." Yashia smirked and raked her fingers through her auburn Senegalese twists. "Don't forget to sell your fashion tickets. How many did you get anyway?"

"I got twenty, but they're already sold because my dad is going to pay for all of them and let me give them away to my family and friends since he knows our project is going to win. So I'm good."

"Cool."

Kela wiped her mouth with a napkin. "Call us later to let us know how your appointment goes."

"I will." Nahima turned her attention to Ryan. "Please take care of that with Rashawn for me."

"I got you, girl."

"Thank you. Okay, ladies, I'm out."

KiKi replaced the cordless phone in its cradle and looked at Jay again. "She's still not answering, King, It's not three o'clock yet, so school ain't out."

Jay nodded from the examination table where she lay on her side hooked up to an IV. "Try again right after three."

"Okay, I will."

Gracie was standing at the bottom of the examination table, massaging Jay's swollen feet. All three ladies had agreed that they reminded them of elephants' feet because of their puffiness. Jay could tell her older friend was worried about her, and it warmed her heart.

"I want my auntie to know what's going on with me, but I don't want to scare her. Besides, I think it would be better for me to wait until Dr. Dalrymple comes back in here and gives me my test results."

"I agree, Kang. Ain't no need to call your auntie, upsetting her when you don't even have the whole story. Let's wait and see what the doctor has to say."

"I think that's a good idea too," KiKi added.

"Thank y'all for taking care of me. It's a damn shame I've got more support in prison than I have on the outside. That shit hurts." Jay wiped her tears with the back of her hand. "I owe Sheftall a million dollars for letting y'all skip work detail to stay with my raggedy ass. I swear y'all treat me better than my brother, who don't give a shit about me."

"Relax and don't think about what or who you don't have, Kang. You need to focus on positive stuff like your chirren and what that law student is gon' do for you. I pray to God they can get you up outta here soon."

Jay closed her eyes and imagined Jalen's face. He was a day old the last time she saw him in the flesh. He was such a gorgeous baby with the most exotic gray eyes like his father. Jay wondered what he looked like today. Before she'd asked Aunt Jackie to tell Jill to stop sending pictures to the prison, some of her facial features had begun to take over his angelic face. Jay remembered his lips were full like hers, and he had her dimples, too. None of that mattered now. All Jay cared about was getting out of Leesworth so she could touch her son one more time and let him know who she was. Children needed to know who their birth parents were, especially their mother. She believed if she had known the love of her mother, her life would've been much different. A real maternal bond was greater than any other bond between human beings.

Nahima may have been Jay's biological child, but she had not conceived her in love like she'd done with Jalen. And she had not carried her in her womb, sharing her body with her for nine months, either. The maternal experiences of her two children were as different as the moon and the sun. The way Jay saw it, Jalen was her child, her flesh and blood. He was the product of a man and woman who'd been very much in love. Nahima, on the other hand, was simply her offspring, a product of an egg she had donated to her ex-lover so she could have the baby she'd always wanted. That was why Jay couldn't connect with her no matter how great an effort she had put forth initially when she had received that first email from her nearly five months ago. They just didn't click at all, although they were so much alike, too much alike in fact. However, as it had been from the beginning, Jay felt nothing for Nahima, but she couldn't sever ties with her just yet because she needed her. Her wish to leave prison and spend her last days with the child she loved rested in the hands of the child she'd never loved and never would.

"Call Nahima again, KiKi. I know it's after three now."

"No, it's not, King. I'll call her again in seventeen minutes."

"Okay."

Chapter Twenty-one

"So, you ain't getting the ol' snip, and it's a no from Ramona on having her tubes tied?"

"Correct."

"How the hell are y'all going to keep from getting pregnant again then, bruh?"

Dex was four inches shorter than his best friend of twenty-five years, and he outweighed him by at least fifty pounds. It was obvious that he was struggling to keep up with Zach's long strides as they trekked down Jesse Hill Jr. Drive Southeast, headed back to Grady Hospital. They'd had a taste for fish and grits, so Uncle Chuck's Diner on Armstrong was where the friends had eaten lunch after the morning session of a special training they'd signed up for. The short walk on such a nice early spring day was a way to get a little exercise in along with a good ol' down-home meal.

"We agreed on a compromise," Dex managed to say, huffing as he took giant steps to keep up with Zach.

"I'm listening."

"Instead of either one of us getting fixed or Ramona taking the pill or injections, we decided on a low-hormone IUD that's good for five years called Kyleena. It's ninety-nine percent effective."

"That's what's up, bruh."

"Yeah, I'm glad we settled on something we both like. Her appointment is next Thursday."

"Cool. I'm just happy y'all ain't about to hit my pockets with more godkiddies."

"Hell, we can't afford any more crumb snatchers. That's why we had to do something about it."

Zach opened his mouth to say something, but his cell phone chimed and vibrated in his pocket. He removed it and checked the screen. It was a text message from Patricia, his stepmother. Zach stopped walking in the middle of the sidewalk filled with moving bodies traveling both ways. Dex stopped too.

Pat: Tag number was traced to Oscar Floyd Wilson B/M DOB: 02/19/1951 Age: 63 Raleigh, NC. That's all I have. On my way to court now. Luv u!

Zach: Good looking out. Thx.

"Bingo! It's on now."

"What's on? Who was that?"

Zach smiled at Dex, rubbing his graying goatee. "Stepmom came through. I got a name on Aunt Jackie's low-key lover."

"Ah, shit. What you plan to do now?"

"Call Wallace and see if he's ever heard of him and go from there."

"And if he don't know him or ain't ever heard of him?"

"I'll hire a PI to get the goods on Mr. Oscar Floyd Wilson's ass for me."

"Bruh, I think you're doing too much. Why don't you just tell Aunt Jackie you know she's seeing some old dude and ask her to introduce y'all? You know she ain't about to lie to you. So man up and take the direct route."

"Nah, I like my plan better. If Wallace don't know the cat, I'll go with the investigator, because Auntie is obviously too sprung to see anything wrong with creeping around with some man like some undercover, sanctified THOT. Let me find out if he's legit, and then I'll confront her." Zach started walking again.

"Okay, do it your way, bruh. But let the record show that I don't like your plan."

"It's on the record, and I don't give a damn."

Patricia placed her cell phone on the end table and rubbed her hands together. Pressing her teeth into her bottom lip, she looked down into Wallace's eyes as the back of his head rested on her lap. "It's done. Now what?"

"I suspect Zachary will be calling me real soon, definitely before the day is over."

"He has the information he needs now, so why do you think he'll call you, babe?"

"I know my son. Time in prison and distance didn't change our connection. Zach is still the same meddlesome and stubborn boy he was when I went away forty years ago. He's going to call me and ask if I know Oscar or if I've ever heard anything about him."

Patricia shifted on the sofa, still looking down at her husband's face. "And what will you tell him?"

"Oscar asked me the same thing this morning when he called, and I still don't know. I ain't no lying man. You know that like you know Jesus saves, baby. But to be honest, I wish Jackie would let Oscar call my boy up and introduce himself so they can get together and talk man-to-man. It's the right thing to do. Jackie and Oscar are two level-headed, respectable Christian adults who don't need Zachary's permission to be in love. This situation is turning into one big mess. I kind of regret hooking up my friend with my former sister-in-law now. It seemed like a good idea at the time, but maybe it was a mistake."

"How can you say that when they're so happy, Wallace? The man proposed to Jackie, and she said yes. That ain't no mistake right there. It's love."

"It's definitely love all right. If Oscar weren't in love with Jackie, he never would've asked her to marry him, because he's not that kind of man." Wallace sat up on the sofa and turned to meet his wife's gaze. "He told me the day after he buried Florence that he would die a widower because he couldn't ever love another woman the way he'd loved her. He swore he would never marry again, and he was sticking to that plan until he met Jackie. I don't know what she did to him, but it sure has made him very happy. Now every time I talk to him, which is just about every day, all he talks about is Jackie this and Jackie that." Wallace chuckled.

"See? That's your evidence right there! Hooking them up was not a mistake. It turned out to be a blessing to a pair of well-deserving people. Don't you let the devil steal your joy. Do you hear me, Wallace King?"

"Yes, honey, I hear you loud and clear," he answered with a slight smile.

"So stop worrying about Jackie and Oscar, because they're going to be just fine. God's got His hand all over this. Zach can't touch it no matter how hard he may try. Besides that, Oscar ain't no punk, and you know that firsthand, Wallace. He is one of your closest friends. You were his vice principal, working side by side with him at the roughest high school in Raleigh for eight years. Oscar didn't take no shit from those crazy kids, and he won't take any shit from Zach either."

"My God, Patricia! Watch your mouth, girl. There ain't nothing worse than a woman with a filthy mouth."

"Oh, really now, Reverend King? You don't have a problem with my filthy mouth when it's doing something else."

The most devilish grin lifted the corners of Wallace's mouth, and he reached over and squeezed his wife's thigh. "You're right about that, baby."

"No, no, no, honey, there will be none of that right now," Patricia fussed, swatting his hand away. "I still need to know what you're going to say to my stepson when he calls you and asks if you know Oscar Wilson."

"To tell you the truth, I haven't made up my mind yet. Let me pray on it and see what the Lord has to say about it, and when Zach calls, I'll speak accordingly."

The sight of bright red blood in the commode sent Jay into panic mode. It wasn't her period. She knew that for sure because it came regularly in the first week of every month, which had already passed. Dr. Berger, a nephrologist Jay saw twice a month, had warned her that this would happen someday, but she hadn't expected it so soon.

"Kang!" Gracie knocked on the door of the tiny restroom right outside examination room three. "Dr. Dalrymple is back. She needs to talk to you about your test results."

"All right, G. Tell her I'm coming. Let me wash my hands."

"Okay."

I'm not going to cry. I'm not going to cry. I will not die until I get out of here and have a few days with my son. I'm not going to cry.

Jay silently chanted those words over and over again while the warm water ran over her soapy hands. She had to believe her own declaration, because if she didn't, she would give up the fight against the diseases that were gradually taking her down, and die before she made it out of Leesworth.

After she dried her hands with the hard gray paper towel, she tossed it into the trashcan and left the bathroom. When she returned to the examination room, waddling on swollen, achy feet, she was surprised to see

Dr. Berger. He wasn't supposed to be at Leesworth today, and Gracie damn sure didn't mention he was with Dr. Dalrymple.

"Dr. Berger, what are you doing here today? I didn't expect to see you again until next month." Jay waddled past KiKi and Gracie on her way to the examination table, where she took a seat.

"Ms. King, Dr. Dalrymple called to tell me you weren't feeling well today. I became concerned and decided to come and check on you."

"Dr. Berger and I need to talk to you about the results from the tests we administered earlier, Ms. King."

Both doctors looked equally concerned, which was a sign that whatever they had to say wasn't a good report.

Jay clapped her hands together one time, and the loud sound bounced off all four walls in the small room. "Okay. Give it to me straight, no chaser and no bullshit. What's the point in beating around the bush anyway?"

Dr. Dalrymple's eyes shifted from Jay over to Gracie and KiKi, who were standing by the door, before returning to Jay. "Are you sure you want—"

"Yeah, I'm absolutely sure I want my friends to stay. Those two women over there are more like my blood than my own damn brother. That's how come the warden gave them special permission to hang out here in the infirmary with me. So whatever you have to say to me, you can say it in front of KiKi and Gracie."

"Okay, your friends may stay." Dr. Dalrymple opened the folder in her hand and skimmed it briefly. "We've done all we can do for you, Miss King, but the results from all of your tests indicate that you're dying. I'm very sorry."

"Oh, God, don't say that! Lawd, have mercy!" Gracie broke down.

KiKi didn't respond verbally, but tears began to flow down her cheeks as she wrapped her arms around a distraught Gracie.

"How long do I have, Doc?"

"Don't you want to know exactly what's going on with your liver, kidneys, and now bladder, Ms. King?" Dr. Berger asked.

"Hell nah! What good will it do me for y'all to fill my head with a bunch of medical mumbo jumbo that I can't understand when y'all can't do shit to save me? Just tell me how long I got and get the hell out of here!"

"You have three months at the most, but maybe longer if we transfer you to the medical prison in Augusta."

"I ain't going down there to that goddamn death trap! I'm staying my ass right here so I can be close to my son and my aunt."

"It's not up to you, Ms. King. That's a decision that Warden Sheftall and her boss will make based on my recommendation and Dr. Berger's as well."

"It doesn't even matter, because I'll be at home soon anyway."

Without another word, Dr. Dalrymple walked toward the door, and Dr. Berger followed her out of the room. Gracie and KiKi walked over to Jay and hugged her. The three women cried in a huddle as several minutes passed before Jay finally broke the silence.

"I don't want to talk about it, y'all. So don't ever bring up the subject." She wiped her eyes. "KiKi, call Nahima again. She should be at home by now."

Chapter Twenty-two

"Damn," Nahima mumbled under her breath when she heard her phone vibrating in her purse again.

For some weird reason, Jay had been calling her from an unfamiliar number at the prison ever since Venus had picked her up early from school. Of course, she hadn't answered for obvious reasons, but she damn sure was curious as to why she was calling her during school hours on a Thursday, a day that she'd never called on before. Everything about Jay reaching out to Nahima today was very peculiar. Something was up, no doubt. She was being overly persistent, too. Every time the phone stopped ringing, it would start ringing again within seconds.

Nahima had enough on her mind already after filling out the medical questionnaire that Venus had insisted on helping her with. She had refused to let her, though, because she knew her mom was just trying to be nosy. Nahima was hip to her game. Therefore, she'd gotten up and moved to another chair in the lobby of Dr. Avery's office so she could complete the form alone and in peace. And she'd wanted to be able to answer the phone just in case Jay called so she could find out what was going on with her. But she didn't call back until Nahima was in the examination room with a nurse who didn't look all that much older than her. She was getting her vitals checked at the time, so she could only peep at the phone's screen to see it was definitely Jay calling. And she had been calling nonstop ever since. The phone was even buzzing in her purse now.

"Nahima, I need you to place your feet in the stirrups at the end of this table and scoot all the way to the edge down here toward me."

She followed Dr. Avery's instructions and looked at the young-looking nurse out of the corner of her eye. Nahima held her breath when she felt the doctor insert his finger inside her vagina. He was talking to her the entire time, telling her step by step what he was doing. She wanted him to shut the hell up and get it over with already so she could get her prescription for birth control and go home. Once there, she could answer the phone the next time Jay called and find out why she had been blowing up her damn phone for the last hour and a half. Whatever was up must've been pretty damn important. Hopefully, it was some good news about her early release. Nahima could only pray that was the case.

"Girl, ain't nobody checking for Chad Moore! I don't care how cute he is. All his stud stock went down when he got with Willow 'the Ho' Brady."

"I know that's right!"

"You ain't lying, girl!"

Two other girls at the bus stop and Ryan laughed and slapped palms with Kela.

"She might be a pretty little cheerleader and dress fly as hell, but she done fucked and sucked the starting five on the basketball team and half of the football team! Yashia will stomp that ho to sleep if she even looks at the baseball team, and I would help her."

All four girls cracked up and passed around high-fives again.

"What about Killian Woods, though, Kela?" Ryan asked with a smirk. "Are you checking for him?"

"Hell yeah! You already know he can get it anytime, anyplace, anyhow, all day, and every day!"

Just as the girls exploded with another round of giggles and hand slaps, they heard the bus rounding the corner, headed in their direction. They all turned around. Ryan's mouth went completely dry when she saw the shiny black Ford Mustang cruising in front of the bus. The top was down, so she could see the driver clearly. Ryan could hear Quay's "Black Velvet" pumping through his stereo speakers, too. The bus skidded to a stop, but the Mustang kept moving, stopping directly in front of her and her friends.

One of the girls with them—Ryan didn't know if it was Amber or Satin, and she didn't care—asked, "Who is that fine-ass nigga in that Mustang?"

"Girl, that's Rashawn Gibson." Kela rolled her eyes and waved her hand. "He's too rich and bougie for us Pine Tree Hills chicks. So stop drooling and looking thirsty, honey."

Just then, Rashawn lowered the volume on his music and blew his horn. "Hey, Ryan and Kela, y'all want a ride home?"

"Nah, we're—"

"Yeah, we—"

Rashawn's handsome face balled up, obviously with confusion, because of the different half answers from Kela and Ryan.

Amber and Chloe said goodbye and walked away quietly from their friends to get in line to board the school bus. Kela stepped to Ryan and stared her down with a deep scowl on her pretty milk chocolate face.

"I don't want to ride nowhere with Rashawn Gibson. You know rich niggas like him always think they gotta do favors for girls like us. I ain't no poverty project for him to try to rescue from the hood. I rode the bus to school, and I'm riding it home."

"I'm not a poverty project or whatever the hell you said either. But I know Nahima needs me to ask Rashawn if he'll pretend to be her date to the Quay concert. That's why I'm about to cross the street, hop in his whip, and handle that for her."

Rashawn honked his horn again. "Are y'all riding or what?"

"I'm riding!" Ryan walked off and never looked back to see Kela's reaction.

I may not be rich, and yes, I'm from the hood. But Tasha Monique Mathis didn't raise no fool. Nahima only wants Rashawn for one night, but I want him period.

Nahima looked down at her phone and saw it was Jay calling her again. But this time it was from the usual number she'd memorized. The phone didn't accept incoming calls, but Nahima knew it was located in Jay's office where she worked as the inmates' accountant and business manager. Even in prison, education gave you an advantage. While all Jay's inmate buddies mopped floors, cleaned toilets, and washed other inmates' dirty drawers, she was sitting behind a desk crunching numbers.

Jay called again just as Venus got off the exit that led to their subdivision a few miles away.

"Who is that calling you back-to-back like that, Nahima? I hope it's not some little horny-ass boy, especially not the one you've been screwing and smoking weed with. He's the reason you had to get that injection today."

Nahima rolled her eyes and snapped, "It's not a boy, okay? Not that it's any of your business, but it's one of my female friends."

"If it's a girlfriend, as you say, why won't you answer the phone?"

"Do you really think I want to have a conversation with anybody in your presence?"

"If you don't have anything to hide, you can talk in front of anybody."

"Well, I won't talk to anybody, girl or boy, in front of you." Nahima looked around when Venus pulled into the Publix parking lot. "Why are we stopping here?"

"Not that it's any of your business, but I have a few things to pick up for dinner this evening and breakfast in the morning. Are coming in with me?"

"Nah. You go ahead. But can you please get me some chips and some more of those ice cream sandwiches I like?"

Venus sighed. "Yeah, I can do that."

"Thanks."

As soon as her mom closed the car door, Nahima stared at her phone, willing it to ring again. It was just like Jay to call her a thousand times when she wasn't able to answer but ghost her now that the coast was clear for her to talk. Timing was everything in life.

While Nahima waited for Jay to hit her up again, she tapped the Instagram icon on her phone and started scrolling through it to check up on her friends. All she saw on Yashia's page were pictures of Dondrae and her. Kela hadn't been on the Gram in a minute. The last thing she had posted was a picture of the two tickets to the Quay concert that her granddaddy had bought for her and Ryan from last week. As expected, Ryan's page was boring as hell with pictures of her with her brothers and sisters everywhere. There were six Mathis siblings in all, and they were tighter than tight. They weren't rich, and they didn't live in the 'burbs, but they always looked happy whenever Nahima saw them together. Maybe once Jay got out of prison, she could get custody of Jalen from Zach and Jill, and then her little brother, their birth mom, and she could become a happy family. Nahima was so deep into her thought of being with Jay and Jalen that when her phone rang, it caught her off guard and she almost dropped it.

"Hello?"

"Nahima, I've been calling you for hours. Why didn't you answer?"

"I had a doctor's appointment today, and I couldn't pick up. And when I got in the car with my . . . with Venus, I didn't want to talk in front of her. She's in the grocery store now, so we've got to talk fast."

"Okay. Look, you've got to give me the name of my resource person today. We don't have time to waste, Nahima. Do you understand?"

"I do."

"Good. I need another reference, too. My warden is one, my resource person will be one, and then I need one more. Can you take care of that, too?"

"I think I can, but why are we rushing? Why does it have to be done today, Jay?"

"Time is running out, damn it! You said you had my back, and now it's time for you to prove it! Now find me a resource person and another reference so Jalen can start visiting me. I hope soon after that I'll be able to get up out of this hellhole. I've already emailed you the link to the form the references need to fill out, along with my ID number and other information. I sent another link to the form that the resource person needs to complete ASAP. You may have to make up some shit about how I met the people and how long we've known each other, but you're smart enough to do that. I really, really need you to make it happen, Nahima. Promise me you got me."

"I got you, Jay. I promise on everything that I got you."

"Okay. I'm going to call you tonight at eight sharp, and I expect you to have the name of my resource person and references."

"I'll take care of everything. I promise."

"That's my girl. I'll call you tonight."

"Okay."

Nahima sat there for a little while wondering why Jay was rushing her to find the resource person and references all of a sudden. It was going to be hard for her to get it done by eight o'clock, but she would do it even if it killed her. And Santana would help her. She started dialing his number, but she stopped when she saw Venus walking toward the car with a few bags of groceries. She would call him as soon as she got home, because Jay was depending on her to come through for her, and she would.

Chapter Twenty-three

Venus stopped in the middle of the foyer, holding the grocery bags and her briefcase. "Where are you going, Nahima?"

"I'm about to go upstairs to do my homework and study. Why?"

"I need you to put away the groceries while I get dinner started."

Nahima blew air from her cheeks in frustration and dropped her purse and backpack on the couch in the den and marched in Venus's direction. She took the grocery bags from her mother and headed toward the kitchen. She didn't waste a second removing the food items from the bags and placing them in the refrigerator and cabinets all around the kitchen in silence. The only thing on Nahima's mind was taking care of Jay's business before she called her at eight o'clock. But she couldn't get anything done without first talking to Santana. He was the only person who could help her, although she was pretty sure that Aunt Jackie wouldn't have a problem stepping up to be Jay's resource person. Why wouldn't she? Everybody, including Jay, knew how sweet Aunt Jackie was. There was nothing she wouldn't do for her family. Nahima had no idea why Jay wouldn't just ask her to help her. It just didn't make any sense.

"I'm done."

Venus turned away from the stove and smiled at Nahima. "Thank you, baby girl. Dinner will be ready

around six. Your dad should be home by then. I want us
to eat together tonight, okay?"

"Yeah, okay."

Nahima left the kitchen, gathered her stuff from the
den, and ran upstairs. She locked her door once she got
inside her room and took her phone out of her purse.
Then, after hitting the number three on her speed dial,
she waited for Santana to answer.

"What's up, shaw . . . shawty?"

Damn, his ass is drunk!

"Hey, bae, I need a big, big favor."

"What'chu need? I . . . I know what I need from y . . .
you."

"Santana, I'm not playing! I really need you to be
serious and listen, okay?"

"I'm sorry. I'm listenin'. Damn."

"I need you to ask one of your female family members
who's over eighteen and has never been to jail to serve as
my birth mom's resource person."

"What's that?"

"It's someone on the outside who'll work with my
mom's case rep to help her get out of prison early through
this special organization. They won't have to do all that
much, but she needs them to take my little brother, Jalen,
and me to the prison to see her soon and sometimes meet
with her case rep."

"Damn, girl, that's gon' cost you some money. I . . . I
don't know nobody who gon' do some legit shit like that
without gettin' paid plus gas money."

"No problem. I'll pay the person and give them gas
money. Who do you have in mind who'll do this for you
to help me, Santana?"

"My sis . . . sister, Avila, will do anything for a few bucks.
I'll even let her use my car. But she's gon' need a . . . a
babysitter for her bad-ass kids."

"Shit, bae, can't you keep your own nieces and nephews for me?"

"I ain't got no damn nieces, just three nephews all under the age of . . . the age of eight. Them li'l niggas got warrants and shit." Santana laughed, and the sound of it grated Nahima's nerves.

"Has your sister ever been to jail or had any run-in with the law?"

"Nope. Never."

"Okay. What's her full name and birthday?"

"Her name is, um, Avila Marie Bridges. Shit, I can't remember her birthday, though." He hiccupped and laughed again. "But she's three years older than me."

"Can you call her for me please? I really need to talk to her right away, Santana. It's important."

"I'ma give you her number, and when you call her, tell . . . tell her you my girl. Explain this shit to her, and she'll help you for me."

"Okay, I will." Nahima searched through her backpack for a pen and a piece of paper. "All right, what's Avila's number?"

"Hold up now, shawty. I need you to sew something for . . . for my cousin. She's pregnant."

"Huh?"

"Sew my cousin a baby-doll dress. She's pregnant."

"What cousin are you talking about, Santana? You have never mentioned your pregnant cousin to me before. What's her name?"

"Never mind all that. You want a nigga to do somethin' for your, um . . . birth mom, so you gotta sew my cousin a baby maternity dress. She wants flowers and shit, fancy shit to wear over some fuchsia tights for her baby shower."

Nahima sat quietly for a moment, confused and trying to make what Santana had just told her make sense in her head. He had assured her that his sister, Avila, would help her with Jay's business, and now he was asking her to sew a maternity dress for his cousin. He had mentioned his sister to her a few times and had even called her from her house before. But who the hell was this pregnant cousin he had never talked about? And why did he want Nahima to sew a maternity dress for her? It sounded kind of suspicious.

"Shawty, you still there?"

"Yeah, I'm still here. When is your cousin's baby shower?"

"Shit, I don't know! Maybe in two weeks, I think. You gon' hook her up or what?"

"She wants a baby-doll maternity dress with flowers or some other pattern to wear over some fuchsia tights. Is that what you said, Santana?"

"Yep. Flowers or p . . . paisley or some shit like that. You gon' make it for her or what?"

"Yeah, I'll make it for her as long as your sister will help me out with my mom. Deal?"

"Deal."

"What size is your cousin?"

"Ummm, make it your size but bigger in the ass. She's five or six . . . six months pregnant."

"Okay, I've got some pretty cream fabric with different colors of paint splashes all over. Some of the splashes are fuchsia. Do you think your cousin would like that?"

"Yeah, I think so," he slurred like a typical lush.

"Cool. Now can I have your sister's number? I really need to talk to her."

"It's 404 . . ."

Ryan had been nervous and excited about riding shot-gun in Rashawn's smooth Mustang from the moment he offered her and Kela a ride home. As she crossed the street to take him up on that offer, her eyes nearly popped out of her head when he got out of the car to open the passenger's side door for her to get inside. That was the first time Ryan had ever seen any guy do that Hollywood-type of move for a chick in real life. It had really blown her mind, so it was on from that point on.

Ryan's nerves and shyness had kept her quiet when she'd first settled into the butter-soft leather seat. The fact that Kela had been watching—no doubt with smoke blowing out her nose and ears—only made matters worse. She had felt Satin and Chloe's eyes zooming in on her from their regular seats in the back of the bus, too, but that hadn't bothered her so much. And after Rashawn put his whip in drive and took off around the corner with Quay rapping about some boss bitch he called Black Velvet, Kela instantly became an afterthought.

With the top down, the light springtime breeze had lifted Ryan's long sandy brown hair and tossed it all around her face and shoulders. And to her surprise, she hadn't cared at all. There was something about Rashawn that made everything feel right no matter who was watching. It was kind of funny that she had never paid him much attention before today when they'd held that short conversation at his locker. For sure, Ryan had somehow missed how fine, suave, and handsome Rashawn was, because all she'd made him out to be was a thirsty dude stalking Nahima only to be rejected by her every time he stepped to her. He wasn't looking thirsty at all at the moment, sitting across from her in a corner booth at Wings Wizard.

As they'd cruised closer to the Pine Tree Hills community with Ryan giving him directions, she had begun to feel sad that their time together, regardless of how platonic the scenario was, was about to come to an end. That had been her cue to state her business.

"Rashawn, I need to ask you something very important, but you can't judge me on it. Okay?"

He'd looked in his rearview mirror before his eyes slid to rest on Ryan. Then he'd pushed the button on the dashboard to lower the music. "Oh, yeah? Ask me then."

"Well, Nah—"

"Hold up. Are you hungry? I am for sure. I was in the chemistry lab during lunch, working on an experiment for extra credit. My dad acts a fool when I bring home a B in math or science. So I knocked out that little experiment, and now I'm starving."

Ryan had laughed, but it wasn't loud and ratchet like she laughed with her clique. "I wouldn't mind eating something sweet like a slice of cake or some doughnuts."

"This is your territory. Name the spot where you can get some dessert and I can eat some real food."

"Okay." Ryan had checked her surroundings, looking from left to right. "Make a left at the next light."

Ryan's directions had brought them to the Wings Wizard, where she was enjoying a thick slice of double-chocolate cake with two scoops of vanilla ice cream on top while taking in the sight of her dream man devouring a twelve-piece lemon-pepper wing meal with fries and veggies on the side. She had talked him into trying the small diner's famous cranberry lemonade, her favorite beverage in the world. He was on his second refill, so there was no mistake that he liked it.

Rashawn dropped another meatless bone on his plate and wiped his sticky fingers covered in sauce and smiled at Ryan. "I thought you had something very important to ask me."

"I do."

"I'm waiting."

Ryan's nerves made her belly flop, and her shyness returned under Rashawn's intense stare, but she fought it off because she couldn't let her girl down. "You see, Nahima's uncle bought her two front-row tickets to the Quay concert. One was supposed to be for Yashia, but Dondrae surprised her with a ticket so they can go together. And because Nahima didn't want to choose between Kela and me who she would give the extra ticket to, she decided to take her boyfriend."

"That makes sense. But why did you need my opinion on Nahima's business?"

"I didn't." Ryan shook her head. "I need you to do a favor for Nahima for me. You know, since you like her and all."

"For the record, I don't like your girl anymore. Believe that. But what's the favor?"

"Nahima's boyfriend is some twenty-two-year-old man who Yashia said is a thug. I don't know if that's true, because I've never met him. Hell, I didn't even know his ass existed until the other day."

Rashawn frowned. "What does any of this have to do with me, Ryan? I don't get it."

"Nahima needs you to pretend to be her date to the concert to throw her parents off. All you got to do is ride with us to her house and act like you came to pick her up. But once we get to the concert, she'll meet up with her boyfriend, and everybody else will sit in the seats they paid for. Then after the show, we'll all go to IHOP and take Nahima home afterward. You'll see her to the door just in case her parents are still up. The end. Can you please do that for her?"

Chapter Twenty-four

Rashawn laughed out loud in Ryan's face, but he regretted it as soon as he did. Right away, he could tell he had pissed her off, which was the last thing he'd wanted to do. But he wasn't laughing at her. It was karma that he found funny as hell. It had turned around and bitten Nahima Lawson-Morris dead in her ass after all the times she had been rude and nasty to him.

"You know what? Don't even worry about it, Rashawn." Ryan dropped her spoon onto her saucer and grabbed her purse. "Forget everything I just told you, and you better not tell anybody, either."

When Ryan slid across the bench and stood up from the booth, Rashawn got up too. He gripped her wrist loosely with care. "I'm sorry, Ryan. Please don't leave. I was wrong, and I shouldn't have laughed at Nahima's situation. But you've got to admit this is some wild shit your girl is on."

"Maybe it is," Ryan mumbled, poking out her bottom lip and folding her arms. "But Nahima is one of my best friends, and I don't appreciate you clowning on her like that."

"I said I'm sorry. Look, if I agree to help your girl out, will you sit back down and finish your dessert? I was enjoying hanging out with you, and I'm not ready for it to end yet. Please stay."

Ryan didn't really want to leave. It was easy for Rashawn to tell that by her body language. And something in her sexy light brown eyes told him she was feeling him just as much as he was feeling her. Sure, she was definitely salty about him laughing at Nahima's fucked-up love life, and he shouldn't have done it. But he'd be damned if he was about to let this madness mess up his chance to get close to Ryan.

"Are you going to stay with me and finish your cake and ice cream or what? I'll help Nahima out only because you asked me to. Just sit back down so we can finish talking, all right?"

Ryan gave Rashawn the answer he wanted when she quietly slid back into the booth. It didn't matter to him that she didn't give him an audible answer, because his dad had told him a long time ago that actions always spoke louder than words. If that was true, Ryan was exactly where she wanted to be—with him. Only a fool wouldn't take advantage of a golden opportunity, and Rashawn was much too damn smart to be anyone's fool. So he retook his seat across from Ryan.

"Okay, now that we've solved Nahima's situation, how about we work on ours?"

"Our what?"

"Our situation, of course."

Ryan smiled, and Rashawn could've sworn the lights in the little hole-in-the-wall restaurant seemed brighter. How the hell had he not noticed how beautiful this girl was before?

"I didn't know we had a situation, Rashawn. Tell me about it."

"I like you a lot, Ryan. I think you're cool. You're very pretty, stylish, and funny. You must be smart, too, since you're in Mr. Knight's Advanced Placement Biology class. I took that same class last year from him, and it kicked my ass. If my dad hadn't hired a tutor to help me out, I wouldn't have made that B-minus."

"Well, I'm maintaining a strong A-minus right now, and my mama couldn't afford to hire me a tutor even if her life depended on it. I just take lots of notes, ask plenty of questions in class, and study like crazy all the time. I have to set a good example for my younger brothers and sisters since I'm the oldest child at home now. My big brother, Chase, is in the army. He's stationed in Germany. Man, we miss him so much."

"You just gave me another reason to like you, girl."

"When did you first start liking me?"

"Believe it or not, that brief conversation at my locker today opened my eyes."

"I believe you, because the same thing happened to me. That's why when you pulled up and offered Kela and me a ride, I didn't think twice about saying yes. Keeping it real, I saw it as the perfect time to ask you to help out my girl like I had promised her, but I wanted to spend some time with you, too. And I'm not ashamed to say I'm happy I got in your car."

"I'm happy you did too. But I must admit I was nervous as hell when I rolled up on y'all."

"Why?"

"Guys have feelings just like girls do. Rejection stings us the same way it stings y'all. Thanks for not embarrassing me in front of Kela."

"You don't ever have to worry about that."

The newfound chemistry and attraction between them were powerful and thick. Only a machete could slice through it. Rashawn felt it down to his core, and he hoped Ryan could feel what he felt. The way his heart was beating all wild and fast in his chest at the moment was something he had never experienced the few times he had held a one-on-one conversation with Nahima. Looking back on it and considering what he now knew about her, she was a bullet that the universe had helped him dodge. Somebody up in the sky was looking out for him.

Rashawn reached across the table and placed his hand on top of Ryan's. Her silky cocoa skin made him want to touch her everywhere. "Tell your girls I'm in on the bogus date plan. Let them know I'll drive my dad's Lincoln Navigator so we can all ride together. It seats eight deep comfortably."

"Cool. Everybody will be glad to hear that so we won't have to squeeze in Dondrae's mom's Jeep Cherokee." Ryan laughed. "Oh, don't forget we're going to IHOP after the show. Will that be a problem?"

"It may be a problem for you and me because we'll probably still be full from an early dinner at the restaurant of your choice. I'm going to ditch my boys and the plans we had just for you. I'll pick you up around four o'clock so we can spend time together alone over some good food. Then we'll scoop up everybody else and go to the concert. How does that sound?"

"I'm down with it. I ain't ever been on a real date before."

"For real?"

"Never."

"Well, a brother's got to roll out the red carpet for you so you'll never forget your first real date. I want to meet your mom first, though. She needs to know that her little girl ain't sneaking around with a thug or a grown-ass man. Just tell me when I can visit you at your crib."

"My mom will be home all day Sunday. That's the only day she doesn't work."

"That's a plan. I'll call you when I get home from church." Rashawn reached inside his pocket and handed Ryan his phone. "Dial your number and let it ring so I can lock you in. Lock me in too so you'll recognize my number when I call you tonight."

Ryan flashed another smile that Rashawn wanted to kiss off her full and luscious lips, but he reminded himself to take things slow and easy with her, because she was too special for him to move too fast.

Zach shut down his Google search on Oscar Floyd Wilson on his cell phone, mad as hell with a million questions swimming through his head. The main question was for Wallace. He felt like calling him to cuss his ass out and Patricia too for pretending like they didn't know anything about the man Aunt Jackie was dating on the sneak. A simple online search on Oscar had taken Zach to the website of an organization of retired African American educators in Raleigh. One of the first mugs he'd spotted front and center was the infamous Oscar Wilson, aka Aunt Jackie's secret boo thang. Apparently, dude was vice president of the organization. Zach didn't know for sure if that information was current, because he had no idea if the man still lived in Raleigh and was only visiting Atlanta periodically or if he had relocated. The latter could save the old cat's life, because that would mean he had his own house or apartment in the A. But if he was doing the visit-commute thing on occasion, he was more than likely staying with . . .

No, no, no! Aunt Jackie ain't letting no nigga lie up in her crib! Oh, hell nah!

Zach pushed that thought out of his mind and shifted his anger back to Wallace. He was a part of the retired educators' organization too. After a little cross-referencing, Zach took a sucker punch to the gut when he discovered that his old man and Oscar knew each other very well. How could they not when they'd worked as a principal and vice principal tag team at the same school for eight years before Wallace retired and Oscar followed him a year later? That was some sneaky bullshit right there. Zach couldn't prove it in a court of law, but his hood instincts told him that Wallace had played cupid for his former boss and former sister-in-law. And for some inexplicable reason that he would never, ever accept, the three senior citizens had colluded to keep him in the dark about it. If that was the game the two old cats and the kitty wanted to play, Zach would play it too, but harder.

He picked up his cell phone from the bed and relaxed on the stack of pillows piled up in front of the headboard. Zach was about to see how many times he could make Reverend King lie in a single phone call. He scrolled through his contact list and dialed his old man's number. Zach almost started laughing as the phone began to ring when he thought about how he was about to mess with Wallace's head.

I'm about to make this Negro sweat.

"Zach, how are you, son?"

"I'm all right. I was off work last night, but I'm tired because I had a mandatory training at the hospital today. How are you?"

"I can't complain. I was lazy today, just relaxing and watching movies. I cooked, though, so Patricia wouldn't have to once she returned home from work. She loves my beef tips and rice, so I put my foot in some for her."

"That's good, because you know a happy wife ensures a brother a happy life."

"Amen. I agree, son."

"Speaking of Patricia, where is she? I want to thank her for matching that tag number to an actual person."

"Oh . . ." Wallace cleared his throat. "Patricia is resting right now. What did you find out from the information she gave you?"

"Nothing but the man's name. He's some old-timer named Oscar Floyd Wilson, and he's from Raleigh just like I'd suspected. I'm surprised you and Patricia don't know him. Ain't that the craziest thing?"

"It's something, all right. What do you plan to do now that you know the man's name, son? Are you going to confront Jackie?"

"Nah, I can't confront Auntie about it because I'll have to confess that I've been snooping around in her business. I've got a wife and kids to take care of, so I ain't trying to die. I'll sleep on it a couple of days and then make a decision on my next move. I might need some help from you and Pat, though."

"Um, I'm not sure what either one of us could do to help you, Zach."

"I'll think of something and punt the ball to y'all when it's time to execute whatever plan I come up with."

"That sounds kind of shady, don't you think?"

"Yeah, it is, but what else can I do?" Zach faked a laugh. "If only Aunt Jackie trusted me enough to be straight up, I wouldn't have to plot behind her back. She's too damn old to be playing silly games, and this Oscar dude is too. I guess just because a person is over sixty, it doesn't mean they're mature. I'm glad you always keep it real with me."

Zach covered his mouth and snickered when Wallace didn't voice an immediate comeback. He could only imagine how uncomfortable he was. Zach hoped he was close to pissing on himself.

"Well, I won't hold you any longer, Pops. Tell Patricia I called to thank her for the information. Let her know I'll be in touch soon."

"I sure will. I love you, son."

"I love you too, old man. Later."

Zach ended the call with his father and clasped his hands together behind his head. He had just launched his first bomb in the war of the young versus the old. He hoped Jackie, Oscar, and Wallace were ready, because he was about to go hard on them until he broke one of them down and they spilled all the tea. As a betting man, Zach would put his money on Aunt Jackie to be the one to throw in the towel. Wallace was a little stronger than she was. Oscar was the one he didn't know shit about, but that was all about to change.

Chapter Twenty-five

"Shit!" Nahima threw her cell phone on the bed and started biting her nails. She had called Santana's sister, Avila, six times over the past hour and a half, and she'd left her three long messages, but she hadn't returned her calls yet. It was a few minutes past seven thirty, and Jay had promised to call her at eight sharp to get the information she needed. If Nahima didn't have those names for her, shit was going to hit the fan, and she couldn't deal with that tonight. Jay had a way of making her feel like the crud at the bottom of the sewer whenever she was mad. It was like she didn't have a filter and couldn't control her anger. Nahima wondered where that kind of rage came from. Maybe it was a result of all the pain and misfortune Jay had experienced in her life.

Nahima picked up her phone to check the time before she hit the redial icon again, calling Avila. She was so angry and worried that Santana's drunk ass had made a promise to her that he couldn't deliver on. If he had, Jay was going to lose it. She had sounded close to the edge when they'd spoken earlier, but if Nahima didn't secure Avila as her resource person, all hell was going to break loose when she called at eight o'clock.

Nahima ended the call without leaving another message and hit the redial again. She started pacing the floor on her bare feet. Usually, she loved the feel of her toes sinking into the thick tan carpet, but because of the heavy pressure she was under, she barely even noticed it.

"Hello?" a female answered, screaming over loud music in the background.

"Avila?"

"Yeah, this is Avila. Who is this? If it's a bill collector, I ain't got no money."

Nahima laughed nervously. "I'm a friend of Santana's. My name is Nahima."

"Yeah, he told me you were gon' call me, and he already explained what you need me to do for your mama so she can get outta prison early. I told Santana to let you know I was down with it. All I need you to do is let me know ahead of time when we gotta make the trips. I'm asking for a hundred dollars each time I drive you up there."

"Okay, I can handle that. Can you please text me your email address so I can send you the forms you need to fill out? My mom needs those forms submitted as soon as possible."

"I can do that."

"Thank you so much. I really appreciate this, Avila."

"It ain't no problem. Any friend of my brother's is a friend of mine."

"My mom should be calling soon, so I've got to hang up now. Don't forget to text me your email address as soon as we hang up."

"I won't. It was nice talking to you. I can't wait to meet you, Nahima."

"I can't wait to meet you either. Thanks again. Bye."

"Bye."

Nahima did a backward flop on her bed and squealed in relief. A few seconds later, her phone chimed with a text alert. Avila had kept her word. She shot her a quick text back, thanking her. Then another text message came through, but this one was from Ryan. It said she had talked to Rashawn. He had agreed to be her pretend date to the Quay concert, and he would drive the whole crew to the arena and IHOP after the show in his dad's Navigator.

"Yesss! Yesss! Yesss!" Nahima cheered, feeling like the weight of the world had been lifted off her shoulders.

She needed to secure one more reference for Jay before she called in fifteen minutes. On a whim, she dialed Ryan's number.

"Hold on, Rashawn. It's Nahima calling."

"I thought you just sent her a text."

"I did. Maybe that's why she's calling."

"Don't leave me on hold too long or I'll hang up."

"I won't." Ryan clicked over to the other line. "What's up, Nah-Nah?"

"Girl, you know I hate when you call me that."

Ryan laughed. "I know. That's why I do it."

"Thanks for talking to Rashawn for me. I owe you a big one."

"You sure do, and don't think I ain't gonna make you pay up."

"And I will. But right now, I need another favor."

"Uh-oh, what is it now?"

"Remember last year how you used your mom's email address to look like she gave Kela and Cree reference letters to that beauty camp?"

"Yeah. Why?"

"I need you to do something like that for me for my ma . . . my auntie. She's in prison, but there's a chance she can get out early because of her bad health with the help of a special program."

"I didn't know you had an auntie in prison."

"Duh! She's been in prison for the past nine years. That's why you didn't know about her. How many people do you know who walk around talking about their incarcerated family members? That ain't nothing to be proud of."

"That's true. Okay, I can help you because my mom never checks her email. You know how she's always at the shop working like a slave. I'm the one who has to keep up with all my little brothers' and sisters' schoolwork and stuff with their school. My mom is a damn good parent, but she don't have time to do certain things because she has to work a lot to take care of us by herself since our dad got killed."

"Yeah, Ms. Tasha is cool, and she really loves all of her little ratchet-ass kids."

Ryan laughed. "Whatever, heifer. So what's the plan? What do I need to do to help your auntie?"

"I'm going to email a link to you for a reference form that you need to fill out like you're Ms. Tasha. Make up some shit like your mom used to style my auntie's hair ten years ago and they became friends or something like that."

"I can do that. But what if they call my mom?"

"Put down your phone number so if they call, they'll reach you instead of Ms. Tasha. Then you can verify whatever information you put on the reference form. Okay?"

"I got you, Nah-Nah."

"There you go with that stupid name again." Nahima laughed. "Anyway, I'm expecting a call from my auntie, so I'll let you go. Thanks, Ryan."

"No problem, girl. That's what friends are for. I'll see you tomorrow."

"Okay. Bye."

Ryan clicked back over to her other line. "Rashawn, are you still there?"

"Yeah, I'm here, but I was about to hang up on you."

"You knew better."

"Oooh, you think just because you're fine and sexy and a brother is feeling you that you can put me on hold for thirty minutes and I won't hit you with the click?"

"No. And it wasn't thirty minutes, Rashawn, so quit lying."

The two teens shared a laugh before the line went quiet.

"I know this thing we got going on between us is new and all, but sooner or later, you've got to tell Nahima and the rest of your girls what's up. No, Nahima and I never hooked or anything, but I was trying to make something happen, so she might feel some type of way when she finds out we're kicking it."

"Yeah, I know. But can we wait until after the concert before we put it out there please? We're all looking forward to seeing Quay, and I don't want anything to mess it up."

"Cool. We can put it on hold until after the show. But then you're going to have to let all your girls know I'm your man."

"I will tell all of them. I promise."

"King, are you awake?" KiKi tiptoed over to the cot in the corner of the small room and touched Jay's shoulder. "Wake up, boo. I've got some good news for you."

Jay's heavy eyelids fluttered open, and she tried to focus on her friend before they closed again. All the medication she was on kept her sluggish, so it was hard to concentrate because it also slowed down her gross motor skills. That was the reason Jay had been under observation in the in-patient ward of Leesworth's infirmary for the past four days.

KiKi kneeled on the side of the bed. "Open your eyes, King."

After a few more attempts, Jay managed to fully open her eyes and look at her friend. "Hey."

"Hey, girl, how do you feel?"

"Like shit.'"

"Well, maybe my good news will make you feel better."

"What are you talking about?"

"I checked your email, and you got a message from Amanda that said the JUP has agreed to take on your case."

"Are you serious?"

"Yeah, I'm dead serious. Now I ain't no lawyer or even a law student, so I didn't understand all those legal terms, but I memorized everything I understood so I could tell you word for word. They said your case was accepted for representation because you're an inmate currently being treated for one or more terminal conditions, and due to your mental health after the birth of your son, you relinquished your parental rights to him without counsel under stressful circumstances."

"That's true." Jay winced and rubbed her stomach in pain. "What's the next step?"

"They need Nahima to submit a video to the JUP, telling the judge why she thinks Jalen will benefit from having you in his life once you're released. It didn't really say Nahima had to do the video. It said a family member familiar with your case. And since she's the only relative who's willing to help you, I figured it has to be her."

"Why can't she just appear in court with Amanda?"

"I don't remember the exact words, but it said something about if the person was under the age of seventeen, they needed to say whatever they want the judge to know on a video. I remember the email address where Nahima needs to send the video."

Jay struggled to sit up in the bed before KiKi reached out and helped her. She was winded and exhausted, using every ounce of energy to sit up straight without toppling over.

"That's good. Now I need you to go to Sheftall and get permission to call Nahima from my office this evening. She'll say yes because she wants me out of here. Let Nahima know what's going on with me and why I haven't called or emailed her in a while. Tell her to make the video and send it to Amanda pronto. Above all that, I need her to bring Jalen up here next Saturday. It's too late for her to pull a visit together for this weekend, but I don't give a damn what she has to do, Jalen better visit me next Saturday. Make sure Nahima understands that, KiKi."

"Okay, King."

Jay relaxed her body on the cot again and closed her eyes. After a moment, she realized KiKi was still there. Jay opened her eyes and noticed how worried her friend was.

"Don't worry about me, girl. I'm an old-ass bird. Believe me when I tell you I've seen tougher days than this one. It'll be many months past the three Dr. Dalrymple said I have left before I take my last breath. Just watch and see."

"I ain't worried about that. I've got something else to tell you, but it ain't good news."

"Go ahead and tell me then."

"You were right when you said Sheftall wants you out of here, but it ain't for the reason you think. The word around here is she's been waiting for you to die because your health is costing the system too much money, and that's why she can't get the big raise she's been past due for when she arrived here. But since you keep holding on, she just wants you gone any way possible. I hate to tell you, but she already put in a medical transfer request for you to be moved to the medical prison down in Augusta. As soon as a bed becomes available, you're out of here."

"That fat-ass, dwarf-looking, evil bitch. I've been busting my ass trying to save money around here every way I can to please her, and this is how she treats me? Fuck Sheftall! I hope she'll swallow her tongue and die." Without warning, she sat up straight on her own. "Never mind calling Nahima for me, KiKi. Help me get out of here so I can take care of my own motherfucking business."

"Are you sure, King? You're so weak."

"Wrong. I was weak. You just fired me up, KiKi. I feel like I can go outside and run a marathon now. Let's go."

Chapter Twenty-six

Nahima stuffed a pillow under the dress after she pulled it over her head and down her body to try it on. Then she walked over to the full-length mirror on the back of her closet door to check out her reflection. Striking a side pose, she rubbed a hand over the expensive fabric in the tummy area that looked like a big baby bump. Any pregnant woman would look and feel fabulous in a maternity dress like the one she was sewing for Santana's cousin. Nahima was pleased with her work so far, but she still had to tweak it a little bit before it would be perfect.

Carefully, she pulled the colorful baby-doll maternity dress over her head and wiggled out of it. After deciding she would complete the split-shoulder butterfly sleeves tomorrow, she put the dress on a satin hanger and hung it in her closet.

With her homework and studying out of the way, Nahima's thoughts immediately shifted to Jay. She hadn't spoken to her in a few days, and it bothered her. Their last conversation had been all about rushing to secure Avila as her resource person and one of her references along with another reference from someone else. Nahima had taken care of everything, and she'd waited by the phone for Jay to call her so she could give her the good news. But that call never came. Now Nahima was worried that something bad had happened at the prison. Was Jay sick, or had she gotten into some trouble and was sent to the hole like those hard-looking female inmates she'd seen in prison movies on Netflix and HBO? All kinds of crazy, scary ideas had been keeping Nahima on edge since the night Jay was supposed to have called her but never did.

Bored, Nahima sat down at her desk and pulled out a sketchpad and turned to a blank page. It was hard to dive into creative mode with so much on her mind. She was worried about Jay and disappointed with Santana because he seemed more excited about the goddamn dress she was working on for his pregnant cousin than he was about meeting her at the Quay concert. Every time she mentioned anything about the show or the outfit her mom had ordered from Nordstrom online for her to wear, he would change the subject to some stupid shit. And whenever she called him out on it, he would say he was excited, but it didn't seem like he was.

With a blue charcoal-tip pencil, Nahima began to draw a scarf that after a few seconds started to look like an African headdress. The long horizontal strokes made it appear like it was flowing in the wind. It inspired her to add splashes of pink, orange, purple, and green. The more she drew, the more fashionable the piece became. The gift that God had blessed her with was the therapy her troubled life needed. Whenever Nahima was in creative mode she felt alive and free. Nothing else mattered except the vision she was bringing to life. But when her phone rang, it snapped her out of her safety zone and brought her back to reality.

She hurried over to her bed and answered the phone. It was Jay. *Thank God.*

"Jay, where have you been? I've been worried about you."

"You don't need to worry about me. I'm here in this goddamn cage, trying to handle my business."

"I know, and I'm doing my part to help you. I did everything you told me to do, and I waited to hear from you. Why didn't you call me?"

"It's a long story. But I heard you stepped up for me. That's why I'm calling now. Forget about the other day. It's time to move forward."

"Fine," Nahima said a little bit testy on purpose. "What's the next move?"

"I need Jalen here for a visit next Saturday. I don't give a damn what you have to do to make it happen. My son has to come to Leesworth so Amanda and the staff at JUP will know I mean business about flipping his adoption. I'm not going to take him away from Zach. I just want access to my son when I get out of here. Amanda said I can get unsupervised visits so he can know I'm his real mother who loves him. Please bring my baby boy to me, Nahima."

"It's going to be hard, but I'll bring him, Jay. I swear."

"That's my girl. I need something else, though."

"I'll do anything for you. Just tell me what it is."

"I sent an email address to you where you need to send a video explaining to the judge why Jalen needs to know me as his biological mother and how he'll benefit from my early release. You need to do it soon so my case rep can secure a hearing before a judge as fast as she possibly can. Will you be able to handle that, Nahima?"

"Yeah, I can handle it."

"Good. Go ahead and work on getting Jalen up here next Saturday and record the video for the judge. I'll check in on you soon. Okay?"

"Okay, Jay."

Nahima shuddered like a chilly wind had swept through her room when the call ended, but she shook it off. There was no time to allow doubts and eerie feelings to distract her. Jay needed her help, and she expected her to deliver.

***

"What'cha gon' cook for dinner for me tonight, Kela?"

Kela slammed the car door shut and put on her seat belt before she turned around to make sure her little brother, Charmer, was strapped safely in the back seat. He was.

"I'll cook whatever you want me to cook, Granddaddy. What do you have a taste for?"

"How about some fried chicken wings and fried rice?"

"That sounds good!" Charmer said excitedly.

"Okay, that's what I'll cook then."

As Mr. Daniels sped up the steep hill on Ryan's street, Charmer leaned forward. "Look, Kela!" He pointed at the black Mustang parked in front of the Mathis residence. "Ms. Tasha got a new car! It's sweet, too!"

"It is nice, ain't it, buddy?"

"Yes, sir, Granddaddy, but I like your car better."

For ten hot seconds, Kela couldn't move or speak. It was a good thing she'd seen it for herself with her own eyes, because if she hadn't, she would have never believed it. She snatched her phone out of her pocket and dialed Ryan's number and turned toward the door so her granddaddy wouldn't be able to hear her talk.

I knew it! I knew it! I knew it! This heifer done broke the girl code. What happened to bitches before britches?

"What's up, Kela?"

"Ain't nothing going on. What's up with you?"

"We're chillin' and Netflixin' tonight over pizza and wings, girl."

"That's what's up. I'm about to come over there and hang out."

"I thought you were spending the weekend with your granddaddy so he can take you shopping for a concert outfit."

"Yeah, but I'm bored, and we ain't going shopping until tomorrow. I can hop in an Uber and be at your spot in less than an hour."

"You'll be bored here too, because the little ones got me watching some *Captain Marvel* shit. I'm about to go to sleep on them."

"Mmm, mmm. I guess I'll stay where I am then."

"Cool. I'll call you tomorrow evening so you can tell me about your outfit."

"All right. Bye, girl."

"Can you believe she was about to come over here?" Rashawn drew Ryan closer to him on the sofa with his right arm, which was curled around her shoulders. "You need to tell her about us. I can understand why you want to wait until after the Quay concert to tell Nahima. But why can't you go ahead and come clean with Kela and Yashia?"

"I don't feel like hearing all the negativity."

"Negativity? Do you think being with me is wrong?"

"No."

"I don't either. But we'll do it your way and wait. I just don't like it."

Ryan had a feeling that Kela already knew the deal. She had been saying a whole lot of slick shit ever since the day Rashawn offered them a ride home and she accepted it. Ryan and Kela had been like sisters since the third grade. Their mothers were even tight. The two best friends loved each other to pieces, and up until she and Rashawn had become an item, they always told one another their deepest secrets no matter what. This was a different kind of secret, though.

Rashawn was Ryan's first real boyfriend. Her mother had never allowed her to have a boy sitting up in their living room around her little brothers and sisters before. But Tasha liked Rashawn for Ryan, and that made him special to her. She didn't want their new relationship to end over some jealous-girlfriend bullshit before it had a chance to take off. That was why Ryan was going to stand her ground on her decision to keep her love life on lock until she was ready to tell her clique that unlike Nahima, she did have something for Rashawn Gibson.

Jill smiled when Zach walked out of the bathroom and into their bedroom wrapped in a towel and let it drop to the floor. Age and a few extra pounds in his waist and tummy hadn't depreciated the exquisiteness of his body at all. His caramel skin was still smooth and tight for the most part, and his regular workouts had kept the would-be bulging belly and muffin top at bay. Her man's pecs were still firm, and his abs hadn't given up the fight with fluff like other men in their late 40s. Most importantly, Zach's dick hadn't drawn up a single inch, and it was still thick and able to sprout an erection even with a feather-like touch. In other words, in Jill's eyes, her husband was still sexy as hell.

"Zachary, are we going to Callie and Bernard's engagement party Friday night?"

"It's up to you, baby," he said, applying deodorant to his armpits. "I can take it or leave it."

"We haven't been out on the town in a very long time, so I think it would be nice. Don't you think? We could dance, drink champagne, and talk with other adults about anything other than Black Panther, Beyoncé, and *Fortnite*. Let's go please, Zachary. I really need a break from your children."

"I didn't make Zach Jr. or Zion by myself. And you wanted to adopt Jalen even before he was born, and I told you no. But I'm damn sure glad we got my li'l dawg. I can't imagine life without him."

"Can we go to the party?"

"Damn, you really want to go, huh? Who's going to watch the kids for us? The party is an overnight thing at some historic mansion right outside city limits. So we need someone to spend the night with them."

"Ask Aunt Jackie. She won't mind babysitting for us."

Zach sat down on the bed to put his support socks on. "I don't know, baby. Auntie's got a bae now. She ain't got time for the kiddies anymore."

"Oh, Zachary, ask her please."

"Okay. I had planned to stop by her house on my way to work anyway."

"You're trying to catch this Oscar guy over there, eh?" Jill winked and grinned.

"Nah, I just want to holla at her and see how she's doing. But while I'm there, I'll ask her if she can watch the kids for us Friday night. If she can, we'll go to the party. If she can't, we'll have movie night and pizza with our little juvenile delinquents as usual."

Chapter Twenty-seven

Nahima stood outside her parents' bedroom with her ear close to the door, trying to hear what kind of "activity" was happening on the other side. The sun had started to fade a little, but it was too damn early for them to be fucking. She knocked three times and waited.

"Come in, baby girl! It's open," Charles, the kindest, most generous father in the world called out.

Nahima turned the knob and pushed the left side of the French double doors to enter the master suite. She walked farther into the spacious room and stood at the foot of the bed. Her mom was lying down in the middle of the California king watching the evening news, and her dad was sitting in his recliner, flipping through a client's investment file from his job. That was something Nahima and Venus had grown accustomed to, because he was a serious workaholic.

"What's up, baby girl?" Charles asked.

"I really had a good time over at Uncle Zach's house the other weekend. I baked cookies with Jalen, and he slept with me in Zion's room." She laughed like a little kid for dramatic effect. "I miss him, and I wish I could see him more often."

"Zach and I have always wanted you and Jalen to have a close relationship. The only thing standing between you and your baby brother is you, Nahima."

"I know, Mom, but I want to change that."

Charles closed the file. "You should."

"I'm going to, but I wanted to talk to y'all about it first. Would it be okay if I invite Jalen over next Saturday morning to spend the whole day with me? I could take him to the movies and maybe Chuck E. Cheese."

"I think that's a good idea."

Venus sat up on the bed. "I don't know about that, Nahima. Jalen is a certified mama's boy and strongly attached to Zach, too. I can't imagine him being separated from Jill for a whole day. Maybe you should start off with a few hours first and then work your way up to a full day. But it's not up to your father and me. You need to call Zach and Jill. Let them know whatever they decide is fine with Charles and me. We just want you and Jalen to have a good, healthy relationship."

"All right, I'll FaceTime Uncle Zach."

Hmmm, the infamous Oscar Wilson ain't getting his mack on today.

Zach pulled up to Aunt Jackie's house on his way to work. He had left his neck of the woods early enough that he could spend at least thirty minutes with her and then double back and still make it to the hospital on time for his twelve-hour shift. Today, Zach had his key to the house where he'd spent his teen years so he wouldn't have to ring the doorbell. Although he was wrong as hell, he had hoped that Oscar would be visiting Aunt Jackie so he could bust in on them. However, luck wasn't on his side this time, and he was kind of relieved.

Zach killed his engine and hopped out of his SUV and made his way toward the house after locking his doors with the key fob. He noticed that Aunt Jackie's grass was freshly cut, the hedges had been trimmed neatly, and the prettiest purple hyacinths lined the manicured bushes and walkway. Either Oscar had a green thumb or he had paid a skilled landscaper to tighten up Aunt Jackie's yard. Her bootleg yard man, Mr. Ernest, who he had begged her to fire for years, hadn't turned the yard into a botanical expo in the middle of Ridgewood for damn sure.

Just as Zach was about to insert his key into the lock, the door swung open. He stumbled a few steps forward from the shock but quickly regained his footing. He smiled at his auntie, who looked gorgeous and comfortable in a bright orange caftan with zebra-print trim.

"Good evening, Zachary Sean King. I wasn't expecting you, but come on in, baby."

He kissed Aunt Jackie's cheek and eased past her to enter the house. After she closed the door, she turned and left him standing in the front hall. Sensing she wasn't pleased with him for popping up on her again, he decided to play it cool so he wouldn't set her off. Zach soon strolled toward the back of the house where he found Aunt Jackie in the den sitting in her recliner watching an episode of *Greenleaf*. It was the wrong day and time for her favorite drama of all time, so she must've learned how to pull it up on OWN On Demand.

"What brings you by this evening unannounced again, Zach?"

Damn, she's still salty about me breaking up her lunch date with her bae the other day.

"A brother can't just stop by and check on his favorite girl on his way to work?"

"Negro, you had to pass by the hospital to get here, so stop playing, and tell me why you're really here."

Zach sat down on the couch. "Seriously, I just wanted to make sure you were okay and to ask you if you needed anything. You'll never admit it, but I know your money gets a little funny in the middle of the month because you insist on paying twenty percent of Jay's meds tab and you keep money on her books."

"I am doing nothing for Jay in her situation that I wouldn't do for you if you were where she is right now. And because of my sacrifices for your sister, God has been faithful to me, and there ain't nothing funny about my money." Aunt Jackie looked at Zach and grinned like he'd just told her good ol' joke. "But if you want to put something in my hand, I sure 'nuff will take it."

Zach whipped out the folded check he had placed in the breast pocket of his blue scrubs shirt before he'd left home. He faced his auntie, returning her grin, and immediately noticed the sparkle in her eyes. She was actually glowing. *Happiness.* It was the first word that popped up in his mind as he offered her the check for $500. But it wasn't the money that she'd had no idea he had stopped by to give her. It was Oscar, the mystery man she was working overtime to keep hidden from him and the rest of their family. The problem was Aunt Jackie's street skills were kind of rusty now, and righteous living was working against her, too. She had been saved and sanctified so long that she had forgotten how to lie and scheme like all of her big sisters, including his late mother, who had successfully carried on an affair with his daddy's best friend for over a year before finally getting caught and killed.

Zach was experiencing mixed emotions as he watched his auntie's smile widen and her eyes buck at the amount of the check. Naturally, he was happy because he had made her happy, but there was a tiny ache in his heart at the same time. However, he was an accomplished actor, straight out of Ridgewood, so he was able to play it off. Fortunately, for Aunt Jackie, Zach had sharpened his anger management skills, too. Because if he and Dex hadn't recently completed the annual mandatory supervisors training on the job, which had included a short session on emotional fitness and awareness, he would've reached over and snatched his check back and ripped that goddamn engagement ring she'd obviously forgotten she was wearing off her finger.

"Thank you so much, Zach. Auntie is going to surprise Hattie Jean and Bertha with those hats they want from that cute little boutique in Riverdale. The owner is an African lady named Lebechi, which means 'look to God.' Anyway, she's from Nigeria, and she told us that all of her hats and headdresses are made by hand. I'm so excited! Hallelujah! Thank you, Jesus! I'm going to buy me one of the pretty hats too. The ushers better get ready to pick Missionary Holston up off the floor when Hattie Jean and Bertha sashay into Refuge in those hats. She can't stand my sisters, but she likes me because I sang "Sit Down and Rest a Little While," by request of course, at her mama's funeral. That woman went to shouting and screaming until she passed out right by her mama's open casket.

"Lord, I hope Hattie Jean and Bertha won't get to fighting and cussing over that royal blue hat, because both of them want that one. So maybe I should buy it for myself and make them pick out two different hats altogether. Yeah, that's what I'll do. But then I'll have to find a new dress and some shoes to go with the hat. That's fine, because after I take my tithe off the top of this check and buy all three of us a hat, I'll still have enough money left over to treat myself to a new dress from the plus-size boutique over in Morrow. Oh, Zach, you should see the clothes they sell for us thick sisters in that place. The last dress I bought there was . . ."

Zach blinked out of his emotional twist and watched Aunt Jackie's lips moving a hundred miles an hour. Her word count had exceeded tens of thousands since he'd placed that check in her hand. And she was still talking. God must've touched Zach in that moment, because he wasn't even mad anymore. In fact, he was calm. Only Satan could be angry over a sweet and selfless Christian woman in her sixties and a retired high school principal finding love and becoming engaged. There wasn't a damn thing wrong with them being together, especially since an assistant pastor, a man of strong faith like Wallace, had played matchmaker for the couple. He loved and respected his former sister-in-law, and there was no way in hell he would've hooked her up with a looser, a buster, or a player.

Zach stroked his goatee and smiled before he reached inside his pocket for his keys. He didn't like how Aunt Jackie, Wallace, Oscar, and even Patricia had tried to pull a fast one on him, but he had to respect their game. Now he would bow out gracefully and lie low. But sooner or later, Oscar Wilson was going to have to step to him like the OG he clearly thought he was and ask for Aunt Jackie's hand in marriage. Zach would give him a hard time off the rip just to fuck with him as punishment for sneaking around with his auntie behind his back. Then he would give the old cat a break and throw him and Aunt Jackie the nicest wedding he could afford. Hell, he might even dig deep and host the wedding at his beachfront property in Jamaica.

"I love you, baby! Bye!" Aunt Jackie stood in her doorway, waving at Zach until he hopped into his SUV and pulled off.

After she closed and locked the door, she turned around with a smile on her face and found Oscar standing there. His flat expression caused her smile to disappear. She wrapped her arms around his waist and rested her face against his lower chest. Oscar loved Aunt Jackie too much to stay mad with her for more than a few seconds.

Therefore, he didn't even try to resist her affection, although he wanted to.

"I won't park my truck in the backyard again, sweet—"

"Ssshhh. Please let it go, Oscar. Don't let Zach upset our peace. We only have one more week and four days. That's what we agreed on—you, me, and your daughter—before we introduce you to my whole family and announce our engagement here over dinner."

"Look at me."

Aunt Jackie pulled back, maintaining her hold on Oscar, and locked eyes with his.

"If I didn't love you from the depth of my soul, I wouldn't be putting up with this foolishness."

"I know, baby. I know."

"One more week and some change, Jackie. And don't you try to push it back, either. Because if you do, I can't promise you that I'll stick around."

Aunt Jackie broke their eye contact without a word and placed her cheek against Oscar's chest again. His heartbeat was strong and steady, thumping rhythmically in sync with hers. She loved him deeply and wanted very much for him to be happy. And she loved Zach with all her heart, so his happiness was important to her too. But did Oscar and Zach love her enough to do the one and only thing that would make her happy for the rest of her life? Only God knew the answer, and He would reveal it to Jackie in one week and four days.

Chapter Twenty-eight

"What's popping, pumpkin?"

Nahima smiled when her uncle's face filled her phone screen and she heard his voice. "Did I catch you at a bad time? I wasn't sure if you had to work this evening. I just took a chance."

"Actually, I just pulled up at work. I'm walking through the parking deck as we speak. What's on your mind? Are you ready for the Quay concert in two weeks?"

"Yeah, I'm ready. But I called you about something I want to do next weekend."

"All right. How much is it going to cost Uncle Z?"

Nahima smiled, tempted to hit him up for some money, but she decided against it. "It won't cost you a dime."

"Whew! Thanks for sparing my pockets. Tell me about your plans."

"I want Jalen to spend all day with me next Saturday, from morning to evening, so we can hang out. I was thinking about taking him to breakfast, to see a movie, and then to Chuck E. Cheese or maybe Legoland. My mom and dad are cool with it. I just need the green light from you."

"Um, pumpkin, that's kind of heavy. Your baby brother has never spent any time with you away from our house before. An all-day deal might be a little too much. My li'l dawg is addicted to his mommy. If Jalen is away from Jill too long, he starts whining and scratching like a crackhead. Let me . . . Hold up."

"What?"

"Do you have plans for Friday night, pumpkin?"

"No. Why?"

"Jill and I want to go to an engagement party at a mansion and spend the night. Do you think you can watch Jalen and your two cousins overnight in our house so we can go? It'll be kind of like an audition or a trial run before the main event. If everything runs smooth like gravy Friday night, I'll let you take your baby brother to breakfast and a movie next Saturday. Deal?"

"Deal! Thanks, Uncle Zach. I promise nothing will go wrong Friday night. Trust me."

"Okay. Tell your mom to drop you off at my crib around seven."

"I'll be there."

"I'll see you then, pumpkin. I love you."

"I love you too."

Nahima was proud of herself. She still knew how to trick her parents and her uncle into doing whatever she wanted them to do. Jay said all the time that she had inherited the power of persuasion from her, and it was true. Now that the first part of her plan was in progress, she needed to get her hands on some extra cash so she could pay Avila for the trip to Leesworth next Saturday. But at the moment, it was time to dive deep into her acting skills so she could make the perfect video to convince the judge that Jalen's adoption needed some minor changes and Jay deserved to get out of prison early so she could be reunited with her daughter and son.

"Okay, it's almost time to pack up everything and head to lunch, everybody," Mrs. Moran announced. "If you haven't turned in the money for your fashion show tickets, please do so soon because the deadline is Friday.

So far, only Erica, Halle, Yashia, Nahima, Gregory, and Skye have turned in all of their money. Some of you have turned in some money and have promised to pay the rest before Friday. Congratulations are in order for Nahima, who sold the most tickets to date with a total of twenty."

More than half the students in the class applauded Nahima for her accomplishment, and she stood and took several bows. She blew a few kisses and threw up the peace sign, too.

"Girl, I can't with you." Yashia laughed and continued packing up her sewing supplies.

"You know how I am. This class is my domain, so I have to be on top of everything. I'm almost finished with the patches on the denim side of our project. After that, Ryan needs to do her first fitting. She is going to look so good strutting down the runway in our original design. I can't wait."

"Everybody knows I cannot sew. I only took this class so I could be with you. That jumpsuit is your design, and you should own it proudly, girl. You are a fashion genius."

"Thanks, Yashia."

"Has anyone seen my key?" Mrs. Moran asked, searching through her desk drawer. "It's attached to a green spring-like rubber bracelet."

Some students shook their heads, and others gave her verbal answers, but no one acknowledged that they had seen the teacher's key. Everyone continued packing up their belongings, preparing to leave for lunch.

"Okay, it's time to go, class. I need to find Mr. Woodard so he can assign me another key. Everybody needs to head to the cafeteria now. Make sure you don't leave anything, because I'm going to lock up whether I have a key or not. I'll see you all tomorrow."

Nahima and Yashia got their purses and backpacks and left the class ahead of their classmates.

"Girl, I want some fresh French fries hot right out of the grease with my turkey burger, so let's hurry up."

"You go on then, Yashia. I'll catch up with you. I've got to pee, and my feet hurt. I'm going to run to the restroom and stop by our locker to swap out these wedges for my flats."

"Okay. But hurry up, because Kela took a picture wearing her concert outfit, and she is not going to show it until we're all at the table."

"I'll be right there."

Nahima broke out in a sprint, retracing her steps to Mrs. Moran's class. Right before she reached the room, she removed a pair of latex gloves from her purse and put them on her hands. Nahima looked all around her before she slid the missing key from her cleavage and unlocked the door. She locked herself inside the classroom and went straight to the teacher's desk. Within seconds, she found the box of cash and unsold tickets in the bottom drawer. Her hands shook as she quickly counted out $500 and stuffed it inside her purse.

After returning the box and closing the drawer, she inched toward the door and cracked it. Her racing pulse made her kind of dizzy as she looked up and down the hallway. She waited for a group of boys to pass by before she stepped outside and left the door unlocked and slightly open on purpose. Releasing a long breath, she power walked up the hall. Nahima damn near fainted when she saw Mr. Woodard, the janitor, walking toward her with a giant metal ring loaded down with what appeared to be over a hundred keys. She kept head forward as she passed him, going in the opposite direction. When she turned down the hall where her locker was located, she ran to it so she could secure the stolen money in a plastic sewing kit before placing it in her backpack. Finally, she changed her shoes, flung her backpack over her shoulder, and ran all the way to the cafeteria. She would toss the key and the gloves in the food chute before she grabbed her lunch.

"What's up, y'all?"

Kela rolled her eyes at Nahima. "It's about time you got here. These two heifers were getting on my nerves! They tried to make me show them my concert outfit before you got here, but I wasn't having it, Nahima."

Yashia and Ryan started laughing and looking at Kela with surprised, wide eyes.

"She's lying, Nah-Nah! Don't believe her. Kela ain't right!"

"She really is lying, bestie. I told Kela to wait for you to use the bathroom and change your shoes, but her impatient ass was ready to let us see the picture without you."

"Shut up, Yashia! You make me sick."

Nahima sat down next to her bestie and started eating her turkey burger and fries. "I'm here now, Kela. Let's see what you're rocking to the Quay concert."

She scrolled through her phone, which was already in her hand, and then placed it in the middle of the table. Ryan snatched up the phone before anyone else could touch it and examined the picture on the screen.

"It's cute, Kela. I like it." Ryan passed the phone to Yashia.

"It's cute?" Kela snapped. "My shit is fire! Do you know how much my granddaddy dropped at Macy's for that outfit, bitch?"

Nahima and Yashia were looking at the picture together.

"I love it! I'm going to find some red fabric and make me a pair of pants just like those."

"I like it too, Kela. That gold waistband on those cream bell-bottoms is the shit, girl!"

"Thank you, Nahima and Yashia. I'm glad y'all like my outfit. Ryan is over here acting like a hater."

"No, I'm not, Kela. I like the outfit. I really do. I think you're going to look fierce at the concert."

"Chill with all that pettiness, y'all. Here comes Rashawn," Yashia whispered. "Be nice, because he's doing all of us a favor by voluntarily driving our asses to the concert."

"Humph, he's doing even bigger favors for one of us and not the others."

Yashia and Nahima cast curious eyes on Kela, but she shifted her eyes to Ryan and watched her fidget nervously with her fork.

"What's up, ladies?"

"Hey, Rashawn," everyone except Ryan practically sang in unison.

Kela didn't miss that her bestie had yet to open her mouth. As a matter of fact, her eyes were glued to her hands on the table. Being straight-up messy, Kela smiled and said, "Thank you in advance for the ride to the concert, Rashawn. I know you only offered to drive us because you like Nahima."

That comment made all three of the other members of the clique and Rashawn visibly uncomfortable, but Ryan took the hardest hit. She actually flinched and grabbed her fruit punch and started gulping it down.

"You're welcome, but it ain't no problem at all. Nahima is my friend, so when Ryan told me about her situation, I decided to help her out. Anyway, let me leave you ladies so y'all can finish eating. I've got to hit the chemistry lab."

Before Rashawn walked off, he looked at Ryan with lustful eyes and smiled like he could see straight through her clothes. Nahima and Yashia might have missed it, but Kela's eyes didn't miss shit.

***

Nahima checked the email address one more time before she pressed the send button. She hoped the judge would listen to every word she'd recorded and grant Jay visitation rights with Jalen so they could be a family. Nahima had already made up her mind that she would move out of her parents' house to live with Jay as soon as she got settled after her release. She was going to cook and clean for her and sew her beautiful clothes. It was going to be the happiest day of her life to finally have her real mother as the center of her world.

There was a knock on the door as Nahima prepared to start sewing, and it annoyed her. She had been working on the video since returning home from school, and now that she'd finally sent it off, she was ready to finish sewing the ruffles on the hem of Santana's cousin's dress. Her plan was to have it done before Friday. That was why she didn't have time for a lecture from her mom right now, but evidently, Venus couldn't take the hint that she was being ignored. So she knocked again.

"I'm busy doing homework, Mom! I'll be done in about an hour."

"Girl, open the door! It's me, Yashia."

Nahima jumped up from her desk and ran to the door and opened it wide. Yashia rushed past her and dropped down on her bed.

"What are you doing here?"

"I got some hot tea, but you ain't going to like it, girl."

"What?"

"The fashion show has been postponed or maybe even cancelled. Somebody broke into Mrs. Moran's class and stole five hundred dollars of the ticket money. We can't pay for the refreshments, security, the runway construction, the awards, or anything else if we don't have enough money. Some thief robbed us, girl. I can't believe that shit."

Nahima sat down next to Yashia on the bed and laid her head on her shoulder and pretended to cry.

"I'm sorry, bestie. I know how much the fashion show meant to you. It was going to be your night to shine. Our project would've won first place, and everybody would've been talking about your skills. I'm so sorry, Nahima."

Chapter Twenty-nine

"Hey, bae, come and check this out."

When Ryan turned around, she saw Rashawn holding up the jumpsuit she had spotted when they'd first entered the store. After flipping the price tag over, she'd put it back on the rack because it was too rich for her blood. Chase had sent her exactly $200 to buy something nice to wear to the Quay concert, but she didn't want to spend it all. Ryan would scrub floors at a gas station for that jumpsuit, but she was a very practical person who knew her limits. Even with the storewide discount of 25 percent off, she still couldn't afford the jumpsuit and have money left over, which was her goal.

"Try this cheetah jumpsuit on. I think you'll look hella sexy in it. It's a size six, your size, and it's the only one like it in the entire store. God's got His eyes on you, girl."

Ryan laughed hysterically. "Boy, these are not cheetah spots. They're leopard spots."

"Oh, yeah? What's the difference?"

"Leopard spots are black with a brown center. Cheetah spots are all black."

"Thank you for teaching me that, because I damn sure didn't know."

"You're welcome. Now put the jumpsuit back, and come with me to the clearance rack." Ryan grabbed Rashawn's hand and tried to pull him away, but he didn't budge.

"I want you to try the jumpsuit on for me."

"Why?"

"I saw you pick it up when we first got here, and I noticed how your eyes lit up. You want that jumpsuit, Ryan, so try it on."

"No. It costs too much. I mean, I have enough money to buy it, but I always like to put some money aside just in case my mom needs me to help her out."

Rashawn pressed the stylish jumpsuit against Ryan's shoulder. "Go and try it on. I'll be sitting outside the dressing room waiting to see how it looks on you."

A few minutes later, Ryan walked out of the dressing room feeling like a supermodel. The soft fabric of the jumpsuit caressed every inch of her petite figure like a second layer of skin. The halter bodice put her slender neck and toned upper arms on full display. Cool air kissed her exposed back, compliments of the deep dip that stopped right above her ass. It had a tapered waistline that made her hourglass figure pop and accentuated her tight, round bottom, which was firm and demanded attention. Even the wide pants were the perfect length, and they flowed and whispered as she walked.

Bashfully, she did a slow stroll toward Rashawn, who was walking in her direction, smiling and looking at her with twinkling eyes.

"I don't know who the hell Apri Osagah is, but he or she made that damn jumpsuit for you, Ryan Mathis. It's you all day long. I want it to be yours because you look so good in it."

"But I don't—"

"It's not up for discussion. Let me pay for it, and you can repay me in glasses of cranberry lemonade. That pitcher you made the other night at your crib tasted better than what they serve at Wings Wizard. All you have to do is make some every time I visit you."

"My mama taught me not to accept gifts from men, because nothing in life is free."

"Ms. Tasha is right about that, because most men do expect something in return when they shell out cash on a woman, but that's not me. I promise you it's not, Ryan. Trust me to buy that jumpsuit for you, and you have my word that all I want in return is for you to look pretty at the concert and a thousand glasses of cranberry lemonade."

"All right, you can buy it for me. Thank you, Rashawn." Fresh tears spilled from her eyes and rolled down her cheeks.

"Hey, don't cry, baby. I want you to be happy." He reached out, pulled her against his chest, and wrapped his arms around her tiny waist.

"I am happy. That's why I'm crying."

Rashawn laughed and kissed Ryan's forehead.

"Okay, Nahima, you're in charge. Don't let your baby brother and younger cousins run over you."

"I won't, Uncle Zach."

"If anything gets out of hand, please call Aunt Jackie, and if it's an emergency, Dr. and Mrs. Peyton live right around the corner. Their number is on the refrigerator and on the coffee table."

Nahima nodded at Jill. She wasn't about to say a word to her black ass.

"Go ahead and eat the pizza and wings while everything is still hot, and Zach Jr. and Zion will clean the kitchen before you and Jalen start baking cookies. Remember to be careful with the peanut butter because Zion is allergic."

"I know, Uncle Zach."

"Dad, you and Mom can leave now. Nahima can handle it, and I can help her."

Zach looked at Zach Jr. with a hard expression as if he were trying to remember something. "Make sure my li'l dawg takes a shower and brushes his teeth before he starts baking cookies with Nahima."

"I don't need him to help me. I'm a big boy!"

"Zachary, let's go, honey. I think they will be fine. I'm ready to dance."

"Yeah, get out of here! Go!"

"Leave already!"

"Bye, Mommy! I love you!"

Jill hugged Jalen and kissed his nose. "I love you more."

Zach lifted the handle on the rolling suitcase and headed for the door with Jill close behind him. Nahima couldn't have been happier that they were finally leaving. She watched Zach Jr., Zion, and Jalen walk their parents to the door and kiss them goodbye with a satisfied smile on her face. Everything was running as smooth as butter according to her plan.

Nahima straddled Santana and leaned over to brush her hard nipple across his open mouth, teasing him. He growled and raised his head an inch or two from the blanket on the floor, trying to suck one of her breasts. Nahima threw her head back and moaned in her throat when Santana trapped her left nipple between his lips and sucked it hard, scraping it with the edges of his teeth. She sat up straight and tried to make out his facial features—his bronze skin, full gold grill, slanted eyes, and narrow nose—through the thick darkness. Beads of sweat glistened under the hairline of his tapered curly hair as she leaned in again and plunged her tongue deep into his mouth, ingesting the tastes of alcohol and potent marijuana.

Nahima's kisses grew urgent and hungrier as Santana massaged and gripped her bare ass, pushing her leaking pussy closer to his thick balls covered with spiraling hairs. His hard dick, thick and long, tapped against her flat belly as precum seeped from its tip. Nahima gripped it and slid her palm up and down the length of it, causing Santana to grit his teeth and pant for air.

"Put that mouth to work," he grumbled, smacking Nahima hard on the thigh with an open palm.

Without any acknowledgment of his words, she slithered down his sweaty body and started licking his dick while working her palm up and down it with pressure. Now on her knees, head down and ass up, Nahima covered just the sensitive, oozing head of Santana's penis with her mouth. She pulled on it with powerful suction and twirled her tongue slowly around its circumference. He reached down and sliced his fingers through her Afro, pressing her head downward, which forced many more inches of his rock-solid dick into her mouth and down her throat. But like a pro, she swallowed him without gagging and started sucking and slurping. Her head began to bob up and down rhythmically, strings of thick saliva dripping from her throat and onto his pubic hairs.

Growing thicker and more rigid as it slid in and out of Nahima's throat, Santana's dick started to pulsate. She raised her head with force, releasing it slowly, inch by inch from her oral control. She lifted her hips with his wet, stiff dick in her palm and slid her pussy down on it, taking it all the way in until she felt her ass cheeks slam against his nuts. Nahima started bucking, bouncing, and rolling her hips slowly at first before she picked up her pace. The ride was bumpy, but her pussy was popping and creaming out of control because it felt so damn good. Santana's dick was hitting all of her hot spots, and she was tightening her walls around his thickness, making him moan in soprano like a bitch. And she was hissing between his moans.

"Let me hit it from the back."

Like an obedient dog, Nahima rolled off Santana and assumed the position. He climbed behind her, grabbed her roughly around her waist, and rammed his dick into her forcefully with no mercy.

"Ouch!"

"Shut up and take this dick, girl!"

After about five fast and sloppy thrusts with his thumb inserted all the way in her asshole, Santana growled like a wild animal and busted a strong nut, sending a stream of hot semen into Nahima's tight and underdeveloped walls. He then collapsed his full weight on top of her back, trapping her underneath him. Gravelly snores soon followed, and she wiggled and pushed her way from under his sleeping body. Nahima flipped over onto her back next to Santana and closed her eyes. She inhaled the scent of their musky sex and smiled before she dozed off.

"I want my mommy!" Jalen ran into Zion's room crying.

She sat up in bed, rubbing her eyes, before she opened her arms to her little brother. "What's wrong, Jalen?"

"I want Mommy!"

"Where is Nahima? I thought she was sleeping in your room with you."

"I don't know. She's gone." He began to whimper pitifully. "I want Mommy!"

"Don't cry, Jalen. You can sleep with me. Mom and Dad will be home early in the morning, okay?"

"Okay."

Zion lifted Jalen into her bed and placed him on the other side of her, close to the wall. She rubbed his back, attempting to soothe him. She hoped he would soon fall asleep. Zion wondered where Nahima was and why she had left Jalen alone when it had been her idea to sleep in his room with him instead of in hers.

Chapter Thirty

"A'ight, I gotta get out of here, shawty. Bein' over here in Beverly Hills around all these rich folks in mansions and shit fucks with a nigga's nerves. I gotta get back to the hood where shit is real and niggas know each other and look out for each other."

"You didn't act like you were nervous when you were eating my uncle's food and drinking his good liquor. You weren't thinking about your peeps in the hood when you were fucking me either."

"Man, whatever."

Nahima tapped the garment bag draped over Santana's forearm. "Your cousin is going to love her dress. Make sure you tell her it's an original creation. I sewed my signature tag in the back so she can see it."

"Don't worry. She gon' like it 'cause it's a gift from me."

"Please take some pictures of her wearing it and send them to me so I can add them to my portfolio."

"Yeah, I'll do that. What else?"

"Nothing." Nahima reached up and wrapped her arms around Santana's neck and kissed his lips. He grabbed a handful of her bare ass when her short gown inched above her thighs. She released him and slid her palm down his chest. Then she opened the door, and he stepped outside into the night.

"Call me."

"I will, but I got shit to do in the mornin' for Sarge."

"All right. Hit me up when you can then."

Santana looked around as he made sluggish steps up the walkway toward his car that looked very much out of place in the exclusive gated community. The security guard was probably suspicious when he called her on the land line to make sure it was okay to allow him through the gate.

Nahima closed the door and secured the locks. As she was entering the alarm's security code into the keypad, she heard a bumping noise on the steps. She spun around and almost screamed when she saw Zion running up the stairs.

"Come here, you little sneaky heifer!" She stomped toward the stairs.

Zion froze. Obviously frightened, her deep intakes of air were loud enough for Nahima to hear from the bottom of the stairs.

"Get down here now, Zion!"

The child walked down the steps slowly with her head down. She was rubbing her hands together nervously.

"How long were you standing on the steps, and what did you see?"

Zion narrowed her eyes at Nahima and didn't utter a word.

"You better answer me right now!" she barked, yanking the child by the collar of her nightgown. "Tell me!"

Zion snatched away from Nahima. "Don't you put your hands on me. I'll call Mom and Dad and tell them you let a stranger in our house! I'll tell them you left Jalen in his room alone and he woke up scared and crying, too!"

"Okay, Zion, calm down. Look, I shouldn't have put my hands on you, and I was wrong to invite my friend over, but please don't snitch. I'm your big cousin. We're supposed to be girls, right?"

"I guess so. But why is your boyfriend so old?"

"He's not old, Zion."

"Yes, he is. He's twenty-two and you're only fifteen. He's an adult and you're a teenager. He's too old for you."

Nahima walked closer to Zion, pissed the hell off with her hands clenched into tight fists. She wanted to punch the little sneaky-ass kid so bad that she was shaking. "How do you know how old my boyfriend is? Who told you that, Zach Jr.?"

"Nope." Zion leaned against the safety rail with her arms folded over her flat chest. "I heard you tell my brother that your boyfriend's name is Santana, he's Puerto Rican, and he's twenty-two years old. I was standing right behind y'all in the great room when you were talking to him the last time you came over here. And I saw what you were doing in my bathroom when you were FaceTiming him, too. You're nasty!"

"Ssshhh. Be quiet." Nahima reached for Zion, but she moved out of her reach, walking backward up the stairs.

"Are you going to tell Uncle Zach on me?"

"I don't know yet. Maybe I will or maybe I won't."

"Please don't tell. I'll give you some money and bake some more sugar cookies."

"How much money?"

"I'll give you fifty dollars, and it'll be our secret."

"No deal. I already have ninety dollars, and there's a whole bowl of sugar cookies in the kitchen. I'm going back to bed with my little brother now, and you better not try to mess with me either. Bye!"

Zion sprinted up the steps so fast that Nahima couldn't catch her even if she'd wanted to. Her body jerked when she heard the little demon slam her bedroom door. Nahima sat down on the steps with her head between her hands, mad and worried about the bullshit she was now in. If Zion snitched on her, all hell would break loose. Uncle Zach would be pissed, and he would never trust her for as long as she lived. He would definitely tell her mom, which meant she would be grounded again and probably wouldn't be allowed to go to the Quay concert. And she could forget about her plan to keep Jalen overnight so she could sneak him to Leesworth to visit Jay.

"Grrrrrrrrrrr!" Nahima kicked the wall so hard that it hurt her foot. "Shit!"

Think, girl, think! Don't let that little bitch spawn of Jill get the best of you!

Nahima grinned and ran to the kitchen. She lifted the top from the square container filled with peanut butter cookies and picked up one and took a bite. It was so delicious and moist. She bit it again and chewed as she continued to work through the details of her plan to keep Zion's big mouth shut. After Nahima finished off the cookie, she grabbed another one and lifted the top from the bowl of sugar cookies. Taking her time, she rubbed the peanut butter cookie over every damn one of the sugar cookies, front and back, thoroughly before she sealed the bowl shut. Then she stuffed the remainder of the chewy, delicious peanut butter cookie into her mouth, left the kitchen, and trotted up the stairs.

"Thank you," the nurse told the guard after he opened Jay's cell to let her inside.

She kneeled down next to the special cot with an air mattress where Jay lay moaning and writhing in obvious pain. The nurse then placed a medical bag on the floor next to her. Jay was perspiring profusely all over, and her labored breathing concerned the nurse a great deal.

"Ms. King, my name is Althea Searcy, and I'm a new nurse on the night rotation. Some other inmates heard you crying in your sleep and became concerned. They alerted the guards to call the infirmary to ask me to come and check on you."

Jay opened her eyes and looked at the nurse. "Mmmm . . . mmm . . ."

"Ms. King, tell me what's going on with you. Where does it hurt?"

"Everywhere."

"I'm so sorry to hear that." Nurse Searcy removed a stethoscope and blood-pressure monitor from her bag. "I read over Dr. Dalrymple's notes in your medical file before I came up here. Let me check and record your vitals, and then I'm going to give you an injection for the pain so you can sleep. Will that be okay?"

"Mmm . . . yes. . . ."

Nahima ran from the great room when she heard the front door's locks disengaging. She was standing in the middle of the foyer right next to her overnight bag on the floor when the door opened. Her uncle walked in, dressed in jeans and a T-shirt, dragging his rolling suitcase. Jill was a few steps behind him, but she stopped at the keypad to turn off the alarm.

"Good morning, Uncle Zach."

"What's up, pumpkin? I see you survived. Where are my little monsters?"

"They're still sleeping because I let them stay up late to watch movies."

Jill walked up and stood next to Zach. "Nahima, you're up bright and early. How did it go with the children?"

"Fine."

"That's great. Thank you for babysitting," Jill said with a smile before she walked away.

Zach glanced down at Nahima's feet. Jill was sure he was looking at her overnight bag, and she was glad because she was ready for Nahima, the adolescent Antichrist, to get the hell out of their house. Everybody in the family thought her little ass was so sweet, but she was an evil, conniving bitch just like her mama.

"I see you're all packed up and ready to go."

"Yeah, I've got some sewing to do."

"That's right. Your mom told me about the fashion show. When is it now?"

"I'm not sure. It's been postponed for some reason, but I'll let you know the new date as soon as they reschedule it."

"Cool. I'll be right back, pumpkin. Let me tell your auntie I'm about to leave to take you home." Zach squeezed Nahima's shoulder as he walked past her.

Chapter Thirty-one

Oscar placed his coffee mug on the table and reached out to pick up Aunt Jackie's ringing cell phone. "Baby, your phone is ringing! I think it's your niece calling from prison!"

Aunt Jackie rushed into the kitchen, huffing and puffing out of breath, holding a stack of mail, which she dropped on the table. Her cell phone stopped ringing as soon as she took it out of Oscar's hand.

"Doggone it! Mrs. Taylor was outside when I went to the mailbox with her nosy, gossiping self. And you know she stopped me to 'put a li'l bug,' as she likes to call it, in my ear. That old woman knows everybody's business except her husband's. I bet she done told everyone on Southwest Chappy Drive and beyond that I've got a boyfriend, but she ain't got a clue that Mr. Taylor's been keeping company with Roxie Calhoun for nineteen years."

"I don't care anything about what Mrs. Taylor says about you and me as long as she tells it correctly. I am not your boyfriend. I'm your fiancé, baby." Oscar winked.

Aunt Jackie lifted her left hand to gaze at her lovely engagement ring admiringly. She grinned at Oscar. "You got that right, sugar."

The engaged couple shared joyous laughter and the sweetest kiss, but they were interrupted by Aunt Jackie's ringing cell phone. It was Jay trying to reach her again, so she quickly pressed the button to answer her call.

"Jay, how are you, baby?"

"Ms. Brown, this is Iris Sheftall, the warden at Leesworth Women's Federal Corrections Facility. How are you today, ma'am?"

"I'm well and you?"

"I'm fine. However, Jayla King, your niece, according to our records, isn't doing as well as you and I. That's the purpose of this call, ma'am."

"Lord Jesus, please tell me what's happening with Jay."

"As I'm sure you already know, Ms. King has cirrhosis of the liver, and she's a dialysis patient due to progressive kidney disease, which her nephrologist now describes as chronic renal failure. In short, Ms. King is transitioning, and she'll pass away sooner than her doctors had expected."

"Oh, nooo! I didn't know Jay's health was so bad!" Aunt Jackie sat down in a chair at the kitchen table and allowed her tears to fall unchecked. "Whenever she reaches out to me by email, she tells me she's doing all right. I didn't know. As God as my witness, I didn't know."

Oscar stood up, hovering over Aunt Jackie, and massaged her slumping shoulders.

"Ms. Brown, the doctors gave Ms. King her prognosis two weeks ago."

"How long does she have to live, Mrs. Sheftall?"

"As of last night, she'll last another month at the most."

Aunt Jackie began to pray silently within her spirit, refusing to cry. Man was full of limitations, but God's power had no end. If it was His will for Jay to live beyond a month, He could just speak and she would live another twenty-five years or more in perfect health.

"Ms. Brown, we're in the process of having your niece transferred to a medical corrections facility in Augusta, Georgia. I applied for a bed for her as soon as I learned about her prognosis. Unfortunately, they have a waiting list, and there are many inmates in the state and beyond ahead of her. Right now, Ms. King is stable. She even sat up and ate breakfast this morning. The doctors are keeping her comfortable with medication and various therapies until a bed becomes available for her at the facility in Augusta."

"I want to see her."

"You're already an approved visitor on her list, so I can arrange for a special visit tomorrow if Ms. King is strong enough and wants to see you. I'll let one of my staff members check in with her and the nurse. Expect a call from someone here later today."

"Yes, ma'am, I'll be right here waiting. Thanks for calling, Mrs. Sheftall."

"You're welcome. Goodbye."

Aunt Jackie ended the call and burst into uncontrollable tears. Thank God Oscar was right by her side to comfort her.

"What the hell?"

Zach sped down the block and threw his truck into park in front of an ambulance right outside his house. He jumped out, forgetting to close his door, and ran as fast as his legs could carry him up the walkway. The door opened, and a pair of emergency medical technicians—a black female and a white male—appeared, guiding a gurney out of the house. Two white male medics were behind them, and Jill was in the doorway screaming at the top of her lungs, holding Jalen on her hip. He was crying too and reaching for his daddy. Zach Jr. ran from behind his mother, past the gurney, and into his daddy's arms.

"Dad, Zion made a mistake and ate some peanut butter! She stopped breathing! We called you, but you left your cell phone in the kitchen!"

"Calm down, Junior!"

Zach pulled away from his son and started walking fast alongside the rolling gurney. The sight of his baby girl with her face covered with hives and swollen beyond recognition, as she struggled to take in oxygen from a tube that was lodged in her throat, nearly broke him down. Zion's tongue was dangerously thick, three times its normal size, and protruding out of her mouth. Two IV bags hung from a pole, releasing medicine into her tiny veins. Zach prayed to God it would save her life.

"Hey, um, I'm her father. I'm a pediatric practitioner, a supervisor in the NICU at Grady. I need to be with her. Y'all got to let me ride."

"Sir, we—"

Zach grabbed the man by his throat and squeezed with both hands. "I'm riding, goddamn it!"

"Zachary, I need to be with her!"

Zach ran to his truck to get his wallet and his keys out of the ignition. He slammed his door. "Call Aunt Jackie, and tell her to come and watch the boys, Jill! Then come to . . . Wait. Which hospital?"

"Emory Children's Emergency Center on Uppergate, sir," the only female EMT answered.

"Come to Emory Children's Emergency Center on Uppergate, Jill."

"No, Mom! Go now! I can call Aunt Jackie and take care of Jalen until she gets here. Go, Mom, go!"

That was the last thing Zach heard before he climbed into the back of the ambulance.

Jill ran into the house with Jalen in her arms. Zach Jr. was right on her heels. All three of them were crying, but she had to be calm for her sons. She took a deep breath and wiped her baby boy's eyes before turning to her firstborn.

"Call Aunt Jackie, Junior. Tell her what happened to Zion, and ask her to come at once." She bounced Jalen up and down a few times on her hip and looked into his steel gray eyes. "Mommy has to leave you to go and be with your sister. Behave like a good little boy for your brother until Aunt Jackie arrives, eh? Then I want you to pray with her like she taught you."

Jalen nodded his head. "I'm going to pray real loud like Pastor Broadus, and jump up and down and spin around and speak in tongues for Zion. Then I'll fall out in the spirit and get back up and do it all over again three times."

"Thank you, sweetheart." Jill smiled through her tears and kissed her sweet baby boy's cheek before she rushed up the stairs to get dressed.

"Satan, you're a liar! You can't have my family, devil! You can't touch a single hair on their heads, because they belong to the Lord! I rebuke you in the name of Jesus. Satan, I rebuke you!"

Loud, nonstop wails of agony soon filled the interior of the truck. Even the strongest Christian had his or her breaking point. And after listening to Zach Jr. over the speaker phone tell his auntie what had just happened to his little sister, Oscar watched the woman he loved, his beautiful fiancée, have an emotional meltdown right before his very eyes. He pulled over to the side of the road and allowed her to cry and scream manically. His heart ached for her, but he was helpless to do anything to help her. Oscar couldn't even hug Aunt Jackie because her arms were flailing wildly, alternating with her fist banging against his dashboard.

When her voice grew hoarse and it seemed like her energy reserve was on empty, Aunt Jackie leaned over and rested her head against the window. Patient and full of compassion, Oscar waited with his hand on her knee for her to speak. He opened the glove compartment and found a box of Kleenex. When he snatched a few out and offered them to Aunt Jackie, she took them and wiped her eyes and nose.

"What's your nephew's address, sweetheart? Those little boys need their auntie right about now. I want to drop you off, but we need to call Wallace on the way to tell him about his grandbaby. You know he would want to know."

Aunt Jackie nodded. "We have to tell him about Jay, too. God must really have something great in store for our family, because right now, we're in the midst of a mighty storm."

"That's true, but all that means is we'll have a greater appreciation for the sun when it reappears and shines again."

"Amen."

Dr. Dalrymple removed the earpieces from her ears and hung the stethoscope around her neck. Her eyes roamed carefully over the numbers and graphics on the monitor before she turned and walked quietly out of the room. She was surprised to see Warden Sheftall standing in the hall outside of Ms. King's room in the in-patient infirmary.

"How is she?"

"Surprisingly, Ms. King is stable. Of course, she's heavily sedated, but all of her vital signs are much better than I'd expected. I want her to spend two more days in here with the nurse. I'll assess her again when I come back Tuesday morning, and if she's stronger, she can go back to her cell. "

Sheftall smacked her lips. "So I suppose she's not up for a special visit from a family member tomorrow then."

"No, she's not. I want her medicated around the clock and on complete bed rest until I return Tuesday. If all is well, you might need to invite the whole damn family, because her days are numbered."

Chapter Thirty-two

Zion shook her head from side to side. Tears spilled from the corners of her eyes. They were so swollen and covered with ugly hives that she resembled E.T., the alien movie character from the eighties. But Zach didn't care if she looked like freaking Quasimodo as long as she was alive and going to be all right. He leaned over and kissed her forehead.

"Don't cry, sweet pea. Dr. Swanson said you're going to be fine, and you know Daddy checked behind him. He gave you a drugstore full of medicine and got some oxygen down into your little lungs, so tomorrow you'll be as good as new."

Zion's puffy monster eyes shifted all around the room, and she moved her mouth as if she wanted to speak, but she started coughing instead.

"Don't try to talk, princess. That big ol' nasty tube made your throat sore."

When she looked around the room and started shedding more tears, Zach knew she was looking for Jill.

"Your mom is outside talking to Grandpa Orville and Grandma Faye. Papa Wallace, Grammy Patricia, and Aunt Jackie were worried about you, so Jill had to step outside to let everybody know you're okay. Your psycho godfather wanted to come up here, but I wouldn't let him. I had to promise him I would help the doctor take care of you so he would stay at work."

Zion closed her eyes, and Zach wondered what was on his little girl's mind. Did she even realize what had happened to her? Was his baby girl afraid when her throat first started to close up on her? Zach's fake macho exterior had been in place since the moment he saw the medics rolling Zion out of their house, but it was crumbling because he was angry and worried. Hell, he wanted answers that no one, not even Jill, could give him, and she was there in the kitchen with their daughter when she nearly died.

"Oh, she's awake." Jill rushed to Zion's bedside.

Zach had been so absorbed in his thoughts that he hadn't even heard her enter the room. He turned and watched Jill kiss Zion's face and rub her arms. She pulled the cover up to the child's chin to make sure she was warm. Baby girl was fighting to keep her puffy eyes open, but she was too tired. The allergic reaction and the treatments had worn her out.

"Zachary, you need to eat something, honey. You haven't had food since breakfast at the mansion early this morning."

"I'm starving, but I . . ." He didn't want to say it because it would show how weak he truly was. "I'll get something soon."

"Go home, Zachary. I'm going to stay here with Zion. That's why I brought a bag."

Zach looked at his little girl, his only girl, and swallowed the rage and fear that was threatening to break him down. He knew Zion was okay. He had been taking care of sick children for twenty-five years, so he knew the science and the signs. But he couldn't shake the questions that kept gnawing at his nerves and poking him. What if things had gone the other way? What if Zion had mistakenly eaten the peanut butter last night when he and Jill were at the party instead of this morning?

"I'm going home to eat, take care of the boys, and rest. Like I can really rest." He laughed dryly. "Don't be surprised if you see me back up here in the middle of the night."

He walked over to the bed and looked down at Zion. She was sleeping peacefully now. Her breathing was even and steady. The hives and swelling in her pretty face were the only signs that she'd had a brush with death a few hours ago. Zach leaned down and gave his precious daughter a forehead kiss. He turned to Jill and hugged her tight.

"Call me when she wakes up."

"You know I will."

"I love you."

"I love you too, Zachary."

Zach left the room and rushed down the hall at full speed. He was like a ticking time bomb, seconds away from exploding. His eyes were blurry, and every emotion known to modern psychology was choking him, harassing him. The moment he stepped outside into the early evening air, he doubled over and cried like he had never cried before. The fear, anger, confusion, and exhaustion poured out of him through his tears. But somewhere floating in the middle of all of those feelings was gratitude. Zach was so grateful that Zion had survived the allergic reaction, because if she hadn't, he wouldn't have survived it either.

Jill looked at her phone when it vibrated on the arm of the chair that was her bed for the night. She had expected to see Zach's handsome face on the screen at this late hour, but Dex would do just the same. She peeped at Zion, who was sound asleep, before swiping the answer icon.

"Hello?"

"How's my little munchkin, sis?"

Jill got up from the chair and hurried into the bathroom. "She's resting peacefully. The doctor said she should sleep through the night. Zach left, so it's only me here with her now."

Dex sighed heavily. "I know, sis. That's how come I called. I wanted to holla at you, not my bruh."

"Oh?"

"Look, I'm going to shoot straight through the shit, sis. I don't think my goddaughter accidentally ate no damn peanut butter. She's too smart and careful and mature to slip like that. When Zion gets home and the smoke blows over, I want you to ask her exactly what happened. I don't trust Nahima no further than I can piss on her. I can't prove it, but something in my belly tells me I'm right."

"Okay, Dex, I will do what you've asked. I trust you."

"Let's keep this between you, me, and Ramona, because she feels the same way. She's the one who made me call you, sis."

"Of course, I won't say a word to Zachary or anyone else. We will talk later, eh?"

"Good night, Jill. Kiss my goddaughter for me."

"I will, Dex. Good night."

Jill looked in the bathroom mirror when Dex hung up. God had used him to confirm that she wasn't crazy after all. He and Ramona believed exactly what she had felt in her heart the moment she realized Zion was having an allergic reaction. Nahima, Jay's child, had tried to kill her child. But why?

Yashia was standing outside of Nahima's first-period class, dressed to the nines in a red maxi dress, when her bestie walked up. "How come you didn't call and tell me about your little cousin's accident? That shit almost gave me a heart attack."

Nahima did a subtle eye roll. "I forgot. Who told you anyway?"

"My mom saw your mom at Target after church yesterday, and they talked about it. My mom didn't even tell me until I sat down at the breakfast table this morning. She said she thought I already knew. So how is Zion doing?"

"Oh, she's all right." Nahima waved Yashia off with a thoughtless flip of her wrist. "The doctor let her go home last night. She'll be running around the house, getting on Zach Jr.'s and Jalen's nerves tomorrow."

"I'm glad little mama is okay. The way my mom explained it, Zion almost died."

"Well, she didn't. Anyway, I've got to tell you about my night with Santana, girl. He came over to my uncle's house after I put my baby brother and cousins to bed, and it was on."

"For real, bestie?" Yashia's eyes stretched wide.

"Yes! And it was sooo good."

"Well, Dondrae's cousin got a motel room for us Friday night, and we tore some shit up too."

The warning bell rang.

"Let me get in this classroom before Mrs. Fuller tries to clown me."

Yashia started walking backward. "I'll see you in fourth period."

"Yeah, I'll finish telling you about me and Santana then."

Wallace closed his Bible after his morning devotion and looked out the window in the breakfast nook. His heart was kind of heavy over the news Oscar and Jackie had shared with him about Jay's condition. He was terribly concerned about Zion, too. Wallace had called and spoken to Jill, and she had assured him that his little princess would make a full recovery. For that, he was grateful to God. However, the burden of knowing that Jay didn't have long to live was weighing him down.

Wallace wanted to talk to Zach so that they could somehow come together and make amends with Jay. The death of their mother at his hands had caused so many problems for them as a family beyond his incarceration and their orphanhood. Now that Jay was dying, Wallace felt it was time for her and Zach to finally clear the air. He wanted his firstborn son and his only daughter, birthed of the same loving mother, to make peace with one another at last. According to Jackie, the doctor had given Jay only a month to live. Wallace thought that was plenty of time for her and Zach to get it right before she met her Maker.

His plan was to wait a few days for Zion to get fully settled back at home and return to school before reaching out to Zach. In the meantime, Wallace would call the prison to check on Jay and try to arrange a visit with her. Time wasn't on his side, and he knew it. Jay was awaiting a transfer to another prison where, more than likely, she would die. Wallace hoped and prayed he would get to see his precious daughter before she was transferred. More importantly, he wished above all things that he could get her and Zach together before she passed away.

Jackie had promised she wouldn't say anything to Zach about Jay, because their relationship had been a touchy subject for a long time now, especially since Jalen's adoption and the kidney transplant between the siblings. And because Wallace was their father, she felt like he should be the one to try to help restore their relationship before it was too late.

***

"What's up, Jay?"

"This ain't your mama, honey. I'm KiKi, her friend."

Nahima aimed the remote control at the TV and lowered the volume. "Where is Jay? Is something wrong with her?"

"She was kind of sick over the weekend, but she's getting better. I'm calling to make sure you and your little brother are still coming to visit your mama Saturday."

"Yes, we'll be there."

"All praise to the Messiah! I'm glad to hear that, because King really wants to see y'all. I can't wait to tell her. It's going to make her feel a lot better to know her kids are coming up here for sure. That's why I called. I'll go tell her y'all will definitely be here Saturday. Take care, Nahima."

"I will. Tell Jay I love her."

"I promise I'll tell her."

Nahima hung up the phone more determined than ever to make the trip to Leesworth with her baby brother. She had already spoken to Avila on FaceTime and sent her $125 by Cash App for her driving fee and gas money for Santana's car. All they had to do was scoop up Jalen Saturday morning around nine o'clock and roll out. Nahima didn't care how tired she would be from the Quay concert Friday night. It wasn't going to stop her from taking her baby brother to see their real mother. Nothing and no one would keep them from visiting Jay.

Chapter Thirty-three

"Stop crying, Zion. Your mom and dad aren't upset with you. No one is," Aunt Jackie explained. "We're just trying to figure out what happened to you Saturday morning."

"I told you already. I don't know what happened, but I didn't eat any peanut butter cookies. I didn't even touch the jar or the container they were in. I would never do that. I know I'm allergic."

Aunt Jackie was sitting on the bed next to Zion with her arm wrapped around her. Jill was sitting at the foot of the bed, and Zach was standing above his wife. Zion's health was pretty much back to normal, with the exception of the lingering hives, and Dr. Swan and her personal pediatrician had released her to return to school tomorrow. But her parents wanted answers about how the peanut butter had gotten into her system. They had called Aunt Jackie to come over to help them talk to Zion. So far, they hadn't learned a single thing.

"Zion, did something happen here before we got home that you're not telling us?"

A flashback of Nahima and her boyfriend kissing at the door caused Zion's chest to hurt like she was having another allergic reaction. She imagined Jalen running into her room, crying for his mommy in the dark, too. Everything about that night replayed in her mind. Zion wished she could forget all of it.

Her friend Ocean had told her many times that if she kept running her mouth like a track star, something bad would happen to her just like it had to another one of their friends. Zion didn't believe her warnings, so she had ignored the little girl. Sadly, Ocean's words had come true Saturday morning. Zion didn't want anything else bad to happen to her, so she decided not to snitch on Nahima.

"Answer your mom's question, baby girl," Zach insisted.

"Nothing happened that you don't already know," she lied. "Like I told you this morning, I sneaked a sugar cookie behind Mom's back when she was cooking breakfast. I didn't taste any peanut butter on it, though. But my tongue started feeling funny, and I was itching all over. Then when I tried to tell Mom, the room started spinning around real fast, I couldn't catch my breath, and I fell on the floor. That's when Mom turned around and saw me. I don't remember anything else. When I woke up, I was in the ambulance and I saw you, Dad. I'm sorry for sneaking the cookie, Mom."

"I don't care about that bloody cookie, sweetheart. I care about you."

"Nobody is mad about you sneaking a cookie, okay?" Zach grabbed Zion's foot and shook it playfully.

"Okay, Dad." Zion smiled for the first time since the conversation started.

Zach Jr. walked into his sister's room with Jalen acting as his shadow. "Papa is on the house phone, Dad. He said he really needs to talk to you. It's important."

"Okay." Zach left the room to talk to his father.

Jalen climbed on the bed next to his sister and gave her a kiss. "I hate peanut butter cookies. I hate peanut butter everything. I don't want any more peanut butter in our house ever again."

Zach picked up the land line in the kitchen. "What's up, old-timer?"

"Hello, son, how are you?"

"I'm great now that my baby girl is out of danger."

"Praise God my little princess is all right."

"Yeah, praise God." Zach laughed. "What's going on with you, though? Junior said you really needed to holla at me."

"It's about your sister, Zach. She's dying. The doctor has given her a month to live."

Zach sat down on a barstool at the center island. "Man, I don't even know what to say."

"Say that you'll meet me at the prison to see her if she'll agree to put us on her visitation list."

"Um . . . yeah, sure. I can do that. Just tell me when."

"Thank you, son. I'll call Leesworth tomorrow and get back with you."

"Cool."

"Hell nah, I don't want to see his ass!" Jay balled up the request form and threw it across her cell.

"But, Kang, what about your daddy? He ain't got nothin' to do with what's goin' on between you and your brother. G'on 'head and make peace with the man, and then try to find some room in your heart to forgive Zach and Jill. Come on now."

"Ms. Gracie's right." KiKi reached over and placed her hand on top of Jay's as they sat a few inches apart on her bed. "I think you should let your daddy come and visit you, and . . . and Zach too. Let it all go so, when your time comes, you'll meet the Messiah in paradise and be reunited with your mother."

Jay pressed her lips tightly together and breathed in air through her nose. She was tired of crying because she was dying, but her tears wouldn't stop falling. The bitterness in her heart for Zach and Jill constantly gnawed at her soul, yet it had become a part of her, and she didn't know how to let it go. She had never gotten over their betrayal even after they'd adopted Jalen and her brother had given her one of his kidneys. The way Jay saw it, she didn't really owe Zach nor Jill forgiveness. Her pending death made them even. They were happy and in love and were enjoying freedom with their two children and her baby boy. They had everything, goddamn it! All she had were a few more days left above the ground and a dream to see her little boy and to hold him one more time.

Jay didn't give a damn about seeing Zach, and she was okay dying without ever seeing her father again. She did want to hug Aunt Jackie and look into her eyes and tell her how much she loved her before she died, though. Jay hated that she had been too sick to see her over the weekend. Mr. Odom, her corrections officer, had told her how upset her auntie was when he got in touch with her late Saturday evening to tell her she couldn't visit her Sunday afternoon, per Dr. Dalrymple's orders. By the good Lord's grace, maybe Aunt Jackie could come to visit her next weekend. Yeah, that would be awesome. Hell, Wallace could even come too. But nobody but her son mattered to Jay at the moment. In just two days, she would see Jalen for the first time since he was a baby. Nahima had sworn to her on everything sacred that she and some girl named Avila were bringing her baby boy to visit her Saturday. Aunt Jackie and Wallace would just have to stand in line and wait one more week, because the day after tomorrow had already been reserved for little Jalen Gavin King.

"Can y'all believe we're actually going to see Quay tomorrow night? Aaahhh! I'm so damn hyped!"

The three other clique members looked at Nahima like she had lost her damn mind, and started laughing.

"I can't lie. I'm getting excited too. It hit me last night when I looked at my outfit hanging in the closet and my new shoes sitting in the box on my dresser! I mean, this shit is really about to go down tomorrow night!"

Kela rolled her eyes at her girl while she chomped on a mouthful of chicken salad. When she swallowed it, she asked, "How come ain't none of us seen your outfit, Ryan? Everybody else showed theirs. What's so special about yours that you can't share it with your girls, huh? First you hide your outfit, and then you claim your mama ain't gonna do your hair until tomorrow after school. What's up with all the secrets?"

"Don't nobody care about outfits and secrets right now. We're going to see Quay, and I'm happy as hell about it. Damn lame-ass secrets."

"Well, maybe you should care about secrets, Nahima, because I think somebody's keeping a great big one from you."

All four girls got quiet. They exchanged suspicious-looking stares and the air around them seemed too damn thick to even flow. Ryan could hardly breathe, and she felt naked all of a sudden out of guilt. But at least she knew for sure now that she wasn't "just paranoid" like Rashawn had tried to make her believe. He had been wrong, and Ryan had guessed it right. Kela definitely, beyond a shadow of a doubt, knew that she and Rashawn were a couple. How she had figured it out was a puzzle Ryan couldn't even begin to solve.

"Stop tripping, Kela!" Yashia snapped and hit the table one time with her fist. "I don't know what the hell is going on with you and Ryan, but y'all need to fix that shit before tomorrow night!"

"But Ryan is—"

"Shut up, Kela! I'm the oldest and I'm talking now! It ain't fair for you two to let your pettiness ruin a night that we've all been looking forward to for weeks. So lick each other or blow one another's brains out! Shit, I don't give a damn what y'all have to do. The only thing I know is Kela Daniels and Ryan Mathis better be back to being best friends since the third grade, fire-ass bitches from Pine Tree Hills, who live around the corner from each other before tomorrow night when Rashawn picks both of your asses up. Got it?"

"Yeah, I got it," Ryan mumbled.

Kela jumped up with her empty plate, gathering her backpack and purse. "I got it."

Yashia, Nahima, and Ryan watched her storm off, grumbling under her breath as she did. As if on cue, Rashawn appeared at the table, seemingly out of thin air.

"Hey, Rashawn," Yashia and Nahima purred at the same time with big smiles on their face.

He sat down in the chair Kela had just vacated. "Hey, lovely ladies. I hope everyone is feeling good and ready for the show tomorrow night."

"Hell yeah, I am!"

"I am too, bestie."

"I'm ready," Ryan said softly, looking at everything except Rashawn.

"Cool. I stopped by to go over my pickup schedule. I figured I would scoop up Ryan first and swing around the corner and grab Kela and . . ."

Dear God, please let everything work out between me and Kela so all of us can have a good time at the Quay concert and IHOP tomorrow night. Don't let us fuss, fight, or say anything to our other friends that we will live to regret. And thank you for putting Rashawn and me together, because we're very happy. Amen.

Chapter Thirty-four

"Hold on, bae." Nahima swiped the mute icon. "I'm coming, Dad. Let me put on some more mascara!" After unmuting her phone, she told Santana, "Just make sure your phone is on at all times. I'll let you know where to meet me as soon as we park. We'll be in a platinum limited-edition Lincoln Navigator."

"Got'cha, shawty. Damn!"

"Put the tickets in your pocket right now, and please try not to be drunk or smelling like weed."

"Girl, get the fuck off my damn phone. I'll see you in a li'l while."

"Okay. I can't wait to see you."

"Me too. Later."

Nahima picked up her brand-new designer purse from her bed and dropped her phone inside. She walked over to the full-length mirror and busted a little dance move. Her reflection was volcano hot. Nahima looked awesome in her off-white strapless jumpsuit with flowing palazzo pants. The bronze glittery sparkles in the fabric set off her fourteen-karat gold teardrop earrings and matching rope chain with a teardrop pendant. Her mom had encouraged her to apply false lashes to accentuate her bronze, pearl, and sienna eye shadows that made her bronze lips and cheeks pop. Nahima was pleased that she had done away with her Afro by asking Valencia, her hairstylist, to part her soft curls down the middle and slick them back with shiny gel. Santana was going to be all over her tonight.

"Nahima! Get down here, baby girl!"

Satisfied with her appearance, she turned off the light, left her room, and locked her door. She took her time walking down the stairs on her three-inch strappy stiletto sandals. Nahima was surprised to see Uncle Zach standing at the bottom of the steps snapping pictures of her with his cell phone camera. Charles was moving about with his Canon forty-five-millimeter with the zoom lens, capturing her from all possible angles.

Zach moved in close to place a light peck on Nahima's cheek. "I just stopped by for a minute to see you before your big night and to give you this." He discreetly pressed some money into her palm.

"Thanks, Uncle Zach." She dropped the money inside her purse.

"You are so welcome, pumpkin. Wow! You look amazing!"

"I do, don't I?"

Zach, Charles, and Venus laughed at Nahima's lack of humility.

"Don't forget to make sure Jalen is dressed by nine o'clock for breakfast and a movie in the morning, Uncle Zach. I can't wait to see him."

Zach took Nahima by her hand and led her a few feet away from her parents. "Listen, pumpkin, you're going to have to postpone your outing with your baby brother to a later date."

Nahima felt like someone had just poured freezing water all over her. She blinked a few times, hoping her hearing was off. "What did you just say?"

"After the incident with Zion, Jalen has been real clingy and whiny. He won't let Zion out of his sight, and he's sworn off cookies, all kinds, period. He won't even sleep in his room. So Jill said he can't hang out with you tomorrow. I'm sorry."

"Jill?" Nahima repeated furiously. "Okay, she said Jalen can't spend time with me tomorrow. I get it. But what do you say, Uncle Zach? That's my little brother!"

"Calm down, pumpkin. Jill and I are a team. You may be Jalen's biological sister, but we are his legal parents. If Jill says he can't go out with you tomorrow, that's the law."

Nahima stood frozen in place, staring her uncle down. She was so damn pissed that she wished Zion had died Saturday morning. She wished to God that Jay had blown Jill's goddamn head off in that shanty in Jamaica, too. If Nahima thought she could get away with it, she'd go upstairs and sneak her dad's 9 mm handgun out of the house. Then she would request an Uber after the concert, go to Uncle Zach's house, and set the whole fucking mini mansion on fire. And when they all ran out to escape the flames, she'd shoot them between the eyes, one by one, all of them except Jalen. Jill would get the worst of it, though, because Nahima envisioned standing over her, emptying the gun into her body while she lay on the ground begging for her life.

Only the sound of the doorbell snapped Nahima from her wishes of death on everyone who had ever done Jay wrong and had kept them apart over the years with their lies and manipulations. To say she was enraged didn't tell one fifth of the story. Nahima was filled with hell's fiery flames from the hand of Satan himself. She tasted blood, and she wanted to kill Jill for messing up her plans to take Jalen to visit Jay.

Nahima ran toward the front door and ripped it open even as her mom and dad called out and ran after her. She sprinted past Rashawn, who was standing on the front stoop clutching a red rose, acting his part as her date for the evening. When she reached the SUV, Nahima opened the door and threw herself into the back seat with Yashia and Dondrae. Sweat was dripping down her face and back. Her armpits were even damp, although she had applied more than enough Dove deodorant to each of them and sprayed perfume on top of it. Nahima swallowed her anger when she realized everyone in the truck, along with her family standing in the middle of the walkway, was staring at her with strange expressions on their faces. She released a stream of air she'd been holding much too long when Rashawn climbed in the driver's seat and closed the door.

"Oh, my God, I'm so ready to go. Let's get this party started!"

"Are you sure you're going to be okay waiting in here by yourself, Nah-Nah? Kela and I can stay with you."

"No, the hell we can't! Rashawn said she can leave the AC and radio on. She will be just fine until Tito or Santos or whatever the hell his name is gets here."

Everybody but Nahima found that comment funny, so she didn't join in the laughter.

"Yeah, y'all go ahead. He just sent me a text saying he's already here looking for somewhere to park. He's so damn cheap!" Nahima laughed. "He said he will not pay twenty-five dollars for a parking space. So I guess he'll park someplace far off and have to walk to meet me out front."

Yashia, Dondrae, Kela, Ryan, and Rashawn exited the Navigator. They were all dressed like hip-hop royalty right off the pages of *Vibe* magazine. Nahima pressed the button to lower the window with Fantasia serenading her. "I'll be in there soon."

Rashawn looked at her, and she saw genuine concern in his eyes. "Kill the AC and the radio before you get out, and don't forget to lock it up."

"I got you, Rashawn. I promise."

"Here we come, Quay!"

"Yasss, hunty, yasss!"

"Y'all Pine Tree Hills girls are so ghetto!"

Nahima snickered at her friends walking through the parking deck, talking shit to each other. She was so hyped about seeing Quay with her man that she had forgotten all about Uncle Zach, bitch-ass Jill, and Jalen. So what? She couldn't take her baby brother to see their mom tomorrow, but it wasn't going to stop her from making the trip. Nahima had dreamed about meeting Jay ever since their first conversation now five months ago. She didn't know if she was going to simply look at her in awe or if she'd cry. There was no way she could predict her reaction. Nahima just wanted to meet the woman who was responsible for her existence so she could finally feel complete.

Rashawn was pumping his fist in the air, vibing to the music in an atmosphere that was filled with high-power electricity. He was so close to the stage that he could see the sweat pouring down Quay's face. It was almost as if, if he were to reach out a few inches, he could touch those fat-ass emerald-cut diamond studs in the rapper's earlobes. They were so big that Rashawn bet they were at least three carats per ear.

He raised his cell phone for the hundredth time to snap some more pictures. He had already captured a lot of good shots and a few short videos, too. Ryan had made him promise that he'd take plenty of pictures and videos just for her. Rashawn had been attaching some great shots of Quay to text messages throughout the concert and sending them to his girl. He looked up in the section where he believed Ryan and Kela were sitting. If he had connected with sexy Miss Mathis just one week earlier, she would be right next to him in the third row. They would be all hugged up and enjoying the show like Nahima and her man were in their premium front-row seats.

Rashawn craned his neck, looking toward the front. He wanted to lay eyes on his friend and her grown-ass boyfriend. Everybody was up on their feet dancing and waving their hands in the air, so it was hard to see anything. Rashawn decided to walk up there to holla at Nahima. So he excused himself past everyone to the left of him to make it happen. He smiled as he walked, bouncing to the funky beat of the music his entire way up front. He lowered his head as he scurried across the front row. When he figured he'd reached the halfway mark, he found himself standing in front of some Puerto Rican dude with a pregnant chick. She was a very attractive lady, and she was stylishly decked out in a colorful dress. The dude was holding the woman from behind with his hand on her big belly. They looked happy swaying to the music. Rashawn moved past them and hurried to the other end of the row. Then to be sure he hadn't missed Nahima, he doubled back, only this time he walked so slow that some people started cussing and talking shit to him. It was sad that out of all of those angry people, he didn't see Nahima.

Rashawn stood off to the side so he wouldn't block anyone, scanning the front row again. He just couldn't let it go. Where was Nahima? She damn sure was nowhere in the front row. Dondrae had told him that he'd actually seen her tickets, and he confirmed that she had the best seats in the house. It just didn't make any sense. Rashawn was a smart guy, so a couple scenarios popped inside his psyche, but he didn't like any of them. He walked back to his seat and dismissed Nahima so he could finish enjoying the concert. If she had given him a chance, she would be enjoying the concert too.

The entire gang was loudly talking over each other, laughing, and slapping high fives over pancakes. It seemed like everyone in IHOP had been to the Quay concert. The scene around the restaurant resembled an after-party/post-fashion show. Nahima noticed how sharply put together Ryan was. She couldn't remember her girl looking prettier. From her perfect spiral curls down to her black wedge-heel Roman sandals, she won the diva award for the night hands down. Nahima wondered who had applied her makeup, consisting of earth tones with the smoky eyes and lashes. Ryan wasn't into cosmetics like that, so a pro must've hooked her up. But how had Ms. Tasha been able to afford a makeup artist and drop a grip on that Apri Osagah jumpsuit when she could hardly pay her rent some months?

"Let me see your pictures, Nah-Nah. I know you got some good ones with your iPhone in the front row."

Nahima blinked out of her thoughts. "Girl, I was singing and dancing so much that I wasn't even thinking about taking any pictures. Santana took a lot of them, though. He's going to send me all of them tomorrow."

"How come he didn't join us for breakfast? I want to meet Sinatra." Kela laughed at her own dig.

"Santana," Nahima barked. "His name is Santana, Kela. What is your man's name? Oops, you don't have one."

"Honey, I know—"

"How are your blueberry pancakes, Kela?" Yashia asked, clearly jumping in as always to shut down a brewing argument.

"They're delicious. I wish I had ordered bacon with them instead of turkey sausage patties, though. These things are nasty."

"Here. Take a piece of mine." She lifted her plate in Kela's direction for her to get the strip of bacon.

"Thank you."

Nahima rolled her eyes at Kela. It seemed like everybody was coming for her. This was supposed to have been the most unforgettable night of her life, but it had turned out to be her worst nightmare. First, Uncle Zach had disappointed her by allowing Jill to shit on her plans to take Jalen to Leesworth to see Jay in the morning. Then Santana didn't even show up for the concert. She had sat in a truck all night while everyone else enjoyed her favorite rapper's performance. $2,200 had gone to waste. On top of that, Ryan had chosen this night to outshine her in hair, fashion, and makeup. And Rashawn damn sure seemed to appreciate it. He had hardly looked at Nahima since picking her up. Finally, Kela was being Kela, which was fucking nerve-racking. Nahima just wanted to go home and get ready to go see Jay tomorrow. She was the only person in her life who truly mattered right now.

Chapter Thirty-five

"Good night, bestie! I'll call you tomorrow! Bye, Dondrae!"

Nahima pressed the button to raise the passenger's window in the Navigator and then chanced a glance at Rashawn out of the corner of her eye. She had picked up on how he'd made it his business to drop off everyone else first so he could get her in his dad's boss-ass truck alone. Dude thought he was slick. Rashawn still wanted Nahima after all the times she had rejected his ass. And he knew she had a man. Well, she had a man until tonight. Nahima hated to admit it even to herself, but it was time to put Santana in the wind. All he ever did was disappoint her. He never took her out or bought her anything. The nigga had never taken her to his house. The truth was she had been the giver in their relationship, and he'd been the lucky taker.

Every damn thing Yashia had ever said about his piece-of-shit ass was true. Santana was a lowlife, drunk, weed-head thug with no real job. He had a criminal record, too, which suited him just fine since he liked stealing cars and selling drugs. Nahima didn't know what she had ever seen in the pervert. She would never forget what he had asked her to do with Zion. That was the perfect time to cuss him out on the spot, for asking her to tell a 9-year-old little girl to show him her pussy.

But all that was in the past from this night forward. Although Nahima's heart was broken, because she really did have love for the nigga, she just couldn't keep letting him dog her out. Like Yashia had told her too many damn times to count, she needed to get with a dude her own age with a promising future and something to offer her. So as soon as she and Avila got back from Leesworth tomorrow, Nahima planned to call Santana to tell him it was over and to stay the fuck out of her life. She couldn't risk kicking his ass to the curb tonight because he was low-down enough to stop Avila from driving her to the prison to see Jay.

A touch of shyness washed over Nahima when Rashawn parked in front of her house. He hadn't said two words to her during the short drive of two lefts, a right, and another left from Yashia's house to hers. He released his seat belt and picked up his cell phone from the console. He read a text message and smiled before he started scrolling through the phone.

Damn, I guess I'll go ahead and finally give Rashawn my phone number and let him shoot his shot. I wonder if he can kiss good. And please let him have a big dick.

"I know you realized I changed up my drop-off schedule so I could bring you home last, Nahima."

She unbuckled her seat belt. "Yeah, and I know why, too."

Nahima flipped her body, threw her leg over the console, and skillfully straddled Rashawn in the driver's seat. She was like a wild octopus, bouncing on his crotch, running her fingers through his coils, and sucking his lips into her mouth

Rashawn shoved her away so hard that she toppled over into the passenger's seat and hit her head on the window. "Damn, girl! What the hell is wrong with you?" He wiped his mouth with both hands and started making a gesture like he was spitting.

"I'm sorry, but I thought you wanted to get with me. You've been running behind me forever. Don't you like me?"

"No! I mean, yes, but only as a friend. You made it perfectly clear that you weren't feeling me, so I moved on way before the concert."

"Oh, my God! I am so embarrassed!" Nahima snatched up her purse and reached for the door handle.

Rashawn took hold of her wrist to keep her in place. "Don't go, Nahima. And there's no need to be embarrassed."

"Let me go, Rashawn! Let me go!"

"I will after you look at this." He held up his cell phone in her face. "Do you know these people? Tell me the truth now."

Nahima snatched the phone for a closer look. Her eyes were blurry from a heavy flow of tears, but she could still see Santana smiling with his arm around a pregnant woman, who looked like a million bucks in her original design. The baby-doll dress was a perfect fit. Nahima swiped through the pictures and felt her heart rip down the middle when she saw one of Santana kissing the woman on the lips with his hand on her belly. The funny thing was it appeared that neither one of them had any idea that their images were being capture by a camera.

"How did . . . I mean—"

"I walked up front during the concert to holla at you, but I couldn't find you. So as soon as the concert was over, I ran back to the front to check their seat numbers, and when I realized they had been sitting in your seats, I followed them and snapped a few pictures so I could show you. Who are they?"

"That's Santana and, apparently, his pregnant girlfriend or wife. And that pretty dress she's rocking is one of my original designs. He lied and told me I was making it for his cousin." Nahima sniffed and wiped her eyes. "I feel like such a fool. Why is so much bad shit happening to me?"

Rashawn patted Nahima's shoulder. "Sometimes life sucks like shit. Trust me. I know."

"Rashawn, please don't tell my girls about Santana. They will never let me live it down. And don't tell them about what I did to you. I don't know what I was thinking."

"I promise not to say anything to anyone ever."

"Thank you." She reached out to hug Rashawn and started laughing when he leaned away. "This will be an innocent hug. I'm not about to try to rape you again."

"Go, Nahima! Go, Nahima! Go, Nahima!"

She was feeling herself, doing the bounce before transitioning into the snake all while sitting in the passenger's seat of Santana's car. Avila was blasting Lizzo's "Good as Hell" with the windows down, pushing eighty up I-75 North. When the song ended, Nahima reached for her bottle of Sprite in the cup holder and turned it up. Avila lowered the volume on the radio when an advertisement came on.

"So how did you hook up with my brother?"

"We met on Instagram, and because I was young, dumb, and clueless, I fell in love with him. He convinced me that he truly cared about me when he actually saw me as a stupid little girl he could use for money, expensive gifts, and sex. Five months later, I am no longer a virgin, I have no self-respect, and I'm out over five thousand dollars in cash and gifts."

"Damn! Santana's ass should be ashamed of himself. I'ma kick his ass."

"Leave it alone. What goes around always comes around. I was an easy target."

"You remind me of myself when I was your age, Nahima. I was sprung over this older guy and ended up having two babies back-to-back for that fool even though he was beating my ass every morning, afternoon, and evening. By the time I left him for good, I had almost been to jail for cutting his other baby mama over his ass, and I was twenty years old with a tenth-grade education. My credit was bad, and me and my kids were homeless. And I was selling my body because I was strung out on crack. I was pitiful."

Nahima didn't know what to say. She hadn't been through half the shit Avila had experienced. "Where were your parents?"

"My mama was in and out of jail because she was an addict who stole and sold her ass to support her habit, and my daddy was in New York with his new wife and their kids. That's why when Santana called me and asked me to drive you to the prison to see your mom, I said yes. The only reason I charged you was because I sell sandwiches and drinks in my neighborhood every Friday and Saturday. I needed to make up for sales I missed today."

"It's cool. Nothing in life is free."

"You're right about that." Avila looked over at Nahima. "Let me give you some valuable advice, baby. Love yourself first, and always respect yourself so other people will respect you too. Don't expect anyone to love you just because you love them. That shit will break your heart and eventually kill you. Don't give away anything to anybody, I don't give a damn who it is, that you can't live without. It's not wrong to be selfish sometimes. And when somebody shows you the type of person they really are, don't fool yourself into thinking you can change them to be who you want them to be. Accept them for who they are, and take them or leave them."

Nahima nodded and read the sign that said Leesworth was five miles away. "We're almost there."

"I know. Are you nervous or excited? Tell me how you feel."

"I don't know how I'm supposed to feel. I've never seen my birth mom before. I really don't know her. The only thing we talk about is her and what her life has been like, and we discuss all the things people did to her that caused her to be in prison. Hopefully, when she gets out, which I hope will be soon, we'll get to know each other well."

"You look real pretty, Kang. Your hair sure is long. How do you feel?"

"I feel good. I think I'll ride my scooter all the way to the transit area and walk the rest of the way."

KiKi stopped brushing Jay's hair. "King, are you strong enough to do that? Look how swollen your feet are. You've got on flip-flops and socks because your sneakers are too tight. How is your back?"

"It hurts a little bit, but I'm not taking any pain meds until after the visit. You know damn well it makes me sleepy. I don't want my baby boy to see me acting loopy the first time he meets me."

"Kang, you better get on 'round there. Big Baby will help you if she sees you. Her mama is coming to see her today."

Jay hobbled to her scooter and fired it up. "I'll see y'all later," she told her friends before she sped away.

Fifteen minutes later, Jay was third in line to enter the visitation room. Sure enough, Big Baby had made a way for her to avoid the long line. She was standing right in front of her. Jay could feel her heart pounding like a freight train. The moment she had been waiting for would happen soon. She looked through the door to see if she could catch a glimpse of her son waiting for her. Her eyes roamed about the room a few times until she spotted Nahima. She recognized her right away from all the pictures she sent via email all the time. She was talking to a lady sitting next to her. She had to be Avila. But where was Jalen? Jay stretched her neck and narrowed her eyes in search of her baby boy. Her eyes began to burn with fear and then anger.

A guard came to the door and called two names. The woman at the front of the line and Big Baby left the transit area, giving Jay an unobstructed view of Nahima and her friend. They were still laughing and talking. And Jalen was nowhere to be found. Fury shook Jay to her core and made her weak. The pain in her back, stomach, feet, and legs that she'd forced her mind to forget for a visit with her son hit her like she'd run headfirst into Stone Mountain. Gasping for air, Jay signaled for the guard, who came right over.

"You're up next, King."

"I'm leaving. I don't want to visit with those two girls right there unless they brought my son," she said, pointing directly at Nahima and the young lady with her. "I don't see my baby!"

"Hold on, King. Let me go and check it out."

Jay didn't even bother to stick around because she already knew the deal. Zach and Jill wouldn't let Nahima bring Jalen, but she decided to come anyway. Wrong damn move. It took every ounce of strength Jay could muster up to make it back to her scooter. When she sat down on it, she was aching all over and could hardly catch her breath. Blackness wrapped all around Jay, and the room started spinning fast.

"Help me! Help me, somebody! Help!"

Chapter Thirty-six

"Wake up, Nahima, we're almost at your house."

The moment her eyes opened, she started crying again. "I'm sorry I wasted your time, Avila. I still can't believe my mom didn't want to see me. I tried to bring my baby brother. I did everything I could, but my uncle and his evil—"

"Uh-uh. What did I tell you? What did I tell you?"

"Stop blaming one person's actions on another person."

"That's right. Your uncle and his wife have a responsibility and a right to protect their son. And no matter what you or your birth mom say or think, Jalen is their son."

"But what about me? I'm Jay's daughter! Why didn't she want to see me? I have done everything she has asked me to do from day one, and she rejected me! Why?"

"Remember what you told me before you fell asleep? You said when you asked your auntie for your birth mom's address at the prison, she told you to wait and let her find out if Jay wanted to connect with you, because she didn't want you to be disappointed if she didn't. But you found your birth mom's email address and connected with her anyway, right?"

"Yes."

"Nahima, your birth mom does not want a relationship with you. She used you to try to get to your baby brother. The way I see it, Jay and Santana are two of a kind. They prey on the weak and use them up. Stop expecting people to love you just because you love them, okay?"

"Okay." Nahima looked up in time to say, "Turn right. I'm not ready to go home yet. I want to go hang out at my best friend's house."

When they pulled up to the Taylor residence, Yashia was about to get inside her car.

"Where are you going, bestie?"

"Kela made some lemon-pepper and teriyaki wings, and I want some. You feel like hanging?"

"Yeah!" Nahima turned to Avila. "Thanks for everything."

"You're welcome, baby."

"Can I call you so we can talk sometimes?"

"You better. Give me a hug."

Nahima and Avila shared a warm embrace and then smiled at each other.

"Bye!" she yelled over her shoulder on her way to Yashia's car.

Avila honked the horn and pulled off.

Nahima listened to her bestie talk about the concert and all the nice clothes and hairstyles they had seen at IHOP last night. Yashia was on a roll. Nahima couldn't contribute anything to the conversation about the show, but she had a mouthful to say about some of the outfits people had on at IHOP. Ryan was at the top of her list.

"That was a three-hundred-dollar Apri Osagah jumpsuit. I saw it online at Neiman Marcus. How the hell could Ms. Tasha afford to buy Ryan that and then pay for her shoes and makeup?"

"Chase sent her some money. She told us that. You remember, Nahima."

"I guess so."

"Hey, let's swing by Ryan's crib before we go and eat at Kela's house. You know she's always stuck at home with her little brothers and sisters while Ms. Tasha is at the shop serving up hair."

Seconds after Yashia whipped her car around the curve and up the steep hill, the shiny black Mustang was in clear view in front of Ryan's crib. Nahima's jaw dropped. Yashia increased her speed and pulled up right behind it. As if they weren't shocked enough, Rashawn and Ryan were standing in the doorway kissing. The besties just sat there watching. Nahima was already out of the car and stomping up the driveway when Rashawn released Ryan and began his descent down the front steps.

"Stop it, Nahima! Come back here!" Yashia screamed, running to catch up with her bestie.

Rashawn froze on his stroll down the steps, and Ryan was standing at her front door looking horrified.

"What the fuck?"

"What's up, Nahima and Yashia?"

"So you were kissing me in your daddy's truck last night and now you're over here with your tongue down Ryan's throat today, Rashawn?"

Nahima's outburst made Rashawn laugh, but it sent Ryan flying down the steps to stand next to her man.

"You are dead to me, Ryan! You ain't shit! Now I know what Kela was trying to tell us about your sneaky ass!"

Rashawn took Ryan's hand into his and turned to walk her back up the steps. After they walked inside the house, he closed the door.

Yashia pulled Nahima back to the car. She was cussing and screaming every step of the way. When they finally got inside the car, Yashia turned to Nahima with her eyes narrowed to razor-thin slits.

"I can't deal with you right now, so I'm taking you home. We live in the suburbs, but you came to the hood and showed your entire ass, and for what, Nahima?"

"Ryan knew Rashawn wanted me! We're supposed to be girls! What happened to bitches before britches?"

"So you're pissed with Ryan for hooking up with a guy you ain't got shit for? You and Rashawn never got together because you didn't want him! You're too damn stuck on Santana to look at guys your age. So what is your problem? You just made a fool of yourself! And you know you lied on Rashawn. I don't believe he touched you last night. I'm not talking to you until you apologize to Ryan and have a civilized conversation with her."

Once Warden Sheftall contacted Aunt Jackie about Jay's condition around ten o'clock Saturday night, she immediately called Wallace, who broke down in tears. Patricia took over, suggesting that a Zoom meeting would be the best way for the family to communicate. So Aunt Jackie, Wallace and Patricia, Zach and Jill, and Aunt Hattie Jean were staring at each other over cyberspace. Aunt Bertha was technologically challenged, so she would wait for a three-way call between her and her sisters.

"The warden said that her kidneys have pretty much shut down. She's not in a coma, but she's nonresponsive yet breathing on her own for now."

"I want to see my daughter, and I want Zach to see her too."

"Jay denied our requests for visitation. How is that supposed to happen?"

Aunt Jackie hummed and closed her eyes. "The warden said all family members can come to the prison Monday. She has approved special visitation for us."

"Count me out, Jackie. You know I don't do good in these kinds of situations, and Bubba don't either."

"Zachary will go, and I will stay home with the children."

"Yeah, I'll go. Somebody needs to drive Aunt Jackie."

"Hopefully, Jay will still be alive and at Leesworth Monday. The warden said if the facility in Augusta agrees to an emergency transfer, they will medevac her out immediately. But they will notify me, and I'll call you first, Wallace."

"Bless you, darling."

"Well, family, I guess that's all. But before we disconnect, I want to pray for God's will to be done."

"This nigga . . ." Nahima placed her phone under her pillow and turned over.

Santana had been calling her since Saturday night, and she hadn't answered a single one of his calls. It was after midnight, leading into Monday morning, and she was still ignoring his ass. Nahima was done dealing with people who didn't give a shit about her. From now on, she only had time for those who truly loved her and showed her their love on the regular. And Ryan was one of the people who had always loved her and had her back. That was why Nahima couldn't wait to get to school in the morning so she could find her girl and apologize to her for showing her natural-born ass in her front yard.

Ryan was the sweetest and most loyal member of their posse, and she in no way deserved to have been cussed out and accused of doing anything foul. Rashawn didn't either, especially after being so nice and understanding to Nahima. So as soon as she got to school, she was going to make things right with them.

Her phone rang again, and it was Santana. Instead of letting the call ring out, she declined it just to piss his ass off. Nahima wished there were a way she could reject Jay the way she had rejected her when she was born and at the prison Saturday. No one had ever made her feel like shit the way Santana and her birth mom had. They were the two people on earth she had done the most for, including her baby brother, who deserved more from her. It was a damn shame. But it was all good, because Nahima would never let either one of them hurt her again. Ever.

"Fuck them!"

***

Jill walked Zach to the door and kissed him. "Drive safely."

"I will. I'll call you before Aunt Jackie and I get on the road."

"I'll be waiting."

Zach waved at his neighbor, Senator Olan McCord, across the street as he walked toward his car. On a whim, he stopped at the mailbox before he headed for his G-Wagen, since he seemed like the only member of the King family who gave a damn about the mail. He pulled out a thick stack of bills and sales papers. A large, peculiar-looking brown envelope got his attention.

"'Judicial Unlimited Project,'" Zach read out loud.

He unlocked his SUV and climbed inside. Curious, he opened the envelope and pulled out some papers that were stapled together. After reading the top page, Zach started flipping frantically through the other pages, refusing to believe that something this crazy was happening to him.

"This shit can't be real. I know this shit ain't real!" Zach threw the papers in the passenger's seat, started his whip, and secured his iPhone to the dashboard connection. "Call Kirk Orowitz."

Nahima swallowed her pride when she turned the corner and saw Ryan and Rashawn walking down the 11C hall. She also ignored the mean mugs they shot at her before they did a U-turn and started walking in the opposite direction away from her. Determined to do the right thing, Nahima broke out into a power walk behind them.

"Yo, Ryan! Rashawn! Wait up, y'all!"

"Step off, Nahima," Ryan warned, turning around with one hand on her hip and the other one still tucked in her man's grip. "You said enough Saturday for all of Pine Tree Hills to hear, so you can keep the rest of that shit to yourself. You embarrassed me in front of my peeps in my hood where the badges love to come and throw a bunch of us in the back of a paddy wagon and haul our asses off to jail just for being black. But you don't know a damn thing about that now, do you? Nah, you don't, because that's not how it goes down in West Silver Lake."

Nahima started walking fast in their direction. "You're right about all of that. Everything I said and did Saturday was fucked up. I was wrong to get mad at you and Rashawn, and I had no right to cuss you out or accuse you of being disloyal to me. I'm so sorry." Nahima closed the gap between them. "I've been making a bunch of mistakes and bad moves over the past five months, and I've hurt a lot of people. You didn't deserve for me to go off on you, Ryan. I was mad at myself and the people who had actually hurt me, but you for sure weren't one of those people. Will you accept my apology?"

"Yes, I'll accept your apology if you will accept mine, Nah-Nah. I should've told you about me and Rashawn. He and I had agreed to put our truth out there to you first and then the rest of the clique after the concert so we wouldn't ruin everybody's night out together. But when you and Yashia rolled up on us Saturday, I didn't know what to do. Anyway, please forgive me for breaking the girl code."

Nahima wiped her tears and smiled as she shook her head. "You didn't break the girl code, Ryan. Rashawn and I never got together, and he didn't kiss me Friday night, either. I lied because I was pissed and jealous."

"I know he didn't kiss you. Rashawn ain't that dude and . . ."

Nahima searched Ryan's eyes when her voice trailed off, and then she looked at Rashawn. "Oh, my God, you told her, didn't you? Wow, I am so embarrassed." She turned around suddenly to walk away.

Rashawn reached out and took hold of Nahima's elbow, pulling her back around to face him and Ryan. "You gave me no other choice but to tell her when you lied on me, Nahima. What else was I supposed to do?"

"I understand, but I feel like shit just the same."

"Please don't be ashamed, and don't worry about me telling Yashia, Kela, or anyone else. Your secret is safe with me, Nah-Nah. You know I know how to keep a secret, girl."

"Hell yeah, you do."

The two girls laughed and wrapped each other up in a bear hug. Nahima didn't avoid Ryan's intense gaze when she pulled back.

"Nah-Nah, of the girls in our clique, you're the one with the most blessings. You've got a mom and dad who love you to death, a rich uncle and godfather who makes it rain on you just because, you live in a phat crib, you got two closets full of labels and designers I ain't ever heard of, and you have unlimited opportunities to succeed in life because of your designer and sewing skills. And you're very pretty with the kind of body Kela, Yashia, and I wish we could have. By the time you get your car next year, I don't know if I'll be able to stand your ass, but I will celebrate with you. I love you, Nah-Nah, with your bougie, spoiled self. I love you so much that I would do anything for you. But I need you to count all them blessings you got and start loving and respecting yourself. That way you won't make bad decisions that leave you wide open for other people to do you dirty."

Damn, she sounds just like Avila. They both speak the 100-percent, sista-girl truth.

Chapter Thirty-seven

"Thank you, Jesus! I'm happy to hear that, Mrs. Sheftall."

"Dr. Dalrymple said it's nothing short of a miracle."

"Oh, yes, it is."

"Before I let you go, I need to tell you that although Ms. King is awake, she's unable to move or eat, but she's talking. It's only one word, though, and she's been saying it clearly all morning."

"What is Jay saying?"

"Jalen. She's asking for someone named Jalen. Whoever he is, it would be great if he could travel with the family to Augusta tomorrow to see Ms. King."

"I'll see what I can do about that. Thanks for calling, Mrs. Sheftall."

"You're welcome. Goodbye."

Aunt Jackie dialed Wallace's number to give him the good news. Jay was awake and on her way to Augusta to the medical facility where the family could visit her tomorrow. But why was she asking for Jalen all of a sudden? It was strange.

"Jackie?"

"Good morning, Wallace! I've got good news."

Zach stormed out of his attorney's office mad as hell. Some group of law students was trying to help Jay amend Jalen's adoption in her favor as part of a special early-release program. Kirk believed they had a pretty good chance to make it happen, but because Jay was on her deathbed, it wouldn't make a difference. It was the principle of the matter, though. How the hell could a dying woman wreak havoc in Zach's life? In good health, Jay had caused him grief, and in terminal health, she was doing the same. But she was coming for his baby boy now. That was straight bullshit right there. Kirk had told Zach that some chick named Avila Bridges was a support person for Jay and there was a video from someone in the family who wanted Jalen to have contact with his birth mom. Kirk was working on finding out everything he could and would get back with Zach as soon as possible.

Aunt Jackie rushed to meet Zach in the hallway when she heard him enter the house. "Didn't you get my message? There's been a change of plans."

"No, I didn't get your message, but you're right about the plan change. I'm not going to see Jay. I don't wish anything bad on her, but you need to find another ride."

"What happened, Zach?"

"Evidently, before Jay's health took a turn for the worse, she started proceedings to have Jalen's adoption changed, claiming she agreed to Jill and me taking custody of him while she was mentally incapable of making major decisions at the time. Long story short, a group of law students is helping her along with some advocate and a member of our family. I can't wait to find out who it is. A possibility for an early release is her ultimate goal. Nothing will come of it because Jay is dying, but this crap makes my ass itch, Auntie!"

"Watch your mouth, Zach!"

Zach walked to the back of the house, and Aunt Jackie followed him. When they sat down in the den, he started scrolling through the faces of his family members in his head. Who would help Jay interfere with Jalen's adoption? He couldn't imagine who would want to help her do anything good or bad. Zach rubbed his temple against the headache he felt coming on.

"Hey, Oscar, come on out, man! I know you're here. It's time for us to meet!"

Aunt Jackie clutched the collar of her canary yellow T-shirt, lightly scraping the edges of her fingernails over her chest where her jaw had almost dropped. Zach had no idea why he'd done it. Maybe the devil made him. Shit, his evil red ass had already messed up his morning, so it was time to strike back at him by spreading a little humor around.

A moment later, Oscar walked into the den, and Zach stood up with his hand extended. The two strangers, who were aware of each other in a roundabout way, shook hands.

"I'm Oscar Wilson, Jackie's fiancé. It's a pleasure to finally meet you."

"I'm Zachary King, Jackie's nephew, but she raised me as her son. At last we meet. Have a seat, sir."

It was quiet for a moment in the den. Aunt Jackie looked like she had seen Satan.

"How long have you known about me and Oscar, Zach?"

"Let's stop playing games, Auntie. I knew about y'all, and y'all knew that I knew about y'all. You, Oscar, Wallace, and Patricia ain't slick. I figured everything out a while ago, and I was just waiting for y'all to tell me. And you had your engagement ring on the other day I stopped by to give you that check."

"Lord Jesus!" Aunt Jackie looked at her left hand.

"There were other hints here and there, too, but all of that is water under the bridge now. Welcome to the family, Oscar."

"Thanks, Zach. I appreciate that. But just so you know, I don't live here. I live with my daughter, son-in-law, and their three children in Ellenwood. However, as soon as Jackie and I get married, there's a townhouse in a retirement village in Buckhead with our names on it."

"Buckhead, you say? At least Wallace didn't hook you up with no scrub, Auntie. I've got to thank him for that one."

"And you don't have to pay for our wedding, Zach."

"Yes, I do. I owe my auntie that much and more. But please keep it simple, and don't try to cash me out."

"We won't, son. I promise you. Jackie wants something small, short, and simple, and so do I."

"Good." Zach stroked his goatee and looked off into space. "Before we start planning the wedding, we've got to get past this situation with Jay."

"She woke up this morning, Zach. The warden called and told me. She's being transferred to the medical facility in Augusta as we speak. We can visit her there tomorrow. That was the change in plans I left you a message about."

"Oscar will have to take you because I ain't going, Aunt Jackie. Wallace can meet y'all there, but he won't see me. Jay didn't want me to visit her anyway, and you know it. So I'm not going to torture her with my presence on her deathbed like she's torturing me now over Jalen. God and I have an understanding regarding me and my sister, and I'm going to honor it."

"You may have to make a concession on the situation with Jay, Zach. She woke up this morning, like I said, and she started asking for Jalen. The warden said it's the only word she's said. And she's repeating it over and over. She wants to see her baby before she dies."

Zach stood up and started pacing the den and rubbing his goatee. "I don't know about that. My little boy has had some emotional challenges since Zion's allergic reaction. I don't know how to explain Jay to him. He's too young and fragile for this. Damn it!"

"Zach, Wallace and I will be there with Jackie and the boy. Your sister is too weak to say anything that'll upset him. Let Jackie take Jalen to see Jay. I won't let anything bad happen to him, and you know your dad won't either."

"I appreciate that, Wallace, but Jill, my wife, might buck against all of us. When it comes to Jalen, she's the law."

Zach's phone chimed in his pocket. He took it out and sat down on the sofa again. "It's an email from Kirk," he mumbled, staring at the screen. "He sent the video that the mysterious family member submitted to the judge in support of Jay."

"Oh, my God!" Aunt Jackie reached over and rubbed Zach's shoulder. "Let's see who it is, baby."

"My name is Nahima Angelique Lawson-Morris, and I am the biological daughter of Jayla Simone King, an inmate of nine years at Leesworth Women's Federal Corrections Facility. I have a baby brother named Jalen Gavin King. He was adopted by my maternal uncle, Zachary Sean King, and his wife, Jillian Bessette King. My mother wouldn't be in prison today if it weren't for the betrayal of my uncle and his wife, which is a bitter irony because they now are the legal parents of my baby brother. That is why I appeal to you, Your Honor, to consider amending Jalen's adoption so that my mother will be allowed to have unsupervised visits with him and he can learn who she is upon her release. She's his mother, who will protect him against my uncle, who has severe anger issues. No one knows that better than I do, because I have been a victim of his verbal and physical abuse. My uncle, Zachary King, brutally attacked me by choking me and slamming my head against the wall in the home of my legal parents, Charles and Venus Morris, recently. He cursed at me and threatened to kill me, stating . . ."

Jill kissed her husband's cheek and rubbed his back, but he didn't acknowledge her affection. He sat on the sofa in their great room with his fingers linked together in front of him, staring down at the floor. His tears were falling unchecked.

"Venus and Charles agreed to submit affidavits to the judge on your behalf to do away with the turmoil Nahima has caused. No one is going to take Jalen or our other two children away from us. Do not worry, Zachary."

"Why would Nahima do some shit like that? She made me out to be a demon in that video."

"We won't know the entire story until after Venus and Charles speak with her when she returns home after school. All we know now is that Jay and Nahima have somehow been in contact." Jill slid off the sofa and kneeled in front of her husband. She cupped his face between her palms. "Jalen will go with Aunt Jackie and her fiancé to Augusta to see Jay. Papa King will be there too. It is the right thing for us to do, Zachary. God will take care of our little boy. No harm will come to him. Yes, Jalen must go."

Zach wrapped his arms around Jill and wept. His sobs and whimpers were loud and piercing, filling the great room. Zach cried because he was hurt and furious. He cried for Nahima because she was another victim in a long line of people Jay had used and abused, damn near destroying them. His tears were for Jalen, who would never know how blessed he was to have escaped the wickedness of the woman who had given birth to him. Maybe the child and his father, Gavin, were the only human beings Jay had ever truly loved, or maybe she never loved them at all.

Zach loved his sister, and he always had. That was the main reason he was crying. No matter how much love he had in his heart for her, she didn't have any for him. The pain of knowing that Jay did not love him would haunt Zach beyond her death, but the love of his wife, their children, his aunt, his father, and the rest of his family would overcome all of his pain.

Chapter Thirty-eight

"Nahima, what the hell were you thinking?"

"I don't know, Mom! I didn't mean to hurt Uncle Zach! I had forgotten all about that stupid video! Oh, my God, I don't want the judge to take Jalen away from Uncle Zach! I swear I'll do anything!" Nahima fell on her knees. She wanted to die. Her world had crashed all around her. "Mom, please help me stop the judge and those law students from taking Jalen away!"

"Why did you do it, Nahima? Why did you reach out to Jay and betray the family?"

"I wanted to help Jay! That's all. She told me how you all screwed her over and did her dirty! Mom, I didn't know. Aaahhh, I didn't know. I believed everything she told me. I . . . I believed her. How could I have been sooo stupid?"

Upset to the highest degree, Nahima was ashamed. She fell flat on her face onto the carpet. Her heart ached, and she felt like a fool. She had betrayed everyone who truly loved her, for Jay, who didn't give a damn about her. She had hurt and disappointed everyone. Jay was so damn evil and wicked. She hadn't even had the decency to tell Nahima she was terminally ill with a short time to live. She didn't love her or want her. It was only Jalen she claimed to love, and she had used Nahima to do her dirt to Zach and Jill and everybody else to get close to the little boy.

"Nahima, get up, and talk to your father and me, baby."
Venus was on her knees crying and rubbing her child's
back as an emotional Charles stood above them. "Get up.
I need to know everything from the beginning when you
first emailed Jay."

The next day, Zach drove his li'l dawg to Aunt Jackie's
house and put him in Oscar's Escalade for a trip to
Augusta to go and visit a dying woman he wouldn't even
remember six months from now. Jill had stayed at home
in bed, leaving the responsibility solely to his father. Zach
was at peace with the decision and believed Jalen would
be fine because the hand of God was upon his young and
innocent life, and no one could rise up against him.

Zach locked the door behind him and stripped down
to nothing before he eased back into bed next to his wife.
He gathered Jill in his arms and kissed her cheek. The
last twenty-four hours had been extremely emotional
for them, but they were determined to push their way
through it.

"Are you okay?"

"Yeah. Jalen was excited. He thinks he's going on a
road trip like the cartoon movie. He's got all of his snacks,
juice boxes, action figures, iPad, and movies."

"What about his activity books? Did you forget his
activity books and markers?"

"Nope. I packed three activity books and a new box of
markers. Daddy bought his baby boy a new Black Panther
action figure, too."

"That's good." Jill looked up at Zach. "I still can't
believe Nahima almost killed Zion."

"She claimed she didn't realize how serious allergies
could be, but I don't believe her because I told her myself."

"And she stole money from Jalen's bank, invited a stranger into our home, and sneaked to the prison to visit Jay."

"Yeah, she confessed everything to Venus and Charles, and it nearly killed them. Shit, I'm still reeling from it. I'm just glad she turned that worthless pedophile motherfucker Santana Bridges in to the police. His ass is facing statutory rape charges and drug and auto theft charges. I hope some big, muscular dude with a fourteen-inch dick makes him his bitch tonight."

"What's going to happen to Nahima now?"

"It depends on Nahima. Once she completes in-patient treatment at the youth psychiatric center, I hope she'll hook up with a good therapist and continue to put her life back together."

"I will pray for her, but I don't know if I will ever trust her again. I'm afraid for her to be around our children."

"I am too."

Zach squeezed Jill, and she snuggled closer to him. With treatment, Nahima had a chance that her mother never did. Jay had never confessed to any of her wrong-doings or taken responsibility for the messes she'd made. She had always played the victim and believed she was entitled to everything, like the world owed her something. At least Nahima had taken the first steps, acknowledging that she had a problem and admitting all the things she had done. Zach still loved her very much and prayed that she would make a full recovery someday.

"Hi. My name is Jalen."

Jay looked at her son and cried tearlessly because her body was totally depleted of all fluids. She couldn't speak or move. The medications numbed her entire body so she wouldn't feel any pain. But her heart, the emotional part of it, throbbed with unyielding pain because she was dying and wouldn't have a chance to know Jalen, and he would never know her. Jay was grateful that Aunt Jackie had brought him to visit her so she could see him before she died. She was also glad to see Wallace, who had prayed with her and told her he loved her. Once again, he apologized for killing her mother and leaving her and Zach to grow up without him.

Jalen touched Jay's hand. "I hope you feel better, lady." He turned around and looked up at Aunt Jackie. "I'm ready to go now."

Epilogue

Four Months Later

Montego Bay, Jamaica

Zach dipped the beautiful bride low, brought her back up, and spun her around. The small group of wedding attendees at the beachfront ceremony clapped their hands and cheered wildly. Aunt Jackie wasn't much of a dancer except for when she was in the spirit at church, but she was holding her own as she snapped her fingers and rocked to Shalamar's "A Night to Remember." Nahima had done an incredible job designing and creating her wedding dress. It was baby blue with short off-the-shoulder sleeves and a sweetheart neckline. Tiny cream beads and crystals had been hand sewn onto every inch of the lace bodice. The hem fell to rest at the middle of Aunt Jackie's meaty kneecaps, but her chapel train, embellished with cream carnations made of tulle, gave the simple sheath elegance.

When the deejay shifted the music to Marvin Gaye crooning "Let's Get It On," Oscar appeared at Aunt Jackie's side. Aunt Hattie Jean and Uncle Bubba, Orville and Faye, Dex and Ramona, and Venus and Charles joined the bride and groom on the dance floor of white sand. Jill walked up to Zach and tapped his shoulder, but she had to wait for her dance partner while Aunt Jackie whispered in his ear.

"Go now. Go on now, baby."

Zach nodded and motioned for Zach Jr. When he ran over, his dad said, "Dance with your mom. Li'l dawg, Nahima, and I got something to do."

Jill kissed her husband and then wrapped her arms around her son. They started swaying to the music. Zion ran over and started dancing too while Zach went in search of Jalen and Nahima.

"Li'l dawg and Nahima, we've got some business to take care of."

Wallace and Patricia looked at Zach and nodded. Jalen and Nahima had been keeping them company at their table at the back of the white tent. Wallace reached under the table and handed Zach what he had come to get.

"Thanks, Dad." He took Jalen by the hand and looked at Nahima. "Come on, pumpkin."

Nahima smiled and shook her head. "No, Uncle Zach. I'm good. I have peace and joy in my heart, and I won't let anyone or anything take it away. I'm fine right here with Papa and Grammy."

Zach nodded and gave her a thumbs-up. "Cool. Let's go for a walk on the beach, li'l dawg."

"Okay, big dawg." Jalen turned to the table. "Papa, Grammy, and Nahima, stay right here. I'll be back. Then we're all going to dance."

"We'll be right here, grandson."

"Grammy is going to show you and Papa her moves," Patricia promised with laughter.

Nahima laughed too and waved to her baby brother.

Zach and his baby boy left the tent and started walking down the shore. The tide was low, and the sun had just begun to slowly set over the crystal blue ocean. When Zach could barely hear the music, he rolled up the legs of his blue linen slacks. He lifted Jalen in his arms while holding the red urn in his hand and walked out into the water. Jalen didn't say a word. He just watched his dad open the urn.

"When I empty this, um, stuff into the water, I want you to say, 'Goodbye and be free.' Okay?"

"Okay, Daddy."

Zach turned the urn over, and the ashes floated in the breeze and scattered, eventually landing in the ocean.

"Goodbye! Be free!" Jalen looked up at Zach and smiled. "How was that, Daddy?"

"It was perfect just like you, son."